Burning Up

NS

Burning Up

ANNE MARSH

BRAVA

KENSINGTON PUBLISHING CORP.
www.kensingtonbooks.com

BRAVA BOOKS are published by

Kensington Publishing Corp.
119 West 40th Street
New York, NY 10018

ISBN-13: 978-0-7582-6681-1
ISBN-10: 0-7582-6681-2

First Kensington Trade Paperback Printing: November 2012

10 9 8 7 6 5 4 3 2 1

Printed in the United States of America

For Marge. With love.
I couldn't have written
a better mother-in-law or friend.

Chapter One

The DC-3 pulled through the air, heading for the thick, dark plume of smoke boiling up from the park's northeast corner. Early-summer lightning strikes always wreaked havoc out here in Northern California, setting sleeper fires the Forest Service couldn't spot right away. One quick jolt of lightning could shoot an old, dry tree full of electricity and heat, creating a slow burn spotted only when the fire flamed outward to surrounding brush. The spotter crouched by the plane's open door waved him forward, and Jack Donovan moved into position. Feet and arms braced in the open door, fifteen hundred feet of smoky air between him and his target, he had a clear shot down to the small clearing now blossoming with streamers from the plane's previous pass. The red ribbons pulled hard right, so he'd be watching for crosswind.

Overshoot the drop spot, and he'd slam into the ponderosa pines hemming the clearing.

"You ready?" The spotter roared the routine check into his ear. "Watch the drift streamers, and check your chute, or the boys will be fishing you out of the pines when this fire is finished."

"Fuck you." He grinned at the spotter, knowing his face mirrored the other man's exhilaration. He'd be first jumper out the door on what was likely the last jump for his team.

Christ. If it hadn't been for that damned phone call, he'd have kept the team here all summer. Money was good, and, so far, there was plenty of fire. All the makings of a good summer.

"On final, fifteen hundred." The pilot's crackling voice warned that the plane was turning, banking to make the pass over the drop site. The pilot was a former jumper himself, and he knew the DC-3 better than he would a lover. Hell, for most of them, the plane and the fires she flew them to had to be better than a lover, because it was the rare woman who'd share her man with the fires season after season. Jack Donovan lived for the adrenaline rush and the adventure. And so did his team.

That team of eight jumpers was now sprawled out behind him. The seats of the plane were long gone, jettisoned to make room for the gear, so his boys had parked their asses on the floor in jump order. Ready to go just as soon as the pilot hit his sweet spot and the spotter signaled.

Protect and defend—that was the team's motto. Work hard, play harder. Fire always came first, but they'd steal a few hearts, love-'em-and-leave-'em in a heated blaze that was deliciously short-lived because they knew—and the women in their arms knew—that these were stolen moments. No, there was no time for even a summer romance, because you never knew when that call would come.

You accepted that there wasn't a happily-ever-after waiting at the end of your rainbow. The boys you jumped with were family, and that was more than good enough. The men Jack shared a plane with had become his brothers, and it didn't matter that they didn't share a lick of DNA among them. Family was about more than science.

The plane finished its turn, straightening out as the pilot brought her around. The roar of the engines competing with the dull roar of the flames was a familiar song. This was going to be a real bitch of a fire, and there was no stopping the hungry smile spreading across Jack's face. God, he loved his job.

So why had he agreed to put it on hold?

He should have refused to take the call, should have known she wasn't calling for a little hi-how-are-ya. But, no, he'd let the boys hand him the SAT phone back in base camp, and he'd listened to what she had to say when he should have been running as fast as he could.

"You have a minute for me, Jack?" Her familiar voice had crackled down the line.

He'd always had time for Nonna. Always would. Something primal and satisfied unfurled inside him when he heard that voice of hers. Yeah, hearing her voice made him happy. He'd made his peace with that years ago—treasured what they had. Outside family wasn't something every man on his team had, so he recognized his luck. And he'd answered her before considering his words. "I always do, Nonna."

Her little hum of appreciation was part of the ritual. "It's fire season up here in Strong, Jack," she'd said, as sparing with her words as ever. "We've got the station, of course, but Ben isn't sure we can handle it this time. Says the one truck may not be enough."

"Ben said that?" Her words had surprised him. Old bastard had never admitted to not being enough, and he had reason for his pride. Ben Cortez could have taught the hotshots on Jack's jump team a few tricks. A big, hearty man with shoulders worthy of an ox, Ben could out-bluff, out-talk any fire he went up against. Or so it had seemed to a ten-year-old boy with stars in his eyes. Hell, Jack would still fight fires with the man any day.

Ben had been his inspiration to start his own company after he'd left the military. He'd begun by jumping fires freelance, sign-

ing on with whatever crew needed an extra pair of hands. Now he and his brothers had their own company, running three or four teams each season. Good money, but it didn't come easy.

"He did. This isn't your usual summer."

There'd been a pause, and, again, he should have recognized the signs. He'd wished he could see her hands. When he'd been a young boy living in her house, he'd learned that Nonna's hands gave her away every time. Like him, she'd never been particularly good with words, but those hands had always told him the full story. Even though the harsh static of the SAT phone was hardly a visual, he'd known those hands were telegraphing him a message.

"And?" *he'd prompted finally, when the silence had stretched on long enough to become awkward.*

"And people here don't quite know what to do. They're talking about bringing in outside help, but Ben's reluctant."

"Stubborn old man." *Jack had laughed then, even though now he wanted to curse. That was the way he wanted to go out. Larger than life and cussing right up to the end. Just like Ben would.*

Nonna hadn't said anything—just made that small hum of agreement again. He'd have bet good money her index finger was tracing figure eights on her desk. Because she wasn't done with him yet. She was still leading up to what it was she wanted from him. "Ben might take help from you," *she'd pointed out.* "You come up here, lend a hand, he won't see it as outside help. You'll just be one of his boys, come home for the summer. It would make perfect sense for you to stop by, pitch in a little. Come home for the summer, Jack. We need you here."

He'd wanted to quip, "Call the fire department," *but this was his Nonna. You didn't ignore family, not when they stood there and put a hand out for help.* "I'm a smoke jumper, Nonna," *he'd pointed out, as gently as he could. Hoping against hope that she'd see the logic of his words and let him break the connection and go out on the next fire call with his life unchanged.* "I jump out of planes to fight my fires. Ben's place—that's a small-town fire-house with a single engine."

The town's fire department was local and all volunteer. Jack had spent summers himself on the vintage truck. Hell, he didn't even know if it was capable of getting up a stream anymore. Most they'd ever encountered was an oven fire or two, a backyard bar-becue that had hopped the hearth and torn through some zinnias. Those fires could be bad, but only if they got out of hand. And they hadn't. Boring as hell.

"Night and day," she'd agreed, "but he'll accept your help. He won't accept an outsider."

And for some inexplicable reason, she—and the other three thousand residents of Strong—would let a grumpy, sixty-year-old fire chief dictate their fire plan to them.

"I haven't been back to Strong in years, Nonna." Not since that last night he'd come too close to spending in Lily Cortez's arms. He'd run hard and fast, and he was running still. Lily Cortez was more dangerous than any fire he'd ever faced. He still saw those brown eyes of hers, accusing him, when he thought about that night too much. "You think he'll buy this coinci-dence?"

"Ben's not stupid—just stubborn. He won't ask questions. And it's time for you to come home, Jack," she'd said softly. "You've stayed away long enough."

He didn't want to go home and fight Nonna's fires. He could still see that sleepy mining town, and it didn't take a genius to know Strong wouldn't be much of an adventure. Strong got two, maybe three, good fires in a season. He'd wind up sitting out most of the summer, and sitting had never agreed with him.

Nonna knew that. Even as a boy, he'd always been on the move. Restless. Nonna claimed he was looking for something and wouldn't stop until he found it. Sometimes she'd added that he was looking for trouble. And that, he'd had no difficulty finding. When he'd run for good all those years ago, he'd run straight into the military, and enlisting had been good for him. It had knocked

honor and responsibility into a boy who was too damned smart—
and too much of a smart-ass—for his own good. Hell, he was still
an irreverent bastard, but now he knew who and what he stood
for. What was worth defending. Protecting.

"We've already had a series of small fires, a bad start to fire
season."

He hadn't like her word choice. " 'Series,' Nonna?"

She'd hesitated, but she hadn't taken it back. "Yes. I think so.
And I think Ben believes so, as well. The grass fires were first."

"Grass fires are pretty par for the course," he'd said cautiously.

"True." He could almost see her purse her lips as she mentally
ran through his logic. "And that's what we all thought. At first.
Then there was the mailbox. A trash bin in back of Blue Lou's
Diner."

"Sounds like you have a couple of kids on your hands," he'd
said indulgently. Someone still needed to kick their collective
asses, but it didn't have to be him. Even the most harmless of fires
could burn out of control when fire season got well under way in
California and the rains were a distant memory. He figured she
hadn't bothered him with the oven fires and false alarms.

"Maybe," she said slowly. "Maybe not. Ben says he found ac-
celerants. Maybe some of these were accidents or kids' mischief,
but not all of them. Come on home, Jack," she'd finished. "I
think we're going to need you this summer."

"You talk to Evan and Rio about this?" If he came home, his
brothers would come, too.

"No," she said. "I wanted to talk to you first, Jack."

"I'll make some calls," he said grudgingly. He couldn't be gra-
cious, not about this, but Nonna had always been a smart
woman. She didn't call him on his lack of manners. This time.
"I've got three days left on my contract here, and then I'll pull a
team together. We'll come up and park it in Strong for the summer. But just for the summer, Nonna," he warned.

He couldn't go home, not for good.

★ ★ ★

He'd do it. Grudgingly. Not graciously. He wasn't walking away from Nonna, and that meant he couldn't walk away from Strong. He didn't know how he'd get through the fire season or make sure he and his guys all had what they needed. He was a jumper, not a long-term planner. But somehow he'd figure it out. Town needed someone else there 24/7 in the winter months, too. For all the oven fires and home-wiring jobs gone bad. Ben was getting on; he wouldn't be able to manage single-handedly forever. He'd make some calls, put out some feelers, he decided. Somewhere there was a man who was right for the job. But he and his boys, well, they'd be riding out of town at the end of the summer, like they always did.

There was no changing who or what they were.

The plane banked and came back around, the vibrations making the floor shudder beneath his steel-toed boots. The spotter bawled an update, but the engine's roar drowned the man out. Didn't matter. Jack knew precisely what he needed to do. Fire was clear as day from fifteen hundred feet, a Dante-esque patchwork quilt with the jump spot a small bare circle in the very heart of the flames.

Worked for him.

When the spotter's hand smacked his shoulder in the familiar signal, he went out the door, launching himself into the whistling air and driving down toward the ground as he fell away from the plane. The drag chute snapped behind him, jerking him back and up as his ass cleared the wings, the wind tearing at his lungs and eyes. Adrenaline pumping made a man feel so goddamned alive, you forgot there was nothing but a handful of nylon and chute between you and the ground. Head up, feet down, he started the count.

Jump thousand.

Look thousand. The jump site spun up to meet him as he

came down, cataloging the fire's perimeter. So he'd go back to Strong. Do the same thing there as he was doing now. Jump in feetfirst when the call came in.

Protect.

Defend.

The ground rushed toward him. The roar of the plane's twin engines was drowned now by the fire's greedy voice as it devoured acres of prime woodland. *Reach thousand.* Five hundred feet above the ground, he groped and found the rip cord. A man got just one chance.

Wait thousand. Above him, other jumpers whooped as they jumped free of the plane's cabin and plummeted toward the waiting fire.

Four hundred feet. *Pull thousand.* The chute opened, right on schedule, and he pulled hard on the toggles, aiming for the fluttering scraps of the markers. Laughter ripped from his throat as the canopy jerked hard above him, catching the fire's updraft. God, it was a good day. A good jump.

Check your canopy. When he made the mandatory glance up, he spotted his boys coming down hard on his heels. Steering fast around the tall, summer-dry ponderosas, he hit the ground hard and run-rolled, pulling in the chute and shucking the harness as he came up. The powerful heat of the fire hit his face. Whooping, he turned to high-five the next jumper.

"Let's catch us a fire, boys."

Chapter Two

Betsey wasn't any happier taking this particular stretch of highway than Jack was. The old Ford whined as he pushed her up the nearly deserted stretch of highway, but she didn't quit. Maybe he should have bought a new pickup when his fire company had first made it into the black four years ago, but he hadn't. *Sentimental,* his brothers had accused. *Practical,* he'd countered. Truck still ran and got him where he needed to go.

If he wanted fast and sexy, he had a trio of Harleys in the garage of his Northern California base. But he'd brought the truck with him when he'd struck out from Strong ten years ago, so maybe Rio was an insightful bastard and the truck's bed was hauling a shitload of small-town baggage and memories he'd done his best to jettison along the road. Every time he slid into the cab, he came face-to-face with who he was and what he'd come from. Work hard, and the rest would come to you. Hell, he could practically hear Ben Cortez preaching that line. There were no shortcuts in life, and the truck reminded him of that, no doubt about it. As a smart-lipped teenager, he hadn't appreciated the sentiment. As a man and a former Marine, he believed in those words wholeheartedly.

The road curved, and he let the truck follow the bend, hugging the guardrail. At least he wouldn't be alone in his misery. He'd pulled in both his brothers from the other job site they'd been working. Their company could take the financial hit, no problem, but Evan liked his cushion. The kind of fire crew Jack wanted wouldn't come cheap, either—ex-military, all of them. Strong was going to be safer than Fort Knox.

"We'll both come, Jack," Rio had laughed, his brother's mischief carrying clearly even over a bad cell phone connection. Imagining the devilish smile creasing Rio's face had been all too easy. "The fire here is under control, so we can come on back. You'd better hope Nonna knows what she's asking for," he'd warned before signing off.

Nonna knew, all right. That was what worried Jack. She didn't just live *in* Strong—she lived *for* the damned town.

Just like she'd lived for them all those years.

Boys, she'd told him once—early on, when they were all still learning how to live with one another, and there were more bumps in the road than smooth patches—were more like puppies and kittens than the town's mothers let on. You could never have too many, and, after one look into their eyes, she'd been lost. A sucker for all that love flooding back at her, with the desperate plea of *Keep me*. She'd kept Jack. And then she'd kept Rio and Evan. She'd made them promises, and she'd kept every one.

He never knew why she hadn't married, hadn't borne babies of her own, but somehow he and his brothers had been enough for her. Together, they were a family, and he wasn't stupid. He knew what that was worth—and so, here he was, taking his truck up a highway that hadn't been re-paved since he was a boy. She wanted him to put out fires; he'd put out fires. Whatever his Nonna wanted, he'd give it to her. He could leave again at the end of fire season, when the summer was over.

So far, the weather report this summer was your standard-issue hot and dry. Solution could still be as straightforward as getting the word out about basic fire prevention and praying like hell that the storm cells stayed far away from Strong.

A man could always hope.

Town came out of nowhere, just like it always did. One minute, there was nothing but the ribbon of highway shimmering in the California heat. Next moment, familiar signs flashed past, advertising pick-your-own fruit and fresh cherries. His old truck whined harder, the engine complaining about the hot, dry climb up into the foothills of the mountains, but he was almost there. If he pulled over now, he might give in to the urge to turn around. Truck didn't want to be here, out in the middle of nowhere, and neither did he.

The only company he had on this hot, dry stretch of road was a pickup cooling down beside a big sign, tailgate dropped and flats of fresh-from-the-field berries ready for sale. Blink, and you'd miss it.

The past rushed up to meet him as if he'd never left.

Strong's founders had parked the town right on top of a pack trail that had eventually become State Route 49, as if the original townspeople had worried life might just pass them by if they weren't careful. Pulling his truck off the highway, he let the vehicle crunch slowly onto the gravel shoulder in front of the fire station. Just maybe, they'd been right to worry. Everything looked the same. Historic Main Street ambled lazily along both sides of the highway, the clapboard stores painted a cheerful rainbow of pastels. A wide-plank sidewalk sported barrels of red geraniums and white daisies. Hell, he half expected to see chickens scratching or a sheriff's posse saddling up, but there were just a handful of signs advertising a half-off sale at the antiques store and Blue Lou's special of the day.

Christ. It was even worse than he remembered. The new fire station was a simple, two-garage building stand-

ing in for the run-down historic wreck the town had finally abandoned a few years ago and put up for sale. Black-
and-yellow black-eyed Susan crawled straight on up the
side of a seldom-used front door. He'd always known he'd
been made for adventure and not for cottage-cozy in a
small town, no matter how pretty. There was plenty of
pretty in Strong, and it made his feet itch.

When he swung down from the truck's cab, they were
waiting for him. His Nonna and her Ben. Her shoulder-
length hair was tucked into its usual loop, although more
gray streaked it now. He'd never figured out how she anchored the twist, but the hair obeyed. He'd never known
how she got all her boys to listen, either, because she
wasn't a screamer, and she never so much as hollered at
them. She was blunter than hell, but he'd never mistaken
that wry little twist of her mouth for anything but her loving acceptance of life and the boys that life had placed in
her path.

She smiled when he headed toward her, holding out her
arms so he could swing her up and around in a bear hug.

Ben, on the other hand, didn't look anywhere near as
welcoming. Which figured.

The fire chief was the old dog here, and damned if he
wasn't set in his ways.

"Nonna rope you in, boy?" Ben Cortez didn't look as
if he was buying whatever story Nonna had spun about
her boys paying her a little summertime visit. No, he
looked pissed as hell with a side of frustrated. Nonna could
do that to a man, though. Wrap him around her finger
without ever realizing she'd done it. She'd had old Ben
dancing to her tune for years.

"Can't a man come home for a few weeks?" He
slammed the door of the truck behind him. Nonna just
shook her head, but she'd gotten the message.

"Sure," Ben drawled, "but other men might be wondering why it took ten years for him to drag his sorry ass on back."

"Ben . . ." Nonna's voice was pure warning, and Ben threw up a hand. "Apologies." The older man grunted the word as if it hurt.

"No problem." Jack couldn't blame the man for feeling put out that Nonna had gotten around both of them. Again. Problem was, when a man loved a woman, he didn't want to hurt her feelings. "I'm here now. You going to turn away a helping hand?"

"I'm not that stupid," Ben muttered. "Even if some folks might think so." He shook his head. "Come on in, then, and take a look at what we got."

"Let the boy settle in first," Nonna protested. "He just got here, Ben. He doesn't need to fight fires this afternoon, does he?"

"Maybe not." Ben stumped up the stairs to the firehouse porch, the old wood protesting each step. "But, since it's what he came for, he might as well see what he's gotten into. Unless you warned him already?"

Jack shot Nonna a glance, but she was just following Ben up the steps and into the firehouse, for all the world as if she belonged there. And damned if she didn't. If it came down to it, if the town needed her, she'd board Ben's truck and ride out with the boys. Underestimating Nonna was pure mistake. He'd learned that—more than once—as a boy.

The command center was just a bulletin board with a map of the town and its environs held up with three thumbtacks. The bottom corner had escaped its pin, curling up. Low-tech. Jack didn't have a problem with low-tech, but what he was seeing was impossible. Recent fires had been flagged with pieces of colored tape and ringed with black Sharpie, drawing a clear pattern. An unnatural pattern that shouldn't have been there.

"Yeah." Ben watched him. "That's the problem I'm seeing, son. Little fires, lots of them. Maybe they're coincidence, but it's early in the season, and we're already at last year's max, with months to go yet."

"What's this?" Jack stabbed a finger down on the blank spot at the center of the fire marks.

"Farm." Ben hesitated. "Lavender Creek. Lots of little fires around there."

"The old Stillerson place?" The Stillersons had farmed that land for years, but the old man had to be close on seventy now, and farming was damned hard work.

"Not anymore." Ben threw in another one of those little pauses that meant the man was thinking hard and Jack wasn't going to like the topic any, but he finally continued. "Stillerson sold out about a year back. Packed up and took himself down to Florida. We all worried the developers would swoop in and start building, but the farm sold as-is. She came out here a few months ago to run it herself."

"She?"

"My niece. Lily." Ben's steady gaze didn't let up. *Hell.* Jack had forgotten the lack of privacy in a small town. Ben—and everyone else—knew *precisely* what he and Lily Cortez had gotten up to in the Stillersons' lavender fields. "She went down to San Francisco for a while. Did some marketing work there. Now she's come back. That a problem?"

"No," he said, focusing all his attention on the map and the message it was screaming. Most of the fires were centered around that lavender farm. "No problem at all." Lily Cortez back in town—now he knew this was a bad idea. He and Lily Cortez had history. A history that made a California wildfire look tame.

"You sleeping at the house?" Nonna asked quietly when Jack finally left the firehouse. He'd read through the fire reports and asked some fine questions. Jack wasn't happy, not with her or the situation, but she knew her Jack. He'd do the right thing by them all, even if it was the last thing he wanted. Sometimes she regretted pushing him, and she figured she'd have more regrets before the summer was over. "Your room is still there, Jack. There's always a bed for you."

She'd made sure he'd always known that, but still, he hadn't returned. She hadn't wanted to push.

But now they needed him.

Something wasn't right here in Strong, and, whatever it was, she couldn't fix it for any of them. Not this time.

"I know that," he said, turning his head to smile at her, that familiar half grin tugging at his lips. For a moment, all she saw was the mischievous ten-year-old who had stolen her heart away. "But I'll still bunk down in the hangar, Nonna," he replied, referring to the town's old airstrip and its weather-beaten shelter.

Jack hated walls and always had. He'd claimed they closed in on him, and she'd never had the heart to push for the reason why. He'd been a ten-year-old foster child who was decades older inside and who insisted that his real family were the two other foster boys he'd come with. That trio of boys *had* been a family—and someone else, somewhere, hadn't been. She got that, and she'd respected the unspoken boundaries. Some things were off-limits, even for the mother she'd become.

So she never asked. She'd just brought them up, taught them well—but she'd never forced them to talk about what they'd left behind to come to Strong. *Like feral puppies,* she thought fondly. She'd coaxed and cajoled, put out one bowl of food after another and then sat by it, waiting to see what happened. . . . They could come to her or not. They'd all come.

"You'll stop by for meals, though," she ordered lightly.

"Yes, ma'am," he returned, falling into their familiar routine.

That familiarity was comforting, but she wondered if it would be enough. She needed something, she admitted, as Jack bent his head and bussed her cheek, his arm wrapping around to squeeze her before letting go. He'd gone and grown up on her, the years flying past in a blink, just like the other mothers had warned her they would. He was a man now, and while she wouldn't have traded who he'd become for another day lived in the past, still, sometimes she mourned the connection she'd lost. The little boy who would never be entirely hers again. She'd watched his face when Ben had talked about Lily Cortez, had seen the shadows in Jack's eyes.

Jack had unfinished business with Lily.

She didn't need to be a rocket scientist or a mind reader to know that he'd be paying the girl a visit before too long—perhaps even before the day was over—and then things would really start heating up. She might never see sixty again, but she still remembered those days in her own youth. What it felt like to not know which end was up, only that someone else was suddenly, unexpectedly the sun, moon, and stars in your life, whether you liked it or not.

Whether *she* liked it or not.

Maybe, before the summer was over, she'd lose him a little more, this time to Lily Cortez. That didn't have to be a bad thing, she reminded herself, watching him stride down her steps and get into that battered old pickup of his. She wouldn't be losing him. Just sharing him.

Sharing was good.

She wouldn't be lonely. She had her boys and her town. That should be enough for any woman, now, shouldn't it? Sometimes, though, when things got real quiet, she admitted the truth to herself. Waving to Ben, who was crossing the street toward her, she settled back in her chair. Somehow, over the years, it had become tradition for him to park himself on her porch in the late afternoon to share a drink and the day's gossip. Better than a girlfriend any day, Ben was, even if all they drank now was lemonade. She shook her head ruefully. Past sixty and wanting something, something different for herself, even though she didn't have the words to describe what was missing. This was a real good first step, though.

Whatever she imagined was missing, having her boys home and sitting on her front porch would help fill the hole.

Chapter Three

Jack Donovan had a date with his past. As he guided Betsey along the smooth curves of the long driveway, the two-story farmhouse came closer and closer, and his good intentions receded further and further. Hell if he knew what he was doing driving up here. Two days in Strong, and all his good intentions had gone up in smoke.

He'd recognized years ago that hands-off was the honorable approach when it came to Lily Cortez. She was someone special—and even his rebellious younger self had recognized that truth. She was the kind of woman who tempted a man to wrap his arms around her and hold on. At sixteen, she'd been peach sweet, all innocence and passion, and too damned young for the kind of thoughts he had whenever she brushed past him.

He'd left because leaving had been the right thing—the honorable thing—to do, and he wasn't bad to the bone. Not yet. He knew he was hard and experienced. He'd seen things, done things. Life on the streets of San Francisco hadn't been easy. Neither were three tours of duty in the military. He was older now.

And so was Lily.

He killed the engine, letting the truck coast to a gritty halt on the gravel surface of the driveway. No one was on the porch to meet him, which meant he was going to have to get out of the truck and haul his ass over there. Unfortunately, he wasn't half as reluctant as he should be. No, the problem was, he wanted to knock on that door, all right.

Smoke jumping was a dangerous thrill—and a damned serious job. Which was why he was here, he reminded himself, shoving open the door of the truck. The door shut behind him with a satisfying slam. He needed to warn the neighborhood. Wedged square on the California-Nevada border, the town of Strong was pure trouble in fire season. Ben had shown him the hot zones in the nearby wildlands. And this year, with a possible arsonist added into the mix, there was bound to be trouble. He'd put the team on jump alert. Plane could be up in the air in ten minutes.

The hand-painted sign announcing the farm's name—Lavender Creek—was beautiful, all painstakingly lettered, and it was going to burn faster than shit if the sign's owner didn't get her ass into gear and cut back the grass. The front porch wasn't much safer, a feminine spill of lavender and roses. Purple and rich, shocking pink, the silky petals scattered across the ground in a thick carpet, a boldly sensual statement teasing a man to reach out and slide a finger along the fragrant cups of color.

Pure tinder.

He assessed his surroundings with the practiced eye three tours of duty as a United States Marine had perfected. House might sit on a hilltop, but the land dropped away, covered in bone-dry waves of steel blue and green. Lavender. Acres and acres of lavender. At least the fire would smell good.

Worse, the house on top of a low hill sat with its back to the wildlands. To the north and west, fields surrounded the farmhouse and cut off access to the roads. Only way out in a hurry was down the main drive and out to the county road.

As he got out of the truck, the heat hit him hard. He hadn't felt heat like that since the last time he'd gone head-to-head with a wildfire. Maybe he could convince Lily Cortez to hit the swimming hole with him. Relive their high school days. Shucking the flannel shirt he'd pulled on in the cooler predawn hours, he tossed it onto the passenger seat through the open window and grabbed a handful of fire-prevention literature.

Yeah, right. She wasn't going to be happy to see him. He strode across the gravel and took the porch steps two at a time—the boards had warped and needed replacing—and banged on the door.

Through the closed door, he clearly caught the feminine curse on the other side as the door's owner wrestled with the knob. Heat or age or just general poor maintenance—he shot the porch a quick look—had the door sticking. She needed a handyman.

When she finally managed to shove it open, she kept on coming, sailing through the door frame and landing firmly in his arms. The day was looking up. She was even more beautiful than she had been all those years ago. Before, she'd been a pretty girl. Now she was all woman. Still on the short side but all soft curves and long, dark hair. She'd let her hair grow, a riotous mane that tumbled halfway down her back. Heat made little curls out of that hair, curls that clung to his fingers as he gripped her arms to steady her. Filling his arms full of Lily Cortez felt damned good.

"Thanks," she said, and then, "That's embarrassing." Her laugh made his dick hard, and she hadn't even looked up yet. Hadn't recognized him. She was still getting her balance.

"No problem," he said, and he set her on her feet. Those feet were delicate, sun-tanned, and he couldn't have stopped himself from sweeping his gaze up those long, bare legs if he'd wanted to. And he didn't. What he wanted was her.

Then she looked up, and her face froze.

"Oh, no," she said. Yeah. She remembered their kisses.

He remembered those eyes. Always watching. Watching him. Watching him as he horsed around with his brothers. The erotic thrill of those eyes wasn't something he figured he'd ever forget. What she'd made him want should be illegal. She'd driven him crazy with wanting to know what it would take to convince her to stop watching. To join him. He'd masturbated to that fantasy—and felt like an asshole. Because those eyes were both curious and innocent, and even then, before he'd done his tours in the military, he'd known that innocence made those eyes off-limits.

When he'd finally kissed her, that long, sweet, hot kiss after the drive home from the swimming hole, he'd pulled her slowly up against him, drinking in the heat and the scent of her, while he waited to make sure she was sure, that she didn't really want to pull away from him. He'd kissed her and kissed her, and she'd kissed him back, and he'd never managed to figure out what he'd done to encourage her. Or what it would take to convince her to kiss him again. Seeing her now brought all those old fantasies crashing back.

She dressed differently now, no longer hiding beneath her clothes. The snug tank top and cutoff denim shorts were clearly meant for comfort, but she filled them both out, too, and his fingers itched to touch, his mouth watering to taste all that sun-kissed skin. She'd taste every bit as good as she looked. Watching the sexy ease of her body slipping across the porch, he was sure of it.

Once upon a time, she'd looked at him as if he were her prince charming.

The soft slap of her bare feet on the worn wood of the porch filled up the silence, so he watched silently as she slid sun-browned feet into white flip-flops, her toes curling into the rubber. His erection pressed against his jeans, reminding him he had unfinished business with Lily. She was ignoring him, and that pissed him off. So he set out to get her attention.

This time, he wasn't going anywhere.

"All grown up," he drawled, settling his large frame against the low railing of her porch. Those brown eyes widened as she finally looked him in the eye, and he swore his dick got harder.

"Jack Donovan," she said finally, and, no, she didn't sound pleased to see him. He could kiss his fantasies good-bye.

"Why are you here?" She made it sound as if her front porch was off-limits, and that just put his back up. He'd learned a thing or two about holding his ground, and no way she was going to push away him now.

"It's fire season, and there have been a number of small incidents around your farm," he growled. "I need to give you some fire safety pointers." His social skills were rusty, but he expected her to make some polite noises. Ask a few questions. Hell, maybe he'd been expecting an invitation to share a lemonade—he didn't know, because, as always, she had him at sixes and sevens—but what he didn't expect was her reaction.

Her face paled, the sudden white a startling contrast with that golden suntan of hers. She was scared. Not of him, he was betting, because then she would have been backing toward the door. No, her eyes went straight over his shoulder, as if she expected to see a fire burning in the middle of her driveway.

"Where were the fires?" she said, and he wondered if she knew her nails were carving small pink crescents into her palms. He recognized the scent of fear and desperation. He'd seen it too many times when he'd had to confront a homeowner who wouldn't accept that nature had her own plans for that person's house and property and that there was nothing Jack Donovan could do to stave off the disaster.

He reached out and smoothed a hand against her cheek before he could stop himself. He was attracted as hell, and she was scared. That made him, he figured, a bastard of monumental proportions, because he couldn't decide between wrapping her up in his arms to comfort her and hauling her off to his bed to seduce her. He wanted her, but he would never, ever hurt her. They both knew that. So he'd find out what was wrong here, and then he'd fix it. Her skin felt so warm against his hand.

"Baby, what's wrong?"

Larger than life, Jack Donovan filled a space and sucked the air straight out of it. That hard body of his was a weapon and a warning. He'd hold his own with anything life threw at him. His short hair was plain practicality, he'd told her once. Any longer, and fire would just singe it off. Looking at him now, with his dark eyes and sun-tanned skin, she saw he hadn't changed. Not in any way that mattered. He was the sort of man who was always outside; no one could lock him up or pin him down.

She'd always been cautious. Practical. Even back when she'd been ready for a high school sweetheart, Jack Donovan had been a delicious treat—and completely off-limits. He hadn't been a forever kind of boy, and she'd known she didn't really want to pay that kind of price. Flirt with it, sure. But loving Jack would have cost too much.

He was a damned hero, and she needed him off her porch. Now.

She'd heard through the grapevine that he'd done a few tours with the Marines, then started a private firefighting company. Now he was the hired gun on the largest, most dangerous wildfires. He put his men up on planes and then followed them out the door, jumping into the thick of the smoke and the heat to wage war. He was pure trouble.

"Fire." She forced herself to step away from him, but she knew her stiff smile was a tell she couldn't afford. Jack had never been stupid, and the last thing she wanted right now was to draw attention to herself. "You drove out here to tell me there have been fires."

Surely he meant wildfires, and that meant she was still safe. Thank God. Summer wildfires weren't personal. Dangerous as hell, if they blazed out of control. But not personal. *He* hadn't found her.

Jack's dark eyes watched her retreat. God, she'd loved his eyes. Those eyes had made her feel like the center of the universe. "Yeah." He shook his head. "You know what I do, Lily. And it's fire season up here." He hesitated. "Donovan Brothers is filling in."

This summer was even drier than most. She watched the weather forecasts every night, tracking the elusive rainfall with spreadsheets and lists the hot California summers devoured. All the experts in the world couldn't coax a drop from those burning blue skies. She had to sit back and wait, hope and pray that the skies would eventually fill up and spill their bounty onto her fields. And that burning heat was only part of the trouble she had.

"You volunteered, you mean," she said, keeping her voice deliberately light. She knew what his team cost. No way this town could afford them, so he was here because he had a soft spot for his childhood home, after all. That soft spot shouldn't make her want to smile. They weren't children. Not anymore.

"You need to be careful, Lily." She didn't know whether he was talking about the upcoming fire season—or something else. Those eyes of his didn't move from her face. Uneasy, she tugged self-consciously at her shirt, and that made her angry. He was just a man. A childhood acquaintance all grown up. "Maybe think about leaving till things quiet down," he urged.

She took the pamphlets he held out to her, his fingers brushing hers. Before San Francisco, she might have considered seeing where the spark of attraction led. Now all she wanted to do was lie low. She'd come here for the safety and familiarity of Strong. In running home to her roots, she'd found something even better. What she could build here was special. When she finally made it into bed at night, she might still be alone, but she knew she'd found something she needed here. Peace. Space. Healing.

The farm was her life now. She'd emptied her 401K, quit her high-powered advertising job, and bought this. She hadn't known a damned thing about lavender. Hell, she hadn't known a damned thing about gardening. She hadn't been home enough to keep a potted plant alive. The farm was more than money—those fields were a future she'd literally built for herself. Each plant she set into the ground was a promise. No one was running her off.

Not again.

"You're sitting in the middle of a firetrap, Lily." He leaned back where he was sitting on her porch railing, folding his arms over his chest. As if he wasn't going anywhere, even if she hadn't had the decency to invite him inside.

"Thanks for the heads-up." She turned and walked inside, trying to ignore the man on her heels, and tossed the pamphlets onto the coffee table. "Consider me well warned."

He ignored her, of course. The Donovan brothers had always been stubborn. "You need to cut back your grass, for one thing."

She knew that, but her farm crew didn't really get started for a couple more weeks, and she'd been nervous about hiring anyone new to help. There was only so much she could do by herself. "You volunteering to cut my grass?"

"That canyon out there is dry." He came up directly behind her. She hated herself, but she froze. His hands settled on her shoulders, turning her toward the screen door. "Look out there, and tell me what you see."

Most of the farm was planted with thick, mature bushes of Grosso lavender. From where she stood, she had a clear view of the spike-laden plants marching north-south, the tidy rows of plants blurring into rich sweeps of purple. The green and violet flower buds were picture-perfect, curving up into the June sunshine. Dreamy. Otherworldly. The heated press of the sun against her skin and the thick blanket of scent drowned out all other sensations. Almost enough to drown out Jack. That was her farm. Her dreams. The contents of her 401K.

Her lips curved. "Wildfires have been happening all our lives, Jack. What makes this summer any different?"

Pointing to her beautiful lavender gardens, where they came right up to the house, he growled, "There shouldn't be so many fires this early in the season, and you've got a lot of fuel right there. Fire is going to jump from those bushes to here before you can blink. You've given it everything it needs. Food. Opportunity."

"You're not suggesting I lose my fields, are you? This is a business, Jack. Believe it or not, those gardens aren't there because I like picking flowers." She hated how her voice shook. He'd always managed to get under her skin. "Those plants represent an investment."

"It doesn't matter if you think you can make a living growing this stuff. Fire's going to go straight up that damned lavender and into the trees." He indicated the elm trees lining the edges of the field with a strong, tanned hand. "You've planted a damned ladder, Lily. Fire goes up and hops into the trees. From that point, there's nothing between the fire and the house. You're uphill, and that will make the spread even faster. You'll lose the place before you can finish dialing 9-1-1." His breath whispered against her ear. "I can't let that happen. Not on my watch."

"I bet you feel like you're doing me a favor." She eyed him. "I know what fire season is, Jack. I can take care of myself, and I'm not going anywhere. This is my home." *Now.*

"You're not staying here if it's not safe." His voice was implacable.

"I'm not going anywhere. Back off, Jack."

He moved fast, backing her into the screen door so quickly, she didn't have a chance to protest. Part of her wondered if she would have. Trapped between his hard arms and the door, she gave in to her curiosity. Resting her head against screen, she stared up at him.

"You go when I say you go," he growled. "That's how it works, Lily."

"No, it doesn't."

He shot her a look that dared her to disagree again. So she did. Arguing with him made her feel stronger. Better. "Let's see, Jack. This is my property. My house. Oh, and my life." She ticked her points off on her fingers, watching his eyes flare with emotion.

He slid forward, deliberately crowding her. One powerful forearm came up, braced over her head. The other closed around her fingers. "I'm not letting you stay in harm's way, baby."

Raising her fingers to his mouth, he pressed a small kiss

against her palm. Folded her fingers over the palm of her hand. "Don't push me on this one. You need to stay safe."

He'd been tender-strong that night ten years ago, too.

"Thanks for the ride." She'd been nervous about accepting a ride from him—everyone talked about how wild those Donovan brothers were—but she hadn't wanted to walk home in the dark from the swimming hole, either. He'd been the answer to a prayer she hadn't known she'd uttered.

"No problem." He was already sliding out of the driver's seat, coming around to open the door for her. No one had warned her Jack Donovan could be a gentleman.

After he helped her out of the truck's cab, he hesitated. Tipped his head down toward hers.

He was four years older than she, already in college. He'd come back this summer to work in the local firehouse, and the town had had a field day with his return. He was taller, stronger. Darker. Already, he'd seen things no one here ever would, and he was growing away from them.

"Christ," he whispered, and he lowered his head toward her. "I shouldn't do this."

"We shouldn't do this," she argued, because she was here, too. Jack Donovan wasn't happening to her—they were doing this. Together. And, God, she wanted him to kiss her. She'd dreamed about it for years, and somehow she knew that this would be the only chance she got.

So she slid a hand up his shoulder, wrapped her fingers around his neck, and tugged his head down toward her. His dark hair, freshly cut, was deliciously soft beneath her exploring fingertips.

"Kiss me, Jack," she said, and he did. Kissed her with all the expertise and gentleness he had. Slow, hot kisses that had her insides melting and her body wrapping itself around him.

Then he was setting her away from him, watching her with those devil's eyes of his. "I can't stay, Lilybell, not even for you."

★ ★ ★

That had been their first—and only—night of kisses. He hadn't pushed her for more than she'd wanted to give that night, but they'd both known he was miles out of her league. He'd spent a hell of a lot of time embracing life in the back of that pickup truck he worshipped, and she— well, she'd been a shy, introverted girl who'd been handed a shot at living out a fantasy. She'd taken it—and then she'd moved on. She'd lived her life the way she was supposed to live it. Going to college, getting herself a job. Except that, instead of happily-ever-after with a nine-to-five and a man she loved, she'd found herself trapped in a nightmare.

Because someone had decided to watch her. Stalk her.

And then to set fires all around her.

She didn't know how long her stalker had watched before he'd set the first fire, but she did know he'd burned the life right out of her. Six months of that, and she'd run home.

"You tell me what's wrong, and I'll fix it." That strong, capable hand cupped her jaw, and she fought the urge to melt into his touch. He wouldn't stick around, and she couldn't afford the pain. Not again. "Just tell me, baby."

"There's nothing to tell, Jack." She didn't want him mixed up in her business. Didn't want him mixed up in this. He was too large, too dominant. He was a man who *took* what he wanted, and she wasn't strong enough for that right now. The man who'd stalked her had done a number on her. She knew that. Knew she needed to retreat and lick her wounds a little before she rejoined the rest of the world.

Jack Donovan wouldn't ever allow her to retreat.

Once she let him in, he wouldn't let her back away from the sensual heat that was burning up the too-small space between them. So she'd keep him out, despite all those fantasies she'd stored up over the years.

"I can take care of myself." Stepping away from the warmth of that hand was one of the hardest things she'd ever done, but she did it. "You need to go, Jack. There's nothing here that needs your fixing."

Reaching behind her, she fumbled for the latch on the screen door. Pushed it open a little more forcefully than necessary.

The expression on her face must have been warning enough, because Jack just nodded curtly, stepping past her. "I'll be keeping an eye on you, Lily," he growled. "Whatever's going on here, you're going to tell me all about it, sooner or later."

Ten years had only increased his arrogance. "Dream on," she said sweetly, and she slammed the door behind him.

Lying on his stomach, he watched from the cover of the trees as Jack Donovan drove away in a cloud of angry dust, the big truck's tires spitting gravel as the driver took out his frustrations on the gas pedal. His Lily thought she'd been so smart, pulling up stakes and moving here. Across the state and tucked away in a small town. It had taken him several months to track her down, to realize she'd finally run home, but he'd always known it was only a matter of time before he found her again.

She'd rejected his advances.

Deliberately, he'd made the first fires small.

Fires she could dismiss as coincidence. A small grass fire near the beach where she sometimes ran. A car fire on her street. Nothing too personal. Nothing too close. Then he'd made it personal. A fire in the carport of her San Francisco town house, hot enough and *close* enough to singe the paint job on her new car. Then the tiny bonfire in her kitchen. He'd made that fire too close, too carelessly. She'd seen him at the scene, and she'd bolted. Run. It had taken him months to find her again.

Running was unacceptable.

She belonged to him, and it was time she accepted that truth.

He'd given her some time to get used to the idea, because he knew his Lily was a shy girl. A good girl. He hadn't expected her to fall straight into his arms, but her time was up.

Fear always worked. His little Lily needed to learn who was in charge here. Her body had accepted it with her first fear-laced rush of adrenaline.

He inched forward on his stomach, the dry grass prickling against his skin.

His father—before his grandfather had finally admitted that there was a problem and had taken care of business— had taught him how to hunt a woman. How to claim her.

As a child, he'd discovered that setting fires released his tension. Of course, the fires got larger and larger as he grew up, but he blamed that on his grandfather. Bastard had impossibly high standards. On the day he'd finally been accepted into Harvard, he'd set his first wildland fire.

Sliding one hand into his fatigues, he let his fingers stroke the matchbook in his pocket, a touch that shot straight to his cock.

His other hand brought the binoculars to his eyes. Watching his Lily storm through her house was satisfying. Her visitor had pissed her off. Good. He wouldn't tolerate competition for her.

Fortunately, the smoke jumper would be easy enough to take care of. After all, he'd already started a few small wild-fires. Given the weather and the bone-dry vegetation, starting a larger one would be simple. And once the fire started, everyone knew accidents could happen. Maybe the smoke jumper wouldn't come home. Maybe he'd land poorly or end up overrun by flames. He figured he could make any one of those things happen.

Plus, he always felt better after each fire. His emotions cooled off, like he was slipping into the pool on a hot summer day. Too bad the calm never lasted. Within weeks or even days, he was agitated again. Ready to burn something else. He knew he couldn't give in to the need too often; one clever cluster analysis, and law enforcement would finally spot the pattern. He'd been careful, but he knew the odds.

Lily was worth the risk, however, even if she hadn't appreciated his love notes. He'd been careful before, but now it was time to step up his game. To prove how much she meant to him. Opening the plastic bookstore bag, he let the colorful novel tumble out. The title itself didn't matter, only that he'd seen Lily purchase it—and then read it. She'd bought a copy for herself, so he'd bought one, too. And brought it here.

The book fit nicely into the little ring of stones he'd assembled. He'd burn the book—just part of the book—and then he'd leave it where she'd find it. She'd know he was thinking of her.

Watching her.

Next time, he'd take something from her house.

Pulling out the matchbook, he struck a match and dropped it onto the book. This time, the flames wouldn't jump the pretty little cage he'd built for them, but she would get his message.

He was back.

Chapter Four

Airplane hangars were more home than home to Jack. Hell, the Donovan brothers spent enough time in the air to have qualified for frequent-flyer status on a dozen airlines, so hanging at the hangar waiting for the next fire call was second nature.

Right now, the hangar on the outskirts of Strong was full of Jack's team and equipment. When Jack had pulled up outside, he'd spotted the chopper they used for recon and the DC-3 they used for drops. Ninety-five-foot wingspan, and he'd rebuilt her by hand, picking parts with as much care as he'd picked his lovers. His baby could fly.

His brothers looked up as he killed the engine and parked his truck and got out. His brothers were sprawled on the piles of gear and old chutes stored in one corner of the hangar. Fireman's furniture, but it did just fine. Inside, it was pleasantly cool even with the sun baking down on the roof. The lazy swish of the overhead fans stirred up the air some. When he inhaled, he got grease and rubber with a side of fire retardant. Familiar smells. Familiar territory. For the past five years, the three of them had run a private fire management company, contracting out—government, private. They often headed up separate teams, traveling where they were needed, hiring out to whoever had the money to pay for their services. Which didn't come cheap.

They were the best, because they did more than hold their lines. They beat back those fires, jumping into holes too small for other jump teams.

Rio had dragged in a cooler filled with beer, and now they were kicking back, popping a cold one after going through the day's recon reports. Chopper hadn't spotted any local hot spots today, so they were still in the clear. But when fire season picked up—and it always did—they'd be ready.

Dropping down next to Evan, Jack grabbed a can, popping the top. Rio looked like a golden-skinned playboy lounging on the dusty canvas, but, God knew, he was the cuckoo in the nest. On the surface, he was all play and easygoing camaraderie, but underneath he had a mind like a damned computer. Saw the world differently, their Rio did.

Still, the differences didn't matter. They were all together again, the way they belonged. They'd grown up together in this small town, and more than one eyebrow had been raised at the Donovan brothers' unrelenting pursuit of mayhem and girls. They'd done everything together, sharing stories and cold beers and women in the back of Jack's beat-up pickup. Some things never changed. The beer was still cold, and he still had the damned truck.

"You went up to Lily Cortez's place today." Evan didn't talk much, but he was a big-ass, dark bastard. Like Jack, he had no idea who his father had been. He was a scary-looking, too-large male others crossed the street to avoid, even here in their own small town where folks should have known better. Particularly since, on the inside, Evan was a damned marshmallow—not that Evan would have admitted it. He'd seen too much shit before Nonna had gotten her hands on him, and now he didn't let anyone close.

Still, Evan was turning his head, looking Jack over, so he didn't have too many choices. Because, unfortunately, he was starting to suspect that his feelings were written across his face.

Jack shrugged, deliberately casual. "Yeah. Someone had to. I didn't hear any volunteers when we read through the outreach list this morning."

Evan cursed. "Was Lily home?"

Jack considered his options, but he'd never held anything back from his brothers. Not since the day they'd arrived on Nonna's doorstep, three mismatched boys from a foster care system that didn't give a damn what became of them.

"She was."

Rio hooted. "I bet she showed your ass to the door."

"Maybe," he drawled, lifting his can to acknowledge the derisive snickers.

"Thought you had a history there, Jack." The good-natured ribbing was familiar, second nature to them. "Or she's remembering it differently from you."

"She just knows what comes with the job," Evan pointed out in his deep rumble. "We can't any of us stick around."

True enough that you never knew when the next call was coming. Women didn't like that uncertainty, and girlfriends and wives liked it even less, knowing their men were jumping ass-first out of a plane, fifteen hundred feet over a raging wildland fire. So most of the women left first, before the heartbreak and the uncertainty could do a number on them. They *knew* that happily-ever-after didn't wait at the end of that rainbow.

"She was frightened." He ran a hand over his hair, thinking things through. "She was spooked by something, and it wasn't wildfires."

"She glad to see you?" Evan drawled.

"Maybe." Taking another draw of his beer, Jack mentally replayed their meeting. "She still showed my ass to the door."

Rio leaned forward. "I'd heard she'd moved back here. Gave up an advertising job in San Francisco, packed up her car, and headed home."

Rio "heard things" the way the rest of them breathed. He was a living river of information, and what he didn't know or couldn't find out wasn't worth knowing.

"Yeah, Ben filled me in. Would have been nice if you'd told me first."

Rio grunted, dragging the laptop toward him. His fingers were already flying over the keys. "You didn't tell me you wanted to know, Jack. I'm not a mind reader."

No, just the best damned source of intel Jack knew. He wondered sometimes if Rio really had gone to M.I.T. while he and Evan did their tours of duty, but there were some things you didn't ask, because Rio would have told them if he could.

Evan nodded slowly. "There was gossip when she moved back. Town thinks there was a man, something gone south with her job." He shrugged. "She ran home, Jack."

"Left behind a good job." It wasn't a question. He knew his Lilybell. She didn't do things by half measures, and she always got what she went after. If she'd wanted advertising, she'd have been the best damn account exec in the city.

Evan shrugged. "Probably had herself a whole life out there. Boyfriend, maybe. I remember she used to be real pretty."

She still was. Something more than pretty. Looking at her, holding her in his arms, he'd known he'd regret walking away from Lily Cortez. San Francisco was a dog-eat-dog world, but Lily had never been the kind of girl who ran home with her tail tucked between her legs. Whatever had sent her running, he figured it was bad.

While Rio worked his magic, Jack settled in to make a few phone calls. Set the ball rolling. Maybe he should have waited for her to confide in him, but his gut screamed she didn't have that kind of time. Even if the problem was no big deal, it was eating her alive from the inside out. Tapping his fingers on the cell, he snapped it shut. He really didn't want to think about why it mattered to him, but damned if she wasn't still under his skin.

When he finished, Rio was still bent over the keyboard, fingers flying across the keys. "Got something here," he said tersely. Rio had his back, like always. You could count on Rio.

"Shitload of fire reports. Lily spent a whole lot of time phoning in fires that just seemed to pop up around her." Grabbing his beer, Rio finished it and crumpled the can, lobbing it toward the basket on the other side of the hangar. "Unless Lily was damned careless with matches, she was a fucking magnet for fire. Things burned around her."

"She was never careless." Jack figured they were on to something here. A weight lifted in his chest.

"No." Rio was silent for a moment, connecting the dots. "Got a fire log, too. Series of small fires where she lived. Trash can. Debris. Carport. Kitchen fire. That kind of stuff. Small potatoes."

"Damage?"

"Minimal. To her things, at least."

Rio wasn't telling him something. "But there's a pattern to the calls," Rio continued. "And in the last report, she floated the idea to the investigator that she was a target. Those are too many fires to be a coincidence, Jack."

"And?"

"And she wondered out loud to the investigator if she could have a stalker."

"Did she suggest any names when she decided to kick this theory around?" He wanted to howl, wanted to hurt something.

Rio scrolled through the pages. "Not that I can see. Doesn't help any that the fire investigator wasn't in a particularly credulous mood when she made that suggestion. Investigator noted that Lily was likely either a firebug or paranoid."

Someone had stalked her. Terrorized her. "I want information, Rio."

"Working on it."

"What kind of man stalks a woman and sets fires?"

"What makes you so sure the stalker is male?" Evan grunted.

Rio looked up. "Eyewitness reports seeing a male in the vicinity of the last two fires. They didn't get a good look at him but were sure it was a guy."

Whoever he was, he'd set his last fire. Jack was going to hunt him down and make damned sure of that. "Lily didn't have any idea who was after her?"

Rio shook his head, turning the laptop around so Jack could read the report for himself. "If she did, she didn't share. She could have been protecting someone, but I think he scared her, Jack. Bad. Those fires were personal, and she knew it."

"Attention." His voice was rough with anger and a primitive possessiveness he hadn't known he was capable of. "He was demanding her attention. Burned her things and forced his way into her life."

"A disgruntled lover?" Rio suggested.

That didn't feel right. "Not that kind of personal. Maybe he wanted to be her lover, or he was in love with the idea of her. He had to have watched her."

"Down, boy." Rio shot Jack a look. "Nothing you can do."

The unspoken *yet* hung in the air between them. They all knew Jack would take care of this.

He stared at his brothers, making up his mind. He'd watch Lily. Keep her safe. Fire season gave him the perfect excuse. She was alone up there, and that farm was one damned fuel pile, just waiting for the right spark to go up.

Standing up, he said it, just to be clear. "We look out for her."

No one disagreed with him. Hell, their Nonna hadn't raised them to ignore a problem. She'd taught them to defend.

"She's not going to like that, Jack," Evan pointed out. Stacking his arms behind his head, he watched Jack.

"What she wants doesn't matter. This is about keeping her safe."

He tossed his crumpled beer can into the trash. On his way to the door, he made a pit stop at the locked gun cabinet to make a withdrawal. Hell, he wasn't planning on shooting anyone, but no way was he leaving Lily unprotected. If it came down to it, he'd do whatever it took. Fortunately, he was licensed to carry concealed in California.

"You got a hot date?" Evan's eyes tracked him across the hangar.

"I'm not leaving her alone." *Unprotected.*

"So you're planning to stand watch on her front porch?" Rio drawled. "She's not going to put up with that, Jack. What you described—that wasn't an open invitation to return at any time. What makes you think she's going to want ex-military packing on that porch of hers?"

"I'm staying with her," he said, ignoring his brother's smirk. Hell, he'd planned on giving her a wide berth. Leaving her alone because things were too incendiary when they were together. Rio's information changed everything, however.

Lily's stalker wouldn't give up, not easily. Jack's gut was screaming a warning, and he'd learned not to ignore those signals. That stalker had gone to a hell of a lot of trouble to terrorize a woman. And Jack had seen that flash of fear in Lily's eyes. Sooner or later, she was expecting company. She believed her stalker would find her.

What Jack had to do was clear. When her stalker returned, Jack Donovan planned to be waiting for him.

Chapter Five

Lily Cortez should have known Jack wouldn't give up that easily. He was too damned stubborn. The truth was, she needed a rescuer, even if she wouldn't admit it.

"You didn't tell me what was going on, Lilybell." He knew his eyes were all over her as he climbed out of the truck. She shouldn't have been watching, but damned if she wasn't staring at his legs as he swung out of the truck's cab. He smoothed a hand down the well-worn denim, and her eyes followed. Maybe there was hope for him after all. "You left San Francisco because you had a stalker."

She licked those lush lips of hers, almost visibly reminding herself that this was her place and he was the intruder. "We're nothing to each other, Jack," she pointed out. "Not family. You're not part of my life. It was—and is—none of your damned business."

She was so wrong. Shaking his head, he stalked over the gravel toward her. "Now, that's where you're wrong, Lilybell. We've always been something to each other. And someone needs to keep an eye out for you."

Growing up, Strong hadn't been an unhappy place for Jack, but he'd fought the town's pull tooth and nail. Fought for the chance to run and be free. Small-town living wasn't always easy—everyone knew who you were. Where you came from. Where your roots were. You couldn't walk away from your mistakes—just faced them in the mirror morning after morning. He'd never liked being closed in. That last summer, before he'd enlisted, he'd wake up, sure he was suffocating. He wouldn't have come back now, but there were things in this world worth paying the price for. His Nonna was one.

Looked like Lily might be another woman he'd be willing to pay the price for.

"You're not that someone."

"How come you didn't move back in with your uncle?"

The sudden change of subject clearly threw her, because she just blinked at him for a long minute. "He has a life of his own, Jack. And I'm a grown woman."

Regret flashed in her eyes for a brief moment, and then she lifted her chin.

"But you still came home," he drawled. "To Strong. I figure that makes you my business."

"You're the chief of police now?" she guessed sweetly. "Or the town mayor? In addition to single-handedly managing all our fire prevention efforts? Nice try, Jack, but you can march your arrogance straight down my drive and leave."

He shook his head slowly, watching her. "I'm in charge of fire operations here, baby. I have signed orders giving me absolute authority in case of a life-or-death emergency."

She made a show of looking left, then right, before glaring at him. "I don't see any fire, Jack."

He strode toward her, his boots eating up the distance between them as if it was nothing. The pretty pink flush crawling up her cheeks drew him like a fish on a line. She had him hooked and didn't even realize it. There was just one question: Was he going to fight it or let her reel him in? "I'm seeing a life-or-death emergency, though, Lily.

All these fires happening right around you has made it pretty damned clear that someone means business."

She opened her mouth. Closed it. She was pissed, and that pleased him. *There* was the life he'd searched for before. Her anger pushed the fear right out of her eyes. Of course, she was pissed as hell at *him,* but it was all for a good cause.

He was definitely hooked, he decided.

He'd insist she keep him. After all, this was about what she wanted, too. She'd tell him the truth, one way or another. Fortunately, his Lilybell was all grown up now—deliciously so—and prying her secrets free one kiss at a time was fair game. Apparently he'd left his good intentions behind when he'd returned to Strong.

"If you're staying put here, I'm moving in," he stated.

"Jack—" she warned. "I'm not in the mood for your games."

"I'm serious." He wasn't playing games, not about this. Sure, he was looking forward to playing with her—in bed. Out of bed, however, was another story. His priority was keeping her safe. No matter what it took. "You won't even know I'm here." He was already reaching into the back of his pickup, grabbing a large duffel bag.

Arrogant bastard really did think he could move in with her just on his say-so.

Part of her wished she could let him.

The rest of her—the part of her that wasn't drowning in a sea of hormones—knew that letting Jack Donovan through her door would be a big mistake.

She'd always been cautious. Practical. Jack Donovan had been a delicious treat—and completely off-limits. That way why she'd forced herself to keep him at arm's length. Back in high school and now, too.

Her farm, on the other hand, had been a leap of faith she hadn't known she had in her. Driving up that driveway the first time, she'd known she was finally coming home. The girl who'd been dumped on her uncle's doorstep by her own mother had finally found a place where she belonged. Lavender Creek was one hundred percent hers in a way that her San Francisco condo had never been. She loved everything about the farm. The intensity of the colors and the rich, thick scent of the lavender filling her fields. The two-hundred-year-old Spanish oak trees spreading a little shade. Even the copper still she wrestled with inside the barn, because coaxing the oil from her plants wasn't easy even if it was simple.

And now he wanted to move right on in and take over.

"No." She drew herself up. She wasn't going to be a doormat. She'd run once and had sworn she'd never do so again. His tanned forearms swung the duffel out of the truck bed and onto the ground. Effortlessly. Like he'd always done everything. She shouldn't have found that confidence so sexy.

"You need me here." Not waiting for an answer, he started across the driveway, moving silently, like the predator she knew he was. That sensual, lazy exterior was just a front. She'd seen the hard-eyed warrior staring out at her earlier. Letting him move in would just be setting herself up for heartbreak. He was a smoke jumper, a firefighter who went when and where the wildfires were. And she? She'd already lost more than enough to fire, thank you very much.

"No," she repeated, slamming her hand into his chest. "You stay away from me, Jack Donovan."

"Can't do that, baby." He didn't move toward the house, though, so she figured she had a chance.

"Can't or won't?" She shoved her hair behind her ears, cursing the gesture but unable to stop herself. His eyes locked on her betraying fingers, and she knew he understood that he made her nervous as hell.

"You've got yourself a stalker. A serial arsonist." The blunt words were as forceful as the man. "You tell me you have a plan to deal with that, and maybe"—he shrugged—"I'll go. Until then, though, I'm staying."

Slinging the duffel over his back, he wrapped his large hands around her waist. The wicked heat of those hands burned through her thin tank top, making her think of other places he could touch. Carefully he lifted her and shifted her to the side, as if she weighed no more than a feather. Another time, she might have been flattered. Right now, though, the sexy gesture just made her mad. She shouldn't want him—but she did. She wanted those large hands all over her body.

"You called the cops when shit happened in San Francisco," he said calmly, laying in a course for her front porch.

She wasn't stupid. Of course she had. And they'd come, made their reports, and left. "There was nothing they could do."

"Because you couldn't tell them who it was. Only that you thought someone was there, watching you." His eyes studied her carefully, as if he knew she was holding back. She hadn't told anyone about the very end of that horrific night. He couldn't know. Had to be guessing.

"No," she said, her voice tight. She followed him up the steps of her porch, concentrating on the smooth, cool grain of the old wood beneath her bare feet. She was going to stay strong. Ignore the temptation to fold herself into his arms and let him take care of this. He would, she knew, and he wouldn't expect any favors in return. That was the kind of man he was. For him, her stalker was just one more fire to put out, and he wouldn't hesitate. He'd do what was right.

That scared her more than anything. Because she could come to care for a man like him, and yet he'd walk away when the fire was out. Move on. And she couldn't live like that.

"I want you safe, Lilybell."

She shook her head. "I don't need a white knight, Jack."

"Bullshit." He strode into her living room as if he owned the place. "You need me."

"You can't stay here." She knew her voice sounded too desperate. "People will talk," she pointed out. "Your staying here means every busybody in town will weigh in. They'll think we're sleeping together."

"We will be."

Her mouth fell open. He turned around and crossed his arms over his chest, watching her. "We just won't be having sex. Unless you want to."

In one smooth thrust, he braced her against the wall.

Arousal pinkened her skin.

She was still wearing those snug little shorts that had tormented him earlier. Hooking his thumbs under the thin straps of her tank top, he gently tugged her closer.

If she wanted to get away, she could. Not that there was too far to go in the hot, intimate space he'd created for her between his body and the door, of course. He smiled, slow and hot, watching her eyes widen. He wasn't stupid, after all.

So he pulled her up against him. Soft and sexy, she felt even better than he remembered, and he'd done a hell of a lot of remembering. Pulling the soft fabric of her tank away from those beautiful breasts of hers, he thumbed her nipples into sweet arousal. Just imagining the taste of her had his dick stiffening impossibly behind his fly.

"This is not a good idea, Jack," she warned, and he decided that he was done talking. This was the best idea he'd had in a long time, and they both knew it.

So he lowered his head, watching her face. Just in case he'd misread the attraction there. She'd been frightened once, and he would never do anything to hurt her.

Her lashes flickered down as he stroked his thumb softly against her bare nipple. The slightest, butterfly-light touch.

"Tell me to go again, Lilybell," he whispered against her mouth. "Say it like you mean it."

Her lips parted, and he ruthlessly pushed his advantage, because she was a battle he wasn't losing. He didn't know why the woman in his arms mattered so much, but she did, and Jack Donovan never ignored his instincts.

Her skin smelled like cherries and vanilla. Sweet but with a hint of spice. And, of course, like lavender. He'd never smell lavender again without getting an instant hard-on.

His lips devoured her, his tongue stroking an explicit greeting over her parted lips, sinking between them to explore her sweet, hot depths.

When her hands came up, sliding along his shoulders and over the cotton of his T-shirt, he almost came on the spot. He was going to have those hands on his bare skin, he decided. Right now, though, his legs were tangled with hers, pressing her backward against the door until he couldn't tell where Jack ended and Lily began, the pleasure roaring through them both.

"I plan on having you," he growled, drinking in her little whimper of agreement. "Fair warning, Lilybell. Hot and wet and in our bed. I'm going to find out what we could have been together."

Chapter Six

Hell. She ducked under his arm, and he let her go. Just like that and because he could. She didn't want to deal with his arrogance or this brand of crap, but that was Jack Donovan for you. He and his brothers were heroes at heart—even if they were all bad boy on the outside.

Lily had forgotten just how much she'd wanted him. How much he could make her feel when he touched her. Her body hummed with arousal, and her panties were damp, damn it. He'd come home and put his hands on her—and her body was more than willing to welcome him back. She didn't want to do this, though. Didn't have the energy to dig up the past. Not now.

So she took a precautionary step back and looked up at him. "We need to discuss this attraction of yours."

"This attraction of mine?" he drawled. He let her step away from him, though, allowing her to put a foot of space between herself and his chest. He was older now, his body bigger and harder, the boyish edges sharpened into rugged good looks. The stretch of the thin white cotton T-shirt over the muscles of his abdomen had her regretting she'd vowed prudence.

God, he was even more impossibly delicious than before.

There was nothing safe or practical about Jack Donovan. He was, she reminded herself, a delicious treat. Ice
cream for breakfast on a hot day. He'd leave—again—at
the end of the summer, and a wise woman wouldn't
choose to live on ice cream anyhow.

His eyes darkened as he watched her. "You're thinking
too much."

She shrugged and turned away. "One of us has to." Although she was tired of being the practical one, always
planning for the future. Where had it gotten her?

He smiled. Slowly. "I'm thinking, too, baby, and what I
think is that you're too alone out here. You want to come
back into town with me, we can fix you up a place to stay
until we've got a handle on these fires. Nonna always has
a spare bed."

"No," she said. She was done running away, and, damn
it, this was her farm. Her dream. "Lavender doesn't pick
itself, Jack. I have a job here. Things that need doing."

"These things are more important than keeping yourself safe?"

She wasn't going to think about that. God, she couldn't.
She still couldn't forget that last fire before she'd given up
and fled San Francisco. She'd opened her bedroom door to
smoke and a deceptively small fire burning in her kitchen
sink. Just a few romance novels from her keeper shelf.
That had been the kicker. Her stalker hadn't used the stack
of newspapers by the recycling bin. He could have chosen
anything, and he'd chosen those books.

He'd destroyed the books she'd read and loved enough
to keep.

"I'm safe enough," she countered. "There's no raging
inferno of death headed my way that I can see." She'd
wanted Jack Donovan something fierce when they'd been
in high school, when she still believed in dreams. Believed

that he'd hold out a hand to her and sweep her along with him. She'd grown up since then. She'd learned what he wanted and what promises he was willing to make. That was one thing about Jack that hadn't changed.

She closed her eyes and shook her head before she made herself confront his watchful eyes. Jack never broke a promise.

And he'd never offered her happily-ever-after.

"You aren't safe here. Not from what I've heard." He repeated his statement quietly, but there was no mistaking the determination in his voice. The certainty. "So you have a choice, Lily. You can come back with me to Nonna's, or I'll move in with you here. I'm not leaving you alone."

The sheer male arrogance of him took her breath away. He thought he knew what was best for her. And perhaps he might. In bed. But he had no idea about the monster she'd faced down. The monster who just might have tracked her to Strong.

"I don't want you here, Jack." She turned away, staring blindly out the window. The dark sweep of purple covering her hills represented everything she was building here, she thought fiercely. It was all hers, her hard work and plans. Jack Donovan didn't get to charge in and tell her what to do. "No matter what there was, or might have been, between us in the past, I don't need you to drop in and rescue me."

His watchful gaze didn't change, and she'd grown up more than enough to know what that meant. "I told you what I could give you, Lily, and when it wasn't enough, I walked away."

"Yes." She turned back wearily. "Yes, you did, Jack. No one ever said you were less than honest."

"You wanted me then," he pressed on, brutally honest.

"You want me now. So you don't like the fact that I'm going to look out for your safety. That I won't let anyone hurt you." He eyed her. "I won't hurt you, Lilybell. I promise you that. Whatever happens between us is your choice."

"My choice? Not really, Jack. If it was my choice, your fine ass would be climbing back into your truck, and you'd be headed back into town." God, the memories she had of riding in that truck—and what had happened afterward. "You can't use sex and charm to get your way here. It won't work."

His slow smile still made her insides go hot, damn him. "You sure about that, baby?"

"I know all about you, Jack. What I didn't know in high school, I've learned since. You and your brothers had a reputation practically from the day you hit this town." As they'd grown up, Nonna's boys had been wild, sexy as hell, but with a fine sense of honor that ran bone-deep. They played hard but only with those who were willing. Ten years ago, she'd almost been one of that number. Now, she reminded herself, she was out of the running.

"Hell," she grumbled, "you might as well invite me to move into your hangar. People wouldn't talk any more."

The wry tilt of his head acknowledged the hit. "People talk," he admitted quietly. "But they don't always have all the facts, Lily. We both know that. There's more at stake here than a handful of words someone gave you about my brothers and me. If you were concerned about those rumors, you should have brought your concern to me."

"Don't tell me you didn't earn that reputation, Jack."

That slow, sensual grin of his did something to her, and she prayed it wasn't permanent. "We earned it, baby. Damn right. Want to find out why?" He shrugged. "I didn't think that was your kind of thing."

It was that kind of wicked hint that had earned him the reputation he had.

"Rain check," she said lightly, stepping away from him.

His arm shot out, loosely shackling her wrist. She got the message. He wasn't done with her yet. That made her mad. Still, the sooner she heard him out, the sooner he'd get the message and leave.

"This isn't a game, Lily." He shook his head, dead serious. "Until I've got these fires sorted, you and I are an item. Whoever your stalker is, he'll think twice about messing with you if we're seen as a couple. A woman alone is easier to harass. You play along with me, and we'll pull it off. If everyone thinks we've picked back up where we left off, it will be more convincing."

"You mean, if everyone else believes we've finally become lovers."

"Yes." His eyes held hers. "If we're lovers, there will be fewer questions."

"You're not going to give up on this, are you, Jack?"

"You could enjoy this, you know," he pointed out. "It doesn't have to be all about business."

"Are you asking me out, Jack Donovan?"

He paused, those dark eyes warming. "I could be, baby. If that's what you want. We were good together before. We'd be even better now. Think about it." His voice dropped, the sexy growl making her panties dampen impossibly. "Think about us, Lilybell. I'd like more—wouldn't you?"

"And you'll be out of here at the end of the summer, Jack," she said.

"We've got months until summer ends," he growled. "You always did like to plan ahead."

"And you lived for the moment," she snapped. "Fine. You want to stay here, you stay here. Please yourself."

Spinning on her heel, she stalked up the stairs, aware the whole way of the heated presence at her back, climbing the steps behind her. The farmhouse's bedrooms were picturesque, narrow slices of space tucked beneath painted eaves. The open windows brought in the scent of drying lavender as soon as she stepped through the door of one of them.

"Home, sweet home," she said, indicating the bed with a wave of her hand. Jack's shoulders brushed the door as he stepped in behind her and silently took in the antique iron bedstead. The bed was twin-size and impossibly narrow. The patchwork quilt created a soft, feminine space, making her hyper-aware of his large, male body.

"I may be bigger than you remember," he crooned. The space was suddenly too small, and she knew he recognized the heated flush on her skin. There were just too many memories between them for such a small space, and their new kiss was simply one more to add to her collection.

He reached out, his hands descending on her shoulders. He couldn't stop touching her. Little touches, not all sexual. Like he'd missed the feel of her skin or the accidental contact. She waited breathlessly, hating herself for the weakness, for anticipating the next sexy promise he might make her.

"Real pretty view" was all he finally said, stepping up behind her. The move boxed her in between him and the bed and the windows that opened out onto her fields and their purple sea of lavender. *Dreamy,* she thought, but that was an inadequate description; she'd invested a hell of a lot more than dreams in those fields. She needed them to produce.

"But I'll sleep down there." He pointed to the sunporch the farm's former owner had tacked on haphazardly to the main house.

"On the porch? Afraid for *your* virtue now?"

He shot her a look. "I've never liked small spaces, Lily." The tone of his voice warned her the subject was closed. She wasn't getting a heart-to-heart talk from Jack. Not tonight. Leaning forward, he stabbed a finger toward the line of pink and white oleanders edging her lavender field. "You need a fire line. See right there? Those scruffy green bushes with the little pink flowers? That's where I'll start."

"Don't you touch my oleanders," she said fiercely. "I mean it, Jack. Don't you cut my flowers."

"You need a firebreak," he said. "I'm going to make sure you have everything you need, baby." The little shiver in her stomach warned her that Jack wasn't talking about the oleanders anymore.

"You don't know the first thing about what I need." She stepped away from him, refusing to admit she was disappointed when he let her go. "Sleep up here. Down there. Take your pick." What she needed, she admitted privately, was to get herself the hell away from Jack Donovan's bed. She didn't need to be borrowing that kind of trouble.

He sat down on the bed and just watched her, as if he knew something she didn't and he wasn't in a sharing kind of mood. "I'll figure it out," he said, and she knew he wasn't talking about where he was going to end up sleeping tonight. She wondered if he planned on finding her, and that particular fantasy had her flushing.

Jack, damn him, just watched her and patted the empty patch of quilt beside him. A small smile of male amusement at her retreat crossed his face. Clearly, he didn't give a damn about common courtesy, because, as her unwelcome houseguest, he should have been on his best behavior. Instead, he was pushing for all he was worth. "You let me know what you need, baby," he said.

She refused to look at him as she left the room. She

wasn't going to admit that his soft drawl had her thinking about all sorts of *needs*.

And wants.

No, she was going to get the hell out of there.

And go to bed. Alone.

Chapter Seven

Jack wanted to know what she *needed*? Lily had spent the night tossing and turning, because he was an arrogant ass, and the nightmares were back. Every time she closed her eyes, she saw the flames and smelled the smoke. Her condo—and her life—was on fire, and she was helpless to stop it. Awake now, she wrapped her hands around her coffee cup, because sometimes caffeine and the warm sides of a mug were the only lifelines this early in the morning. God, she was tired of feeling helpless. Tired of being a pawn some man decided to move around the board because he could or because he wanted something from her she didn't want to give. She wanted to *do* something, and she didn't want to retreat.

She wasn't retreating ever again.

Knowing Jack was just downstairs hadn't made the night any easier, either. That handful of stairs was nowhere near enough space between them. He was pure temptation, and she could admit that to herself.

So she was nowhere near ready when Jack dropped down onto the porch step behind her. His legs slid around hers, and a hard, muscled arm wrapped around her waist, tugging her up and backward. His other arm rescued her coffee as she yelped.

He chuckled and stole a swallow. "God, Lily." He stared down suspiciously into her cup. "Did you even bother putting coffee in here?"

So she liked her coffee milky sweet, and she used way more sugar than any adult should. Her house. Her rules. "Make your own damned coffee, then," she snapped.

"Are you always this grumpy in the morning?" he teased. "Because, if you are, I'm going to need a few pointers."

He'd obviously been up for a while. She'd heard the front door slam hours earlier as she lay there sleepless. Watched Jack take off down the road, running. Now, his hair was still damp from his post-run shower, but he was wearing his usual uniform of jeans and a T-shirt. Work boots. So close to him, she felt impossibly bare in her cut-offs and tank top, too aware of the contrast between her bare legs and his muscled ones.

His mouth brushed the skin of her neck, his tongue drawing a wicked little pattern on the sensitive skin. His teeth nipped at her, and the erotic sting had her stilling.

When his hand found the back of her neck and rubbed, she wanted to melt in sheer bliss. She should have moved away. Should have told him to keep his hands to himself. But Jack Donovan in the morning was even sweeter than her coffee, and she wanted something to keep her memories of that night, that fire, at bay.

When he pulled her onto his lap, wrapping her in those arms of his, she finally protested.

"I can't do this, Jack." She pushed at him, and he let her put a few inches of space between them. "You don't want to stick around."

"Take a chance, baby," he growled. He nipped at her lower lip, his hands threading through her hair. "You take that chance on us. I would never hurt you."

"Not intentionally," she said sadly.

Her words hung there in the air between them, and there was nothing he could say. Because those words were true. He would never hurt her on purpose, but summer would end like it always did, and he'd move on—like he always did—because staying put just wasn't an option for him.

He tightened his arms around her. "Don't write me off, Lily, and don't tell me what I want. Right now, what I *want* is you, and damned if you're not driving me crazy. You're going to have to give me just a little trust here."

"Why should I?" She shoved against his chest. She knew Jack. He wouldn't hold her there if she really wanted to go. He might coax and tease, but he'd never force. She shut that memory down before she could follow it back to the night of the fire. Jack's hands weren't getting the message, however, because he just pulled her closer to him. She wanted to talk, but sometimes all those words didn't get you anywhere. She didn't see them resolving this matter with a handful of words anyhow. Bottom line was, she didn't trust him to stick around, and she didn't see how he could fix that particular issue.

"I don't think you want to be hiding from what we've got between us," he growled. His hand slid down over the curve of her ass, tracing the line between her cheeks to dip between them. She jumped, then froze, mesmerized by the delicious heat unfurling right there, between her thighs, where he teased the edge of her panties. Then he tucked one finger against the denim seam and stroked. A little, delicate, knowing brush of his finger.

"Jack," she whispered. Before she could *think,* she leaned forward. Giving him more access. His finger teased, petted. Slid forward to explore.

"You tell me you don't want this," he growled. His finger found her swollen clit beneath the denim and pressed, and that sharp burst of pleasure, so sweet, so hot and unexpected, had her sitting there on his lap waiting to see what he'd do next. Pleasure pulsed through her in short, hard beats. She shouldn't do this. Not on the porch. This wasn't like her.

"You want me to pet you right here, baby, until you come? Because," he said, his voice rough with desire, "I'd love to do that for you." His finger slid beneath the edge of the denim shorts, over the thin cotton of her panties. "I think you want me just fine."

"And if you don't, you just come on over here," a familiar voice teased. *Oh, God.* She scrambled off Jack's lap, and this time he let her go, as if he knew there were boundaries she wouldn't cross. Things she wasn't ready to accept, no matter how decadent the pleasure. Rio was watching them. Rio, Jack's playful, golden brother. The man was all liquid grace and sensual curiosity, and she'd *heard* things about him. About Jack, too. The hooded look on Jack's face warned her that those rumors might be more fact than fiction.

Rio winked at her, as if he hadn't just found her wrapped around his brother, with his brother's hand touching her intimately. "Jack here is going to leave you alone if that's what you want, sweetheart."

Arousal warred with embarrassment, and she stared at him, unsure what to say. He just smiled devilishly. "There's nothing to be embarrassed about, Lily. The view was just fine from over here."

"Rio . . ." Jack's warning growl came from behind her.

She hadn't paid attention to the dull throb of a motorcycle pulling into her driveway. When Jack had her in his arms, that was how crazed he made her. Fighting a blush, she looked over at Rio, astride that damned Harley. No one had ever mistaken the Donovan brothers for choir-boys. Someone—a female someone—straddled the back of that cycle, looking for all the world like she'd ride one or all the brothers the same way. Rio's friend was all long, jeans-clad legs beneath a short white T-shirt baring a per-fectly tanned stomach. As Lily watched, the woman pulled off her black helmet, shaking free a long mane of hair. Whoever she was—and a new face in Strong was a nov-elty—the violet shadows beneath her eyes, her slightly slumberous look, said loud and clear that this woman hadn't been to bed yet. Or, Lily corrected herself self-mockingly, hadn't done any sleeping. Next to her, Lily felt boring and plain-Jane.

Rio got off the bike and sauntered over, and the look in his dark eyes was pure mischief. He was enjoying this early-morning get-together a little too much.

"Why are you here, Rio?" Lily asked bluntly.

The laughter went right out of Rio's eyes, and she knew she wasn't going to like what was coming next.

"I took a little ride up the road, along the ridge." He in-dicated the edges of her field with a hand. "Like we dis-cussed, Jack."

"Wait a minute." She frowned. "I don't recall being part of this conversation, *Jack*."

He shot her a dry look. "But you do remember our talking about the job I have to do here, right? Because this is part of that keeping-you-safe deal we have. Argue with me later if that's what you really want to do, Lily, but right now I want to hear what Rio found."

Because, clearly, he'd found something, or he'd have just pointed that Harley straight on back to Strong.

"Fine," she snapped. "We can discuss it later, Jack."

His hand dropped onto her shoulder. If she looked down, she'd see those fingers—those fingers that had been places she had no business allowing them, not on her front porch—and, God help her, she wanted to look. Wanted to touch. Jack had her all tied up in knots.

"Lots of footprints. He was up there, watching." Rio's eyes met hers, waiting for her reaction. "Your stalker."

"He's found you." Jack's voice hardened.

"We thought he might have," Rio pointed out.

"But why?" She asked the question that had tormented her ever since the horror began. "What did I do to make him come after me like this?"

Jack's hands closed around her shoulders, pulling her close. She wanted to sink into that heat. When she was with Jack, she felt safe. Protected. She fought to remind herself of why she shouldn't lean back, shouldn't let the strength and the heat of him hold her up. She'd always stood on her own two feet, done things for herself.

"You didn't do anything, baby," he said. "This isn't your fault. For some reason of his own, he picked you for his sick games. You can't blame yourself for that."

"He spent hours up there," Rio continued. "Looks like he picked his spot and hunkered down. Not ex-military, or he wouldn't have left those footprints. He came up from the other side of the ridge. I can show you the path he took if you want."

Rio hesitated, and Jack nodded slowly. "So he's a watcher. We suspected that. He's been watching Lily for at least two years now. He's fixated enough that he followed her here from San Francisco."

"There's something else you should see," Rio said.

"What?"

"We know he likes to burn things." Rio shot an apologetic look at Lily. "But it's more personal than that. He built himself a fire up there. Just a small one, and he did it really carefully, so he wasn't trying to burn the place down."

The unspoken *not yet* hung in the air between them.

"What did he burn?" Nausea had her swallowing hard. He'd always chosen something of hers, something personal.

Fury flashed in Rio's eyes, and she realized that maybe she didn't know him as well as she thought she did. For just a moment, the man had been all predator. "A book," he said, tossing a plastic bag toward Jack.

Jack's hand shot out, catching the bag and handing it to her. "Is this yours?"

"No." She shook her head. She recognized the book, though. A romance by one of her favorite authors. The top half of the book was charred and black, but she knew that white farmhouse perched on a green hill beneath a sliver of cloud-gray sky. "But I'm reading it now. It's on my bedside table."

"You're sure that book is still there?"

She hated the possibility that a stranger had been inside her house, touching her things. She'd come back to Strong because she *knew* everyone here. There were no strangers. Or—she shot a rueful glance at Rio's unfamiliar companion patiently waiting for him—not for long, at any rate.

"Positive," she said, handing the bag back to Rio. "I saw it this morning. I bought it last week, at the general store in Strong."

"Shit." Jack dropped a kiss on top of her head, and she wondered if he realized what he'd done, or if the little caress was instinctive. "So he's not just watching you—he's following you, too."

Just the thought of having this creep's eyes on her made her skin crawl. He'd watched her before, but the idea of whoever he was *here,* in her home, in Strong, was more than she could handle. Panic seized her, and adrenaline flooded her body. She wanted to run, wanted to scream against the unfairness of it all. Sure, she'd suspected—okay, she'd known on some instinctive level—that her plans to get away hadn't worked. But Rio's confirmation was too blunt, too much. If the stalker was really here . . .

"Breathe." Jack's soft command in her ear had her gulping deep, sweet breaths of air. The simple act anchored her in the here and now, away from the memories she'd hidden even from herself.

"So how does he do that?" Jack asked rhetorically. "Out here, on the farm, he can hide on the ridge. A high-power scope, some binoculars"—Jack shrugged—"he's got what he wants. But I'm betting that's not going to work so well in town. He has to be able to get up close."

"Which means he's definitely local." Rio cursed. "We'll watch for him."

Lily hadn't given these men permission to waltz on in and take over. This was her life—it needed to be her decision.

"Neither of you gets to swoop in here and make decisions for me," she snapped. "I can take care of myself, Rio. I've been doing it for years."

He sighed. "Which is why you hightailed it on back to Strong, then, Lily? Because things were working out so well for you in San Francisco?"

"I'm not responsible for those fires." Jack had said so himself, and she knew it was true. No matter how many regrets, how many coulda-woulda-shouldas ran through her head at night, she knew this.

"No." Rio unslung a messenger bag from over his shoulder, dropping it onto her porch. "Those fires weren't your fault. Doesn't mean, however, that it's not your problem. If someone is gunning for you, Lily, you need to take a little action. You can't just sit here waiting for this creep to come at you. Jack here knows what he's doing, and so do I."

"I didn't ask for your help."

"You didn't ask for anyone's help, baby." Jack's sexy

drawl behind her made her think of a sleeping tiger. "That's your problem, right there. If you'd asked for a little helping hand, you'd have been able to pick your savior. Now, you're stuck with us. Take it up with Nonna and Ben, but I'm thinking you're not going to change their minds."

Flipping open the bag, Rio began pulling out bits and pieces of electronics. There was enough surveillance equipment to start another Cold War. "Because Jack's right, and we all know it."

She wet her lips. "I didn't think he'd find me here."

Rio just looked at her and shook his head. The electronic gear he was pulling out of his bag made his thoughts about that clear. "24/7 surveillance," he said. "Whatever happens down here in Lavender Creek, we'll see it up in the base camp. You won't be alone."

"You're putting me in a fishbowl." Her skin prickled, flushed at the thought of the Donovan brothers watching her. The intimacy felt shocking, although it wasn't—she admitted the truth to herself—anything like the violation of knowing her stalker was out there, too. Waiting to hurt her.

Jack and his brothers wanted to keep her safe. Wanted to *help*. All she had to do was let them. But then she'd have to tell them everything, and there were parts of that last night in San Francisco that were too raw, too ugly to be shared. She didn't think she could face Jack Donovan looking at her and knowing that truth.

"Give me your cell." Jack held a big palm out, gesturing with his fingertips. "I'll program our numbers into it. You see anything down here, you call us."

"Never heard that pickup line before," she said sweetly. Damned if she was going to roll over for him. If he wanted puppy-dog obedience, he could go chase Rio's blonde.

He shot her a look. "Go get it, Lily, or I'll go myself. You won't like that."

"Don't you dare." She meant it, too. She didn't understand why she had this urge to push him, to challenge him, but she wasn't going to let him give her orders. Not now. Not ever.

He didn't say anything, just looked at her and went on back inside the house. Then she remembered the cardinal rule of the Donovan brothers. They'd never backed down from a dare. Ever.

"That was a mistake," Rio observed cheerfully. He was putting a little camera up beneath an eave.

Right. Leaving Rio to assemble the surveillance arsenal on his own, she stormed back inside and found Jack with his hands on her purse. She reached for the white leather in a panic—there were things in there she'd *really* rather he didn't see—but he'd already upended her bag onto the table.

The bag was a disorganized disaster. Makeup and an old comb, hair ties, wads of Kleenex and paper towel. Two paperback romance novels, because she didn't like waiting, and a good book always made the time pass quickly. Sample soaps from Lavender Creek's line.

"You might want to think about a little spring cleaning." He nodded, sifting through the rest of her purse's contents. He shoved a quantity of stuff back inside the bag, but then he found the little pocket-rocket vibrator. God, she prayed he wouldn't recognize that for what it was. That was a whole different kind of fantasy right there.

The knowing grin tugging the side of his mouth warned her Jack knew precisely what he had his hands on. She could feel that damned blush spreading across her face again as he looked over at her.

"Girl like you shouldn't need this." He put down the

small toy and scored her cell from the remaining mess.
Flipping it open, he programmed in a handful of numbers.
As far as she could tell, her ICE number was going to ring
straight to base camp. "You've got us all," he said, turning
the cell around so she could see the screen. "Me, Rio, and
Evan. The base camp." He hesitated but plowed on. "And
a couple more of the team members. You need anything,
you call—you hear me, Lily? Don't keep this to yourself."

She wondered who was on his jump team this
summer—and how many of them had been drafted into
working overtime as her new security detail. She didn't
kid herself. Anyone Jack trusted was going to be big and
mean and determined. She wasn't going to shake them off,
not easily.

Jack reached the bottom of her purse and, sure enough,
palmed the little hand-piece she kept there in a specially
designed holster. She'd had time to think, on the drive
from San Francisco to Strong, and she'd made some ad-
justments. The small handgun was one of them.

"See, this right here?" He nodded grimly. "This tells me
you know *precisely* what we're concerned about, Lily."

She didn't want to talk about it. "Woman alone, Jack,"
she said lightly. "I've got a permit for concealed-carry."

"You're not alone," he answered, his voice tight as he
ran his fingers over the Beretta, examining it expertly. The
gun was a nice little piece, and she knew how to handle it.

"I'm licensed," she pointed out. "I'm allowed to carry."

He looked up. "You know how to fire this? Have you
thought about what happens if you don't have your purse
handy?"

"Yes," she said tightly. "To both your questions." The
look on Jack's face warned her he didn't think this conversation was over. Not by a long shot. Which was too
damned bad. She'd had about as much Donovan as she

could stomach for the morning. She left him to it and went back out onto the porch, almost running over Rio's blonde arm piece in the process.

The woman looked at her and shook her head. "You have the look of a woman who's had one too many run-ins with a Donovan."

Lily stopped, because, honestly, she didn't know where she was headed anyhow. Just away. Away from Jack. Away from the complications she didn't think she could deal with right now. "Jack," she said tightly, "doesn't know when to quit."

"None of them do." The woman smiled. "They didn't introduce us, did they? You were a couple of years ahead of me in school, and then I lit out for a couple of years." She held her hand out. The nails were polished but short. "I came back when Ma's landed in my lap." With a wry twist of her lips, she added, "Not that running a bar was quite the way I imagined my future."

"You're Ma?"

There was no mistaking the mischief in the other woman's eyes. "That's me. If it's any consolation, I didn't pick the name. I inherited it. It's one of the risks of a family-run business. Most folks call me Mimi. It avoids unfortunate Oedipal moments."

"You're seeing Rio?" She had no business asking questions, but this whole morning was headed toward surreal. Besides, she figured the eyeful Mimi had gotten from the back of the Harley justified her curiosity somewhat.

Mimi shrugged. "He's a good man," she said quietly. "Once you get past the playboy-pretty of that face. That kind of man doesn't grow on trees, not even around here. Strong's a decent place, but it's low on excitement. The Donovan brothers—well, they know how to heat things up." Her gaze slid from Lily to somewhere behind her.

Jack. "You know how they are. I wasn't going to say no. Rio's not the sort to ask twice. And he's only back in town for the summer." She made a little face. "So I don't have time to waste."

Rio was playful, but he only played with women who'd agreed to those terms. If he'd hooked up with Mimi, he believed she understood the score. Right now, he was closing up shop, sliding the last bits and pieces into his bag. Slinging the bag over his shoulder, he threw a leg over the waiting Harley and turned to look at the two of them.

"That's my cue," Mimi said regretfully. "Beer truck's coming in a half hour anyhow. Come on down for a drink sometime, and we'll catch up. Or share war stories." She walked over to the bike, all long legs and sexy saunter. Sometimes, Lily decided, watching Mimi slide behind Rio and wrap her arms around his waist, life just wasn't fair.

What would it be like to not worry about anything but the moment? Mimi had decided she wanted Rio Donovan, and she was taking him. When it was over, it would be over. No worries. No regrets.

Maybe she needed to take Jack the same way.

By the time Jack had finished up with Rio's equipment and hit the porch, his temper had cooled, and he was ready to manage Lily. By God, she'd stay safe on his watch—whether she liked it or not. Based on her reaction earlier, he was betting she'd make this difficult. Turned out, Lily had grown a stubborn streak while he'd been away. Or maybe, he admitted wryly, closing the screen door behind him, that stubborn side had always been there, but she'd had him so wrapped into knots, he hadn't noticed.

Lily was already surrounded by buckets of water half-filled with lavender stalks. By noon, those buckets would be chock-full of fresh-cut lavender. His Lilybell cut like a madwoman. Setting down his coffee cup, he fingered a handful of purple and white flowers. She'd cut the lavender long, preserving a tall, flowering spike of color.

"You take all the leaves off?" Flowers were, he decided, pure mystery. These smelled fine, but the bottoms of the long stems were just bare wood. Why take half the plant off?

"Florists don't care about the leaves." She shrugged. "They'll strip all the leaves off the lower ends anyhow, to make up their own arrangements. It's the color that matters most. The color and the length of the bud. The longer, the better."

"Length." His slow, heated grin let her know exactly where his thoughts had gone. "I could be on board with that, baby." She elbowed him, and he grinned right back at the mock indignation on her face.

Her skin was sun-kissed, a creamy gold except when she bent over and he caught a glimpse of a paler area beneath the waistband of her shorts, where a minuscule scrap of a bikini had—barely—covered her. That pale hint of hidden skin was unfamiliar. Exotic. She seemed to glory in the heat. Tipped her head back to soak in the sunshine beneath her battered canvas hat with its whimsical ribbons. He'd have fantasies about what she must look like in that bikini, dream about wicked little scraps of white crochet that came apart in a man's hands.

"How does this work?" Lily's porch had a perfect view of the fields surrounding her little farmhouse. Lavender on three sides, with a woody upslope on the fourth. The outbuildings were close together, which posed a problem. Anyone could wait there, park his ass in the shadows. Lily wouldn't see an attack until it was well launched. "You can actually make a living growing lavender?"

"Not a huge one," she admitted, and he wanted to lean down and kiss that look of chagrin right off her face. Lily, he was discovering, didn't do failure. She just kept on going until she succeeded. "So far," she continued, "it's paid the bills. I do mail-order, and I have an online store. People seem to want lavender buds and bundles clean across the country, so I cut and ship. And I sell lavender soaps. All my lavender comes fresh from these fields," she said proudly. "I've sent my flowers for photo shoots and weddings. All sorts of places."

"But you're not open to the public." He made her nervous, he realized. Ten years ago, she'd been nervous, too, but he'd thought time and distance would erase that sweet awareness. "Promise me you're not open to the public, Lily. I don't want to hear that you put out that kind of welcome mat for whoever's after your ass."

"No." She licked her lips. "I'm not open for tours. I've been thinking about it, but it's not a step I'm ready for yet. Maybe next year I'll do it."

So no public access. That was good. The fewer defensive angles he had to work, the better. "How many people work here?"

"Two, sometimes three." She twisted a tie around the base of the bundle. "The farm foreman and two seasonal hands. They won't really get started for another couple of weeks, but I've got them doing odd jobs now and then."

"How long have they been with you?"

"Since I started, Jack." Her huff of exasperation warned him she was done with this conversation. "They're good men. Good men who can probably prove they've never been to San Francisco." Deliberately, she changed the subject. "You got plans for today?" she asked, for all the world as if they were some old, married couple parked on a porch they'd picked out together. Surprisingly, that cozy little domestic picture didn't have him headed for the hills or dreaming of the next fire call. "This conversation is over, Jack."

"It's not over until I say so," he said tightly. If she wanted him to take the gloves off, he would. "There is someone after you, Lily. He was right out there, watching you. I can take you to see the tracks for yourself if you want, but you're going to listen to me."

"I don't take orders from you," she said sweetly, putting the shears down on the porch. "Whatever Rio found up there on the ridge, it doesn't change the fundamentals, Jack. You're not in charge here."

He squatted down beside her, putting himself on eye level with her. He was bigger and meaner, and he'd use his size to intimidate her if that was what it took to keep her safe. Yeah, but he wasn't stupid. He nudged her pruning shears out of the way and planted his hands on either side of her. "I'll say this just once." His eyes watched her, hard and knowing. "Your ass doesn't set foot outside this house, Lily, unless one of us is with you. You got that?"

"Loud and clear," she said bitterly.

"I mean it, Lily. I'll paddle your ass if I catch you taking risks."

"I know how to take care of myself." She tried to scoot backward, but he tugged her forward. Up against him. Hell, she had to feel the hard press of his erection straining against his jeans. His body was ready to move on to other things. "I lock all my doors, Jack. I carry a gun." Her voice made it plenty clear she didn't enjoy the latter. "I think I'm pretty damned safe."

"He got to you in San Francisco," Jack pointed out, because it had to be said. "Whoever he is, he's not sane. He's gone out of his way to burn things that mean something to you. What makes you think he'll leave your farm alone, Lily? If he's watching you, he knows *precisely* what this place means to you. He'll take a match to it sooner or later, and I'm going to be ready for him."

"Fine." She smiled slowly, and he knew he wasn't going to like what came out of her mouth next. Lily Cortez thought she'd figured out a way to one-up him. He'd set her straight and enjoy every minute of it. "You want to stay here and be my own personal fireman, you do that. I'd be happy to tell you precisely what needs doing around here."

If she thought she'd be giving him orders, she needed to rethink things real quick. He didn't take orders.

"Let me do my job, Lily, and we'll get along just fine. Right now, I'm going to clear a firebreak." Because either he worked off some of his temper chewing through that iron-hard California soil over there, or he took Lily upstairs and showed her what she'd been missing all these years.

"Excuse me?" Those brown eyes of hers stared up at him as if he were speaking a foreign language. This time, when she inched backward, he let her go. He could wait. And she definitely needed a firebreak.

"All this"—he gestured toward the rows of purple that swooped and curved around the field fronting her property—"is kindling, pure and simple."

"That's not kindling." She grabbed a new bucket and a pair of lethally sharp hand shears. She could skewer a man with those. "You're looking at twelve thousand instances of extremely happy Provence lavender. You have any idea how long it takes to turn a mail-order plug into a plant that makes pretty purple flowers, Jack?"

Hell, he didn't even know what a plug was, although he suspected it had nothing to do with chewing tobacco.

"You take a little, stubby, two-inch bit of a plant." She held up a dirt-streaked thumb and forefinger to demonstrate. "And you put it into the ground if you're feeling really lucky. Maybe you keep it holed up in a greenhouse for a couple of months while you coax it along. Then summer comes along and fries the hell out of it, while you curse the weather and the irrigation piping and anyone who comes along and tells you you're a fool for thinking you could make a going concern of a lavender farm." The grin she shot him was pure deviltry. "Then, after you've got that cursing out of the way, you sit back and wait for the lavender to grow up and flower. It takes two years, Jack, before there's anything to cut."

She loved the sheer, cussed stubbornness of lavender. The shrubby, woody clumps of purple and silver were so tough at heart that even the deer didn't bother them. She didn't know why she bothered some days, but there was magic in those plants. The pure heaven of the aroma had convinced her of that with the very first breath she'd sucked in. Yeah. She'd wanted acres of lavender, and that's what she'd gotten.

"I won't let you lose your farm." His hand wrapped around her wrist. She looked down at his fingers for a moment. Maybe he understood. Maybe he didn't.

"It's not up to you," she said. "It's up to me. I didn't plant all those plants down there, but I've got their brothers and sisters sitting in my greenhouse. I will plant them," she said fiercely. "I'm going to be happy here."

No missing that use of the future tense.

"I'm going to clear out some of this grass, then dig a line between your lavender and the trees."

It would be ugly as hell, so he figured she'd protest, but it would make her farm safer, which made it the right thing to do. He'd dug line before, lots of line. The more you trained, the more you reacted correctly when you were in a fire situation. Sometimes thinking was a luxury.

Sometimes a man had to go on his gut, had to trust that all the training would pay off in spades and he'd do the right thing instinctively.

"Don't touch my lavender," she warned. When he didn't say anything, she aimed a trowel at the nearest field. "That one's all Grosso lavender. Over there, behind the house, the previous owner put in some French plants, so I've got Hidcote Giant and Provence, as well."

He narrowed his eyes. Maybe those clumps did have different shapes, colors. Still, lavender was lavender, wasn't it?

The plants she'd pointed out looked pretty damned scruffy to him, woody stalks where the purple blooms hadn't burst through yet. They had the prettiest names, though, and there was no denying that her face lit right on up talking about them. That was enough to keep him nodding.

He'd done more than his share of gut-churning, nausea-inducing runs. If you couldn't make the time, you were off the team. No excuses. Up there on the mountainside, when the fire was roaring all around you, you needed to know that every man jack on your team could run like hell if he had to. Fire didn't care about age or injuries or even just a bad fucking day at the races. Fire burned, and that was that.

"So go ahead and dig." She was fussing with those bushes of hers, all her attention focused on a handful of scraggly gray-green plants poking up out of the dirt. Still, she'd stopped talking about getting him to leave, and she seemed, for the moment, to have forgotten their argument about her ability to protect herself. So he damned sure enjoyed the look of confusion on her face when he made to hand back her little Beretta.

"You certain you know how to use this?" He slid the

safety into place, his fingers running over the gun with easy familiarity. A man didn't spend five years with the Marines without learning his way around firearms. "If not, I'll take you down to the range. You can get some practice rounds in."

He offered the gun back to her, grip first, and she took it. "I know how to use it. I'm not taking any chances, Jack. That's your job."

He just watched her. "Probably," he acknowledged. "But I don't take unnecessary chances, baby."

The little snort of disbelief was out before she could stop it. "Then tell me why you jump. Don't tell me you don't enjoy it."

He wasn't a fool. He knew what the risks were. "It's a love-hate thing," he said. Carefully stacking his tools by the fence, he vaulted over it, one-handed. "Nothing better than the jump itself, the feeling you get in the pit of your stomach as you fall through the air and you're waiting to pull the cord. But then there's the fight waiting for you down below. And it's going to be a good fight, but there are never any guarantees. We might win the battle; we might lose." He shrugged. "But we have to fight it. We can't just let it burn, knowing what might happen to the towns and the people in the fire's way. People have moved into areas nature never intended for us to live in, and now we're paying the price. My job is to keep that price as low as possible."

She nodded slowly, sinking down onto her heels as she pulled on leather work gloves. "But it's dangerous."

"Men die," he acknowledged quietly. "But it doesn't happen all that often, and I know how to jump," he said quietly. "I know the where, the when. How to read fire signs and use the equipment. It's not voodoo. It's science. Practice, training, discipline. And experience."

The sleepy drone of early-morning insects filled up the air around them as the critters checked out the bright orange stalks of daylilies jabbing up into the warming air behind the beds. *God.* Jack talked so matter-of-factly about death and dying, but she didn't want to imagine him facing that kind of threat. It scared her. She could admit that. Not as much as her stalker did, but enough. Jack Donovan was so very alive and confident. She couldn't imagine him caught in a burnover, all that life extinguished in a few agonizing minutes.

He must have read her thoughts on her face. "I don't plan on dying out there, Lilybell."

"Promise?" she asked lightly, trying to move away from the dark tone of the conversation.

He smiled. "Promise. You can take that one to the bank. Besides, I don't jump every day. Today, I'm all ditchdigger." He pulled the shirt off over his head. "We spend lots of time digging ditches. One of the best-paid occupations a man can have in the summertime. But don't romanticize it," he warned. "Unless you'd like to." Winking, he dropped the T-shirt onto the ground. "The goal is to pen the fire between two strips of raw dirt. In the middle of a fire, the faster you dig, the better your chances of containing it. You dig a fire line and pray the fire hasn't gone up into the crowns of the trees, where the heat and flames can flash over and just fly between treetops and screw all your efforts down there on the ground."

Lily's head nodded in all the right places as he gave her Firefighting 101. But those eyes of hers—those eyes were all over him. He hadn't missed the flash of worry when she'd thought about him dying. That little wrinkle forming between her eyebrows assured him he was getting somewhere with her. Slowly. But he was making progress, and that was all that mattered.

He'd dug firebreaks for years, slowly pinching the vee of the line closed until the fire, trapped, had nowhere left to go but out. It was basic physics—pick your point and pick it well, and anchor the line in some unburnable bit of the landscape. Place it where there were too many rocks to burn or the groundcover had already been burned out.

But Lily Cortez had him on unfamiliar terrain, looking to fan a fire instead of put it out. If looks were anything to go by, taking off his shirt had been a damned fine start. Whistling, he picked up his shovel and got down to work.

Loading up the car and heading into town turned out to be harder than it should have been.

Lily had left Jack shirtless, cutting away at the grass ringing her lavender fields. Man was a walking fantasy, always had been. That was the problem.

His truck had been an old, growly beast of a machine, even then. Beat-up but faithful, she'd heard him tell one of his brothers. The paint peeled because he'd put his time and his money where it counted—beneath her hood. That motor purred when he turned the key, and she'd never let him down.

Even at sixteen, she'd been offended at his talk of Betsey, knowing he was talking about far more than trucks. Even then, it was obvious he lumped all females together, as objects to be used, then abandoned if they no longer served his purpose.

When the truck had rattled up to the swimming hole that night, she'd known exactly who'd just arrived to put a crimp in her plans. That late in the summer, the sun stayed up half the evening, but twilight was finally wrapping around the trees surrounding the pond where the local kids swam sometimes. The spot was a popular hangout on the weekends. Up until then, though, she'd had the place to herself.

She'd always loved the pond, even though it was nothing out of the ordinary. Just a swimming hole with ice-cold water and a rope swing for anyone foolhardy enough to launch themselves into the chilly depths. Some years ago, her classmates had liberated a battered picnic table from the school grounds. Part prank and part necessity, the table had become the place for picnic lunches and stolen sips of beer.

The picnic table was also the place for stolen kisses and, after the kisses, hand-carved memorials. That table was the living record of all the couples who'd come here, kissed and cuddled, and moved on.

And now, here came Jack Donovan, right on target to find her here. So she'd been for a swim. Alone. It was no big deal, she told herself. He'd come down here for whatever reason, but that reason wasn't her.

Coming up from beneath the surface of the pond, breathless from its chill, she shook the water from her face, and there he was. Sprawled on the picnic table's bench, one hand playing with her towel. Just watching her.

"Thought you weren't coming up," he said, laughing at her with his eyes.

"I can swim just fine." She treaded water. Halfway through summer, and the water was still cold and getting colder now that the light was going fast. She'd planned on hauling her ass out of there and making for home. Jack Donovan, though, made her shy.

"It's getting dark." He stated the obvious. She'd discarded her sneakers under the table, and his booted feet dwarfed the pale canvas and tangled laces. Those dark eyes of his ran over her face and shoulders again, and she wondered what he saw. He'd never bothered to look at her before.

"You should get out now," he observed, shoving away from the picnic table with that liquid grace that made her breath catch and some other part of her go hot with anticipation. "It's getting cold. And dark. Girl like you shouldn't be out this late. Not alone." Something flared in his eyes, and even she wasn't so innocent

that she didn't understand. He was thinking things. She could almost see those thoughts forming.

"You're not my brother." She swam lazily toward the edge of the pond, and the heat in his eyes grew. She wasn't certain how she felt about that heated look, but she was pretty sure she liked it. Liked him.

"No," he agreed hoarsely. "I'm not your brother. Good thing for you, too.."

"Why?" She levered herself out of the pond and perched on the edge, wringing the water from her hair. The summer night was a welcome coolness against her skin, tightening her nipples until they were pebble-hard beneath her bikini top. His eyes dipped just once and then headed right back to her face. He didn't want to look. But he had. The swell of feminine power was new. Delicious.

Maybe she could make Jack Donovan look twice.

"I'd have a thing or two to say," he growled, starting toward her. "About you being out here, all alone. Bad things can happen, even right here in Strong, Lily."

"Nothing ever happens here," she countered, watching that predatory stride head right for her. Tilting her head back to look up at him, she was playing with fire, and she knew it.

"But they can, Lily." He dropped the towel around her shoulders, holding out a hand to help her up.

That hand was hard and large and callused. That hand was years older than he was. He wasn't a boy, hadn't been for years. Whatever else the town said about Jack Donovan, no one had ever said he was afraid of hard work. He'd spent the summer working alongside her uncle, cutting fire lines and knocking down the brush that threatened to turn Strong into a pile of kindling.

"I don't bite." The hand didn't move.

"That's not what I've heard," she said throatily.

"Lily," he warned. "You're playing with fire."

"Am I?" But she took his hand. Because she was playing, and they both knew it. She was pretty sure the sensation of his

warm fingers wrapping around hers, tugging her to her feet, had branded itself into both her memories and nerve endings. She'd dated. But none of those dates had prepared her for the hot rush of sensation as those long fingers stroked the soft skin of her wrist.

People talked. Girls talked. About the Donovan brothers and the wicked things they got up to. Sensual. Pleasure-loving. Hellbent on tasting every sexual treat Strong had to offer. Those were the Donovan brothers. Now she had her first clue that—just maybe—all of that gossip had been nothing less than whispered fact.

Jack Donovan knew just how to touch her.

Memories were starting to intrude on her work. Shaking them off, she swore she wouldn't let that happen.

If she didn't ship two hundred grower's bunches this afternoon, she could kiss a much-needed check good-bye. A bridal show in Sacramento wanted lavender, so here she was, ensconced in the local flower shop where she rented fridge space when she had a big order to send out. It didn't hurt that the little flower mart, with its flotilla of plastic lawn chairs lined up in the small side alley, was where the women of the town gathered. Those chairs guaranteed she had company while she worked. Sure, the alley wasn't as pretty as the rest of the town, but Miriam had potted geraniums in old planters to spruce things up some. The real business of the town got done here.

She shouldered open the door of the shop and carted in the first load of buckets. She couldn't help stopping by the counter, where Miriam had arranged a pretty display of gift soaps. She got a little thrill of pride every time she passed that display. That was *her* soap. Those delicious squares in heavy cream paper tied up with violet ribbons were unabashedly feminine. Pretty. Sweet-smelling.

Strong and small-town life meant safety. That was what she'd decided when she'd pointed her car away from the mayhem of San Francisco a year ago. Life in Strong was dreamy slow—and she'd wanted that dream then and not the nightmare her life had become. She'd graduated from college and then spent years working in advertising in the city, and she'd been damned good at spinning fantasies, figuring out what magazine readers wanted—and then selling them those hopes and dreams. Finding the one perfect image that flawlessly captured the magic of those dreams, making the possibility of achieving those dreams seem as if it were a simple purchase away.

Illusion wasn't always a bad thing. She knew that. She'd coaxed magazine readers into looking deep inside themselves to find their fantasy lives. And then she'd broadcast those fantasies across the printed page, making the imagined real.

When had she realized that she wasn't chasing any of her own dreams, was too busy creating fantasies for other people? Working the farm had given her the chance to create her own line of lavender products, including the soaps displayed on the counter of the florist's shop. The whimsical, simple packaging made it clear what she sold. Her soaps offered a moment of beauty and self-indulgence for the woman who was working her ass off to keep her family and her home together. A whiff of remembrance. Calm. And a moment of peace and tranquility. She sold more than a bar of lavender soap—she promised a frivolous, stolen moment for women who deserved a lifetime of such moments but had too many other responsibilities. That might seem a lot to lay on a little bar of soap, but damned if she wasn't going to try.

Miriam called a greeting from the back alley. "You bring that lavender on back here, honey. I'm just about done with this first lot."

Married for twenty years, Miriam always doubled up plastic chairs before she'd take the weight off her feet. "I'm too much woman for just one of them," she'd say with a laugh. Miriam was a large, comfortable woman with a pretty face that still lit up when her man, Daniel, came through the door. Those warm eyes watched Lily now while her hands continued to strip leaves off the long ends of the lavender stems.

Dropping onto the plastic chair next to her, Lily pulled a bucket toward herself. The thing she loved about lavender was the plant's live-and-let-live attitude. Lavender didn't mind a little benign neglect. You could plant the hardy purple bushes just about anywhere, leave them baking for sun-soaked hours in clay or sand. But to get the best blooms, you had to feed them, water them, to coax those woody stems to burst into flower. Lavender should have been the official flower of Strong, if the town had been large enough to merit an official flower. People here seemed a little dry and straggly and worn-down, but if you paid them a little attention, took the time to figure out what they needed, they burst right into bloom like her plants.

Like her body insisted on doing at the simple promise of Jack Donovan.

"I heard Jack Donovan came knocking on your door." Miriam's hands kept right on moving, four quick slices to strip the leaves and a twist of her wrist to wrap the rubber band around the ends. Miriam didn't have to help. This was Lily's job, but the last-minute order from the Sacramento florist was good money, and Miriam knew Lily needed the cash. So she'd pulled up a chair and grabbed a bucket.

"You don't have to do this." Lily indicated the buckets with a wave of her scissors.

Miriam just shook her head. "UPS man will be here in two hours. There are a lot of empty buckets here," she pointed out. "Plus, Mr. UPS is mighty fine-looking." Deliberately, she winked. "This gives me an excuse to have a look." Only a blind man could miss the love she had for her husband. "But you were telling me about Jack Donovan and this thing he has for you."

"All he did was come by the house. Why shouldn't he? There's nothing more to it than that."

"No reason at all why he shouldn't." Miriam's rapid-fire work rhythm didn't break. "But that boy had a thing for you before you took off for the city all those years ago. Can't imagine he would be knocking on your door now just because he happened to be in the neighborhood."

"He's a firefighter. You know I don't have any interest in a summer fling." Lily dropped her newly stripped bunch into the water. From the look on her neighbor's face, Miriam wasn't buying that half-truth.

"Sure, honey, and he's hot as hell." A slow smile creased the older woman's face. "I remember what that's like. You see your man standing there in the doorway, and you just melt."

"Yeah," Lily groused. "You remember because, for you, that melting thing happened with the right guy." The smug look on Miriam's face told her the guess was dead-on. The whole town knew that Dan worshipped his wife. "For the rest of us, it's not that simple."

"Of course it is." Miriam nudged her with an elbow. "You just open that front door of yours for him and reel him in. I'll bet Jack Donovan knows what to do with that kind of invitation."

The smell of lavender was overwhelming in the hot, muggy slice of alley. "I can't do it."

"Why not? You had history, the two of you, but I thought it was the good kind."

"We were kids, Miriam." Miriam just looked at her, so

she was going to have to spell it out. God only knew what kind of Romeo-and-Juliet thing Miriam had been imagining. "We kissed a couple of times, and then he put an end to it." He'd walked away from her.

"Of course he did." Miriam nodded, finished filling up her bucket, and reached for the next. "He was a good boy. His Nonna raised him right—and she'd have half-killed him if he'd done anything more than kissing. You were too young."

"Just because we're older doesn't make it any easier now," she pointed out.

"You telling me that boy doesn't want you?"

Growing good lavender required two things. Sun and water. People were more complex. She tossed discretion to the wind. "He wants me," she said. "He made that perfectly clear."

"So what's the problem? You wanted him before— something happen in San Francisco?"

"He's not a keeper, Miriam. You and I both know that he'll leave Strong behind him as soon as fire season finishes. He's never going to put down roots, not here, and he's not looking for any kind of commitment."

Miriam exhaled. "Maybe that's a problem, or maybe it's not. Depends, I guess, on what you're looking for. You want him for keeps, then summer is mighty short. Question is, do you?"

It was a hell of a day when the old women in the town could shock her. Miriam must have read that shock on her face, because she chuckled and dropped the flowers she was stripping, leaning forward with her hands on her knees. "Just because I'm not twenty anymore doesn't mean that I don't enjoy living, Lily. Dan is a good man, and we enjoy each other." That private smile crossed her face again. "The way I see it, you and Jack are adults. If no one else gets hurt, then a little summer fling doesn't have to be a bad thing." She shrugged again. "If that's what you want."

She did. She wanted to let him hold her. Love her. Even if it was only for the summer. "I've never done something like this before," she protested.

"You came here and bought that farm," Miriam said comfortably, heaving herself out of the chair as the familiar brown van pulled up in front of the shop. "That's a chance you took. So far, things seem to be working out for you. Maybe Jack Donovan's another chance you need to take."

Lavender Creek was a sleepy oasis sweltering beneath the remnants of the day's sun. After getting the UPS shipment out with Miriam, Lily had hung out with the other woman, helping her sell a handful of grower's bunches when a tour bus had stopped by, returning from one of the local casinos. Business had been good, and several of the women had purchased most of the lavender wands Miriam had on display.

Surveying the nearest field now, Lily slammed the car door and bypassed the house in favor of confronting Jack about the destruction he'd wreaked while she was away.

Ahead of her, alongside the road that sloped down to the field, a small covey of California quail bathed in the fresh-turned dirt. Dust exploded upward in little puffs as the birds burrowed into the ground, flapping their wings. She'd seen this particular group every day. Recognized their black-and-white striped bellies and black backs. Startled by her approach, the birds took off briefly in an explosion of wings, then settled back down to run. The soft *pip* of their cries filled the hot, dusty air as they called back and forth to one another, scratching at the ground. It was charming.

Too bad for Jack that he was a dead man.

Propping her hands on her hips, Lily strode toward said dead man. Her anger didn't stop the heat unfurling low in her belly, and that just made her madder. She didn't want him to do this to her. Despite the heat, he still wore his usual faded jeans, although he hadn't put back on the white cotton T-shirt draped over a fence. And, God, those muscles. The man was one hard, chiseled masterpiece.

And he had no sense whatsoever.

Pruning oleanders, she'd discovered, was an art form. Cut too late in the spring, and the stubborn bushes wouldn't bloom until late spring or summer. She pruned once in the early spring and again in the cooler fall months, when the bushes became top-heavy. She'd been reluctant to cut away the branches at first, but it was best for the bush. Left alone, the heart of the bush grew woody and stopped flowering.

Jack didn't share those inhibitions.

Hell, the man probably wouldn't recognize an inhibition if the damn thing bit him on the ass.

He'd single-handedly created a wide, ugly strip of stubble around her beautiful field. Decades-old oleanders were just plain gone, chopped down to bare stumps. Maybe those oleanders would come back, but it would take years. Clearly, he hadn't heard a word she'd said. He'd touched precisely what she'd said not to touch, and wasn't that all too typical? He'd taken where he should have asked, and now, judging by the slow, welcoming smile creasing those damned lips, he planned to coax her into a better mood.

Too bad for him she planned on being stubborn.

She forced herself to take a deep breath before she let the words out. "What do you think you're doing?"

"Whatever it takes, Lily." He ran a hand over his head. "That's what I'm doing here."

"This isn't *whatever it takes,* Jack." She gestured toward

the mutilated remnants of her oleanders. "This is carnage. I told you not to touch them. You're no white knight," she pointed out. "You don't need to come charging in here. I don't want that. I don't need that."

"So, tell me, Lily," he drawled, "what do you want, baby?"

God, she was riled up good. Jack shouldn't have found her anger arousing, but he did, and he'd stopped pretending to be a nice man years ago. His hands tightened on the shovel. She hadn't minded his taking care of her before. Hell, she'd been sweet and willing, and he'd had to force himself to walk away before he took something he had no business taking. Somewhere, somehow, she'd changed, and he didn't like hearing she no longer had a place for him in her life.

He missed the sweet trust, the hope in her eyes when she looked at him. He'd wanted to lose himself in those baby browns, and he'd run, fast and hard, because that possibility had scared him. He'd known he didn't deserve that kind of woman—but he hadn't expected it to hurt when she agreed with him.

She crouched down beside the stump of the pink and purple bushy thing he'd cut down. A little frown puckered her forehead as her fingers traced the clean edges of the wood he'd cut through. "Look at this, Jack." She scowled. "You've cut them right back to their roots. They were *beautiful*."

He wanted to talk about what she needed, not about her damn plants.

"Those *beautiful* bushes were going to get you killed." Carefully, he laid the shovel in the bed of his truck and dragged on his shirt.

"Really?" She didn't look up, just moved to the next

stump. "Last time I checked, Jack, these poor bushes of mine didn't have feet. They weren't chasing me anywhere, and I don't want to hear anything more about fire lines and tinder and—and . . ." She waved a hand.

"I know fire." Crossing his arms over his chest, he leaned back against the sun-warmed metal of the truck.

"Yes, Jack, you're the expert," she mocked.

"About this, I am." He leaned forward. "I warned you, Lily. My job here is to keep you safe. It's too damned bad if you don't like my methods."

"And that's something else," she continued, as if this conversation was all one-sided and she didn't want to hear what he had to say. She stood up, all long, sun-kissed legs in those little denim shorts of hers. She was driving him crazy, and he wasn't sure how long he could keep his baser instincts under control. How much longer he could stop himself from pulling her right into his arms and kissing her until she was melting for him and this discussion of theirs no longer mattered.

"You need to stop and listen, Jack. This is my life, and you don't get to come barging in here and take charge of it. Of *me*."

"Maybe you'd like that." He knew damned well that was an erotic game he'd enjoy.

The way her eyes widened, he figured she knew *exactly* what he meant. Her nipples were all tease, hard little nubs beneath the fragile fabric of her tank top. He could tuck a finger into the tempting hollow between her breasts and just stroke that impossibly soft skin while he sucked on those perfect little nipples like they were candy and he was a man with a sweet tooth.

"Don't look at me like that, Jack," she warned. She brushed dirt off her hands, her thighs, and he didn't think he could get any harder. She had to know, too. It wasn't as if his jeans were hiding the evidence. "I'm not some helpless thing you need to take care of."

"Then make the choice, Lily," he growled, frustrated. "Let me do what I can do here. Choose to let me keep you safe."

"This isn't about my choosing."

"It is, baby. Trust me."

"Trust you, Jack?" she cried. "You think I should trust you? I know what your reputation is."

"Is this about my firefighting abilities—or something else? I'm not giving you a catalog of my lovers."

"You tell me, Jack. Is this just another job for you? Do you move in with all the happy homeowners you're hired to protect?"

"You know I don't," he said calmly, loading the neat bundles of oleander branches into the truck's bed. "But we practically grew up together, Lily. Your uncle and Nonna are closer than close. He asked me to help out, so I am. You just have to decide to let me do what I do best here."

"Which would be?" She was spitting mad. He shouldn't have found it endearing. He shouldn't have wanted to keep pushing her, to see what she would do or say next. She'd kept all that fiery passion tamped down, locked up her feelings as if letting herself go would be a bad thing. He grinned. He'd wanted her passion ten years ago. Guess things hadn't changed all that much in Strong.

"Keeping you safe, baby. That's what I'm doing."

"Then leave me alone, Jack," she cried. "You're not helping me, not really. Even if there is someone out there watching me, we don't know that he'll stop just because you're here. I can't do this."

"I'm not leaving." She was headed right for him, but she kept on going, up to the house. She smelled even better than he remembered, and he wanted to lower his head, ease his mouth right on over hers, and kiss her until she forgot everything but kissing him back.

Given what she was muttering, though, he didn't think she'd be kissing back.

Not anytime soon.

Chapter Eight

Ma's was a deliberate hole-in-the-wall. Tucked behind the town's main street so a man had to go looking to find the place, Ma's had the only neon sign in town, with the obligatory light-up martini glass. The bar wasn't precisely flush with martini drinkers—Ben would have bet most of Ma's customers had never tasted a martini in their lives—but the drink was on offer. Live music on the weekends, three pool tables, and an honest-to-God jukebox—a man didn't need much more than that. The owner had talked once about putting in an Internet jukebox, but the patrons had resisted. People here liked the comfort of the same-old-same-old. The world outside might be changing, but there were some things you could still count on. Ma's, a cold beer, and some quarters in the jukebox were among them.

Jack Donovan, now, he looked like a man in need of a real cold beer.

Mimi gave him a friendly smile, deftly sliding a beer across the bar top to him when he picked himself a stool and sat down next to Ben's booth. Jack signaled that he'd run a tab and reached for the cold bottle like it was a lifeline.

"You cut her oleanders down? Man, you do have a death wish." On the other side of Ben, Evan shook his head and smiled. Even Rio, silent Rio, just gave him a commiserating look.

Jack had to know he'd never hear the end of this. "I didn't cut them down," he grumbled. "I pruned them."

"Out of existence," Evan observed. Like any good brother, he was ready to give Jack a hard time. "I didn't know our Lily knew that many curse words. She sure learned a lot living in San Francisco."

Lily obviously had Jack at sixes and sevens. Jack might think this was just a summer gig, but Ben was thinking differently. Still, even if Jack and Lily had a history, that didn't mean she'd want to pick right up where the pair had left off ten years ago.

Even if Jack clearly wished she would.

"She shot him down." Rio nodded knowingly.

"Of course." Evan tilted his beer bottle toward Jack in a mock toast. "He cut down her flowers. Bet he didn't even ask first, just swooped in there, acting all fire chief."

"I asked," Jack pointed out. He didn't lose his death grip on the bottle, though.

Ben shook his head. "Did you spell it out? You don't cut a woman's flowers until you've pre-approved every tiny slice." Ben had spent way too much time in places like Ma's when he'd first hit legal drinking age. More after Lily had joined him in Strong and Nonna had acquired her trio of boys. The pair of them had often hashed out tales of woe—and success—over a beer or two. Christ, those boys had been a handful and a half. He still didn't know how Nonna had managed them.

"It's time we talked about Lily." Ben got right down to the business of their meeting. "Things are heating up."

Jack just nodded. "I agree. I've seen the fire maps. You know what those patterns say. Little fires. Getting closer and closer together. More frequent. Our boy's losing patience, or she's pushing his buttons."

Thirty-plus years after he'd done four tours of duty with the Marines. Three hundred and sixty-five days each of those years. Ben had done his thing, done his best to protect his town from the danger of fire. But, damn, some days he felt like Chicken Little squawking at a bright blue sky. There wasn't always smoke. But he knew firsthand just how fast a blaze could grow.

And lately there had been too many little fires for a town this size. Little, harmless fires you could dismiss as someone being careless. Those fires you put out and moved on from. No worries. But when his Nonna worried, Ben worried. That was why he hadn't put up a fuss when Jack showed up. He knew that Nonna had pulled some strings behind the scenes. And he was okay with having some extra help on this one.

"Someone has a real big issue with our Lily. Question I've been asking myself is, who? Who'd want to hurt her like this, bad enough to follow her from San Francisco?" His baby girl was hurting, and he hadn't forgotten the look on her face when she'd first come home. *I was ready for a change,* she'd said. Hell, he'd known then that there was more to her story.

Much more.

He might not be her daddy, but he was her uncle. They had blood in common, and he'd raised her since she was five years old, when her mother had decided she couldn't do it anymore. He knew Lily, and he damned sure knew when she was running scared.

Jack leaned forward. "So who do you think is behind this?"

Ben considered for a moment and then had to admit the truth. "I don't know. If I knew that, Lily wouldn't be constantly looking over her shoulder. But we've got to figure it out. Fast."

"What makes you think we'll do any better than those cops in San Francisco did?"

Ben snorted. "You taken a good look around you recently? This is as small-town as it gets. We look after our own here. And any new face sticks out in Strong. No matter how careful our guy is, he'll make a mistake at some point."

Jack shook his head. "I don't think this is a stranger, though. I think she knows this guy."

"You sure her stalker is a guy?"

Jack thought for a moment, set the bottle down on the table, and ticked the reasons off on his fingers. "Most arsonists are white. Male. Under the age of thirty. Maybe our arsonist here is female, but I don't think so. This feels personal. I haven't told Lily that she probably knows who it is. It's an ugly thing to accuse anyone of."

Rio nodded slowly. "Any new faces in town? Other than ours? Because I'm assuming you're letting us off the hook for this one."

"None that stick around. People come and go—that's what happens when you live in a historic town."

"This stalker of hers, he's sticking to her. He's watching her, Ben." Jack ran a hand over his hair. "What about family?"

"I never knew who her daddy was," he said regretfully. "Just a mistake—that's all her momma told me. Mistake for the two of them, maybe, but Lily was the sweetest mistake that ever happened to me. I had no idea what I'd been missing out on when she landed in my lap. Thank God for your Nonna," he added, laughing, "or I would have been washed up the first week. I didn't know jack shit about little girls, and Lily was none too happy about being dumped here with an uncle she'd never met. I didn't realize a five-year-old could think of that many ways to say no," he said fondly.

"She was lucky she had you."

"I'm still here for her. She'll always have me. That's a given." Ben gestured for another round. He'd go all out tonight. Make it three beers instead of his usual two. "You have any thoughts on who might be stalking our girl?"

"Ours?" Jack raised an eyebrow, the bottle frozen in his hand.

"Ours," Ben confirmed. "We both know it, Jack. She was yours before you left all those years ago, and some things don't change."

"Lily might have something to say about that."

"Well, I figure you're every bit as much hers," Ben said. Christ, the seats in the bar didn't get any softer as he got older. "Two-way street and all. But she took it pretty hard when you left, followed that road right out of town damn quick."

"We were just kids."

"Maybe," Ben allowed. "You did the right thing there, holding back. You were both too young to handle a serious relationship."

Jack shot him a look that didn't take much interpreting. "She wasn't my first girl, Ben."

"First one that meant anything to you," Ben pointed out comfortably. When Jack didn't say anything, he figured he had that one right enough. "She needed to do some more growing up before she could give what you needed from her. She was a sexy little thing but not old enough to do some things."

Yeah. That was definitely a flush on Jack's face. Maybe it was truth hitting home or simply the fact that Ben wasn't dead and buried yet. Lily was like his own daughter, but there was no skirting some truths. She'd been a pretty, pretty girl. Pure trouble. He'd been glad enough when she'd taken an interest in Jack Donovan, because he'd known, even then, that Jack was on track to be a good man. He hadn't taken advantage of Lily.

"You did the right thing, Jack. You left, because sticking around would have meant trouble. She was too young. You weren't old enough, either. Question really is, what are you going to do now?"

Jack's eyes measured him, and that face of his didn't give away a damn thing. "I'm going to find her stalker, Ben."

"That all?" Ben raised an eyebrow, just to see what Jack would do next. He wasn't looking for the man to pop out a diamond ring—not yet—but damned if he'd loose the man on Lily without getting some kind of commitment from him. "I figure you'll do the right thing by Lily. No matter what folks here had to say about you boys, I always knew you were good at heart. Honorable men," he said pointedly.

"I'm not going to hurt her."

"Good to know." He nodded. "But I wouldn't expect any less from you. Question is, what happens if she needs more than a strong pair of hands, someone to beat the crap out of the bastard making her life hell?"

Jack sucked down his beer and tried desperately to pretend Ben hadn't just dropped the conversational equivalent of the bomb that had hit Hiroshima. For a long moment the only sounds filling up the silence were the country music playing on the jukebox and the soft clack of balls colliding on the pool table. Mimi chatted up a newcomer who couldn't drag his eyes from the tall blonde's face. Her pretty voice was giving a shout-out to the local eateries, but Ben figured her audience wasn't too interested in dinner unless the bartender was along for the ride. Which meant the newcomer was plain out of luck, because he'd seen Mimi ride into Strong on the back of Rio Donovan's Harley. He knew what that meant.

"Don't push me, Ben." Jack went on the offensive, which was usually a move Ben would have applauded. But since this was Lily they were discussing, the tactic wasn't going to fly.

"I'm asking you to tell me whether my girl is a little

summertime fun for you, or if there's something more going on between the two of you." Blunt but to the point,
he decided. He didn't have Nonna's more delicate touch,
but Jack had always appreciated the straight-up.

"I have a job to do here." Jack slammed the bottle back
down on the bar, and Mimi stopped her heart-to-heart
and looked over. *Shit.* He didn't want an audience for this
conversation, or Nonna would hear about it. "Lily is up to
her sweet little ass in trouble, and we both know it. She
needs someone to keep an eye on her, to keep her in line
before she goes and does something that ends badly. Fire-
boy isn't sane. I don't think he's going to go away, and neither do you, or you wouldn't have welcomed me in here
in the first place."

"So you're keeping her safe." Ben took a long sip of his
own beer and decided, *what the hell.* He'd go for broke in
this conversation he was having. "There's no romance.
Just a whole lot of business."

Next to him, Rio snorted and just about fell off his bar
stool trying to hold in the laughter.

Jack glared at his brother, but then he pulled it together.
"I don't know."

That was honest enough. Ben wasn't surprised his Lily
had the other man all turned around.

"The way I see it," Jack continued, "we have some unfinished business of our own. I'd like to see Lily, but you
know me, Ben. You know the job. At the end of the summer, I'll be shipping out again. There will always be another fire."

Chapter Nine

Two days. She'd managed to avoid Jack for two days, but Lily figured she couldn't run forever. After all, they were sharing a house. Her house. He knew damned well she couldn't hide much longer.

All he had to do was wait her out. The devilish gleam in his eye was warning enough.

He wouldn't wait much longer.

She should have been fighting him harder, but she couldn't hide from the delicious sense of anticipation building in her. God, it was going to be so good when they finally landed in bed together. They both knew it. She just wasn't ready to admit it yet, wasn't ready to end this game they were playing.

So, when he pulled up in that beat-up old pickup of his, she was waiting. The fire he'd been called out on had been every bit as small as he'd expected. She'd called Ben to find out. Typical small-town stuff. The guy four houses down from Nonna's hadn't cut back the grass around his barbecue pit, and the whole world—with the notable exception of the mad barbecuer himself—knew the man was no grill master. Too much lighter fluid, and the corn the idiot had decided to grill became tinder. At least he'd had the presence of mind to dial for help when the shooting flames had leaped the pit and gone for the grass.

"Fire out?" she called through the screen door while he stripped on the sunporch.

"Yeah," he hollered back, just as if they were Miriam and Daniel, married for thirty years, with a backyard full of grandkids. "Man's got himself a big black bald patch in his backyard, his wife's still hollering at him, but his house is standing. Not even scorched," he added, and there was no missing the satisfaction in his voice. He'd won another round.

Whistling, he dropped his gear on the floor, Nomex fire pants following his steel-toed boots. She didn't know why he couldn't leave his stuff at the firehouse or in that damned plane hangar where his brothers and the rest of their team were camped out. Instead, he left it all right there on her porch, like a dog or a big predatory cat marking his territory. She could absolutely imagine him as a tiger, rubbing his cheek against the wood of her house to mark it as his. Mark *her* as his.

When he came in, he still had soot on his face, as if he'd scrubbed a hand over it in the heat of the moment. The little breeze from the open door brought her the too-familiar, woodsy scent of fire.

She couldn't shake the memory, couldn't forget those little fires that had upended her life. Just a whiff of smoke was enough to send her over the edge. Someone was out there, watching her. Choosing what to take away from her. He knew what she was reading. He had probably brushed elbows with her in the general store. He was coming for her.

"Baby?" His eyes went straight to hers. "You going to tell me what's wrong?"

"I'm all right," she lied.

"Like hell you are," he said, starting toward her.

She flinched and took a step backward before she could stop herself. He was too much, too overwhelming.

God, she wasn't ready for this.

Maybe, she thought despairingly, she never would be ready.

Standing there in Lily's pretty little living room, Jack froze. He'd wanted to push her, wanted to make her burn for him the way he burned for her—but, Christ, he didn't want to hurt her. Or scare her. Never that. She was looking at him like a skittish kitten. All big eyes. Later, when she rethought what was happening now, she'd hate that vulnerability, but, right now, it felt almost like trust to him. Whether she'd meant to or not, she'd let down her guard. He was seeing a part of Lily Cortez that she kept well hidden, and Ben's little heart-to-heart in the bar kept replaying through his head. *Don't you dare hurt her.*

"What's wrong, baby?" He backed off immediately—still sensual predator, but now all that interest was focused on her fear. Not her body. Part of her was disappointed. The rest of her was aroused, intrigued by that rough tenderness, protectiveness.

"You smell like smoke."

Yeah, he smelled of fire. And she looked as if she hated herself for not being able to dismiss a flash of fear.

He didn't move, hand braced on the door frame, leaning a hip against it. "You don't like the smell of smoke?" She shook her head mutely. "It reminds you of the fires in San Francisco, doesn't it?" he growled.

"Yes. The smell of smoke." She shrugged helplessly. "It takes me right back."

"So I'll shower." He turned, stripping off his T-shirt as he headed toward her ground-floor bathroom. "Baby," he warned as he hit the bathroom door, "I'm coming back, though, and this conversation is just getting started. I thought you'd want to know that."

★ ★ ★

When Jack emerged from the bathroom, she'd done her thinking and then some. She didn't doubt Jack would be every bit as sensually wild in bed as she'd fantasized—and this time, he wouldn't hold back. Even more seductive was the man she was coming to know, strong and honorable, a natural-born protector who would defend her. If she let him. And, she had a sinking suspicion, even if she didn't want to let him.

He padded barefoot into her living room, wearing just a pair of sweatpants and a battered old T-shirt.

"Smell," he coaxed, holding out a hand to her, his eyes dancing with laughter. "I even used that damned lavender soap of yours."

"All better," she agreed, but she didn't come any closer. Her senses were humming, hyper-aware of him. The lush warmth of the evening air surrounded her as the day's heat mellowed into something softer, less searing, but no easier to ignore. She burned for Jack Donovan with each breath of scented air she took.

Her commercial fields—those were lavender. The garden spilling around her porch and her front door was pure play. Lavender tangled with heirloom roses, catmint, and the odd hollyhock. A sweet explosion of scent that greeted her each morning when she opened the door, and, when she left the windows open as she had tonight, the pungent scents drifted through her rooms, getting right under her skin. Right now, the heady aroma of night-blooming roses mixed with the potent scent of the man filling up her house.

He shook his head mischievously. "Not good enough." Moving with the speed of a striking panther, he crossed the floor and wrapped his arms around her waist, swinging her off her feet.

"Jack," she gasped, arms circling his neck reflexively.

"Now, that's better." He smiled down at her. Cheek to

skin with him, nothing between them. Just the warm, masculine scent of him. He smelled so right. Nothing frightening about the arousal humming lazily through her.

"I'm waiting," he invited.

Why not? she thought fiercely. Inhaling, she pressed her cheek against the hollow of his shoulder. Let her lips rest against his skin and felt the shudder go right through him.

"Lilybell," he growled warningly, lowering her to her feet.

"I thought you wanted to play," she whispered.

"Dance with me." He put a little space between them. "We haven't ever shared a dance." The radio was playing country music, the low, throbbing twang of the singer promising heat and heartache.

Just like her Jack.

Damp and soap-scented from his shower, his short hair curled a little on the back of his neck. And she was dancing with him. Moving slowly in the circle of his arms as he waltzed her barefoot around her living room. Focused on her.

Why not? she thought again. The sun was just going down outside, the room sliding into shadows and twilight. The moment was deliciously tempting.

She slipped her hand into his. Callused and warm, careful, his fingers closed around hers and tugged teasingly, pulling her closer to his big body. Toward the warmth and heat of him.

"We'll go just as slow as you like, baby." Heated promise filled his voice. "Just tell me what you want."

"I want to dance." To start with. She stepped closer, sliding her body into the protective curve of his. Perfect fit.

His husky groan was the perfect reward. "You're going to kill me, baby." Heat washed through her, followed by the now-familiar, soft pulse of desire. Oh, how she'd missed him.

"You remember that night we had together, Lilybell?" His question was a husky whisper by her ear. His large hands wrapped around her waist, settling on the waistband of her shorts. "I do. I've thought about that night every night since, dreaming about what would have happened if I'd stayed there at the swimming hole with you instead of taking you home. I wanted you something fierce. Ten years haven't changed that."

Dancing in his arms made it all too easy to remember. He'd chosen to keep her safe, when she'd been dying for the sweet, sweet danger of his touch. He'd coaxed her out of the water, sure, but then all he'd done was put her into his truck and driven her home. Well, he'd kissed her, but that was all.

"But I'm back now, baby. And I think we've both grown up enough to make this turn out all right. I want you. I want *us*."

His hand on the small of her back rubbed coaxing circles, and she was melting into him as if it was high school all over again. She should have been pissed he'd just waltzed back into her life like this, but she wasn't stupid. It might be no more than some really great chemistry, but most people went a lifetime without experiencing this. Even if he was just a summer fling, did she want to miss out on it? On him?

Jack Donovan could be her treat to herself.

Yes.

She liked that idea.

"Baby," he whispered, those wicked hands of his still sliding up and down her back. Coaxing. "You've got to choose for us. Say yes, baby, because you're killing me."

Rough and sexy, his words rocked through her, a sensual promise she wanted to hold him to. Sliding her arms around his waist, beneath the cotton of his shirt, she pressed a cheek against his chest. The beat of his heart was reassuringly fast, his breathing harsh. Jack Donovan wanted her, and he wasn't afraid to let her know what he wanted. Who he needed.

She smiled slowly, before she could stop herself or hide the little sign of feminine pleasure. The radio cowboy was winding down his song, missing his girl something fierce as the night closed in around them.

"Yes," she whispered, reaching up to pull his head down to hers. "Yes, Jack Donovan. Show me what we missed out on that night. Show me how you would have touched me."

"It's a damned good thing you're sure, baby, because I'm not ready to let you get away from me tonight." Lifting her up into his arms, he crossed the room swiftly, lowering them both into her wicker armchair. "We've got all night, and I plan to be very, very thorough."

"Promises, Jack?" Tilting her head back, she smiled slowly as she wrapped her legs around his waist. The summer night unfolding outside the open windows was thick with the scent of lavender and the drowsy hum of crickets. The perfect accompaniments to summertime romance. She'd never felt like this before. The lush heat building so slowly inside her demanded more. She needed Jack, needed his kiss.

The heat spread, building, as she squirmed on his lap, feeling the strength of his thighs and the erotic rub of the worn denim against her bare legs. Just his closeness, the erotic possibilities of the slowly darkening room, had her panties dampening. Making out in the dark like a couple of high school seniors, only there was no one to walk in on them. No reason to stop. The throaty purr of pleasure and acquiescence slid from her throat before she could bite back the sound.

From his answering groan, he liked it.

"God, yes, baby." One hand slid up her back, then cupped the nape of her neck, angling her face for his kiss. His fingers tangled in her hair, sending erotic shivers down her spine. "Tell me how much you want this."

His other hand moved to her waist, playing with the edge of her tank top before slipping beneath it to stroke her bare skin. A slow, heated promise of pleasure and all the time in the world.

His hand cupped one breast, stroking its softness. "You're so beautiful." His mouth lowered, brushing her with a teasing kiss. "You like this, don't you, Lily? You're wet for me, for us, aren't you?"

God. She was going to come from the sound of his voice, the sexy growl of satisfaction he made as he pulled her shirt off. His fingers flicked open her bra, nudging the lacy cups aside.

"I don't hear an answer, baby." He licked a hot, damp path down one breast, rolling the stiff little nipple in his mouth. The pleasure threatened to overwhelm her, suck her down into a heated maelstrom of pleasure. He was pure wickedness. Every bit as delicious as his reputation had promised.

"I owe you something for that night," he whispered, his hands cupping both her breasts now. Teasing her nipples knowingly. "Do you have any idea how many nights I came, remembering how hot you were? Just thinking about what we could have done next?"

Gently, he pinched her nipples, his dark eyes watching as the pleasure tore through her.

One hand slid to her waistband, flicking open the little silver button. Opening her up for him. When he saw the glint of her white lace panties in the gathering shadows, he sucked his breath in. "Better than my fantasies," he groaned. "Let me touch you now, baby. Please."

Leaning forward, she captured his mouth. He wasn't the only one with fantasies. She ate at his mouth, devouring him. Swallowing his harsh groan of pleasure as her tongue dueled with his. Took his mouth with long, slow, heated strokes until there was no part of that mouth she didn't know. All hers.

His hand parted her thighs wider, covering the scrap of white lace concealing her aching flesh. His hoarse groan was her reward as she arched her back into his touch with a wordless cry.

He touched her there, there where she burned. The pleasure was a bright bolt tearing through her as he teased and stroked. Coaxed her higher with each wicked pass of his fingers over the cotton soaked with her juices. Wicked, teasing strokes that traced the needy folds, promising ecstasy with each touch. With each brush of his fingertips, the heat built, her flesh growing wetter, tighter.

She shattered, crying out, rocking against his hand.

Chapter Ten

He was smart enough not to get caught, but the tension was humming through him, and his dick was viciously hard. It had been too long since the last fire.

Bitch had moved a man into her house.

She'd never done that before. When he'd teased her back in San Francisco, she'd done a little screaming. Called the police and purchased a home security system that he could have warned her wasn't worth shit. Those systems only kept out the stupid. This new place of hers didn't even have that, just a few cheap locks on the windows and a forty-year-old lock on the door. Hardware store had spare keys for all the houses in Strong—that small-town neighborliness thing—and he'd helped himself.

Simple.

He went where he wanted to go, as the women who'd filed the restraining orders peppering his college career had learned. All carefully swept under the rug by his grandfather's money while his fires kept right on burning.

Clearly, though, his Lily needed another lesson. Another reminder he was coming for her real soon. Dropping the dirt bike behind a convenient stand of thick grass, he considered his options. He could set her fields on fire, but that would bring out the insurance adjuster double-time, and then he'd have to finish his little game too quickly. Ditto for burning the farmhouse. He'd save those for later. When he was ready to be done here.

Humming, hand in his pocket, he scuffed up the edge of the driveway, scattering the gravel. The little purple and white sign advertising fresh-cut lavender—that would do. Close enough to frighten her, but not too close. His Lily wouldn't get burned.

This time.

Setting the fire was simple. Beneath the fresh paint, Lily's pretty sign was old wood. Once the fire caught, it'd go right up. The little pink and white flowers she'd planted around the sign just made the job easier, as did the woody stalks of lavender. All he needed was a little newspaper and lighter fluid.

Trembling with anticipation, he struck the match and dropped the flaming stick into the little nest he'd made for it. Wrapping his fingers around his dick, he massaged his swollen shaft, keeping time with the flames slowly licking up the painted wood.

Tearing his mouth from hers, Jack buried his face in Lily's throat, drinking in her small shivers as she came for him, tiny, bright pulses of pleasure beating against his fingers like butterfly wings. Her pleasure was so damned beautiful, he wanted to take her there again and again until she was limp and boneless in his arms. God, he needed a bed, needed to lose himself inside her and love her the way she deserved to be loved.

The familiar, acrid whiff of smoke creeping in through the open window was an unwelcome alarm. There shouldn't be smoke. Not here.

Swiftly raising his head, he pulled Lily closer and looked out the window into the darkening yard. There. A familiar orange flicker and a smoky haze. He'd spent the better part of a decade spotting smoke, but this cloud was surprisingly small. Yet too damned close. *Christ*. Rising to his feet, he tucked Lily back into the chair and headed for the door and the familiar tang of burning wood and tinder.

"Call Rio," he barked, tossing her his cell as he took off at a dead run for the farm's sign at the bottom of her driveway. Orange flames were licking straight up the white posts, paint peeling away in dark curls. The little pink flowers and curling vine that she'd planted were already gone.

Too long, he decided, to get the hose unwound. He didn't want to lose that sign. Lily had painted it. That sign mattered to her. It was a symbol. Grabbing a shovel and a blanket from the back of his pickup, he got to work. Smothered what he could with the blanket and then covered over the rest with dirt.

"Oh, God," she said, right behind him, pulling her clothes back on. He wanted to order her back into the house. What if her stalker had progressed from fire starting to sniping? He didn't want her out here where someone could take potshots at her.

Hell. Already, the remaining flames were dying away beneath the weight of the blanket and dirt. Behind him, he heard Lily dialing.

"Get your asses over here. Now," he barked as he heard Rio pick up. He shifted another shovelful of dirt onto the flames. The paint had barely blistered, and the fire hadn't jumped the neat little garden bed Lily had dug around the farm's sign. Plenty of tinder, but there hadn't been enough time for it to catch. There was hardly any damage.

Thank God.

His eyes narrowed, his head coming up. "Get into my truck," he snapped, tossing her the keys. "Take it down to the road, and wait for my brothers. You see anyone else headed your way, you drive like the wind, Lily. You got that?" He couldn't send her back into the house. When they'd seen those flames, they'd both run outside. That meant anyone could have slipped in behind them.

He dropped the shovel, running his gaze over the woods. Bastard was in there. Watching them. He knew it.

"What's wrong, Jack?" She came up behind him, snapping the cell closed.

"Get into the truck, Lily," he repeated, pressing the keys into her hand. "Just do it."

She tucked her hair nervously behind her ear. "You think he's out there."

He filed away her unconscious reference to the gender of her stalker. He'd hash out that telltale sign with her later. For now, he turned toward the strip of woods nearest them, on full alert. Whoever this bastard was, his days of terrorizing Lily Cortez were over.

"Fire's out." He didn't take his eyes off the woods. It was hard to see in the gathering shadows. There. The grass at the edge of the trees shifted a few inches. There was no wind. If there had been, he'd have been facing a much larger fire. "Get into the truck, and go wait for my brothers."

Without turning around, he ran his fingers along her cheek. His hands were ashy from the fire, covered in dirt, so he knew he should have waited. But he had to touch her. Had to feel for himself that she was right there beside him. Safe.

She must have caught his tension, because she stopped fighting him. He savored that little moment of trust. "All right," she said, her fingers closing around the keys. "When you're done here, though, Jack, I want answers."

Gravel crunched as she moved away. Her little hiss of pain as the stones bit into her bare feet only fueled his anger. This bastard had hurt her for the last time.

He waited until the truck's door slammed shut and the lock clicked into place. Then he sprang into action, his legs tearing up the ground between him and that stand of grass.

The hiding place was two hundred yards out and well chosen. Bastard must have brought binoculars with him to enjoy the scene he'd staged, and Jack made a mental note to check the windows in the house. Lily was living in a fishbowl, and he didn't like it. Hell, half the time out here in the country, nobody pulled down a shade. No neighbors and plenty of privacy. God only knew what the bastard had seen.

The grass in front of him suddenly exploded into life. A man ran, his features concealed beneath layers of expensive hunting gear. Man was a walking L.L. Bean catalog with camouflage pants and an olive-green T-shirt. The glossy black helmet with the visor jammed down made a shadowed blur of the face hiding behind the protective panel. Medium build, Jack noted. Caucasian, from the coloring of his forearms.

Ran like a jackrabbit.

Bastard had a dirt bike waiting for him behind the stand of trees. He didn't make any attempt to keep it quiet—just punched the electric starter, let the engine rip, and took off. Jack tried to keep up, even though it was pointless. He was on foot; all he could hope for was to see where the bastard headed. And realize that the other man knew his way around the dirt trails through these woods. Real well.

Lily's stalker was definitely local.

Chapter Eleven

The fire wasn't a big one. Lily grabbed on to that thought as if it was a lifeline in the sea of chaotic, tumbling images burned into her memory. Jack, beating back flames, putting them out. Treating her small grass fire like it was of national importance, and, damn it, she shouldn't have found that *sweet*.

Ten minutes after she'd made the call, Rio and Evan were charging up the driveway, Rio on his Harley and Evan in a pickup that was—impossibly—even more decrepit than Jack's truck.

Whatever they'd been doing, they'd dropped it and hightailed it over here. She curled her fingers over the edge of the truck's rolled-down window and wondered how to explain the unexpected warmth that filled her. It almost felt like belonging. Rio and Evan exchanged a glance she'd have taken objection to under other circumstances, and then they split up.

Evan loped toward the remains of the fire, moving fast and with purpose. His big, booted feet finished up the job Jack had started, methodically stamping out the last embers. Orange licked feebly at his feet and his jeans-clad legs. She wanted to whimper, but that wasn't helping, so she thought about pointing her feet toward the hose. She needed a bucket. Needed to be *doing* anything but just watching.

But Jack had been damned clear about where he wanted her. In his truck.

Rio dropped the bike and headed her way anyhow.

Reaching in the window, he put a hand on her shoulder, as if he understood that she needed to know she wasn't alone right now. Needed an anchor. "You okay?" he asked quietly. His eyes watched those leftover little embers, assessing Evan's progress.

"I've been better," she said quietly.

"Right. Stay put," he warned. "Stay where we can see you." Reaching into the truck's bed, he grabbed a pair of shovels and tossed one to Evan.

"You've got to watch the small ones," Rio said, throwing another shovelful of dirt onto the smoldering embers. "The small fires are the ones that creep up on you, find themselves some fuel, and get damned big real fast. Burn out of control before you know it. So, yes, this fire matters. All fires matter."

God. She *knew* that. The slow tears leaking from her eyes horrified her, but there was no holding them in. How long could she be expected to keep it together?

When Jack returned from his sudden sprint into the woods, she got out of the truck and attached herself to his side. She wasn't stupid. He'd chased someone off.

Jack moved swiftly toward her. "Baby." His voice was a husky growl as he put a hand on her shoulder. She looked down at those fingers, so sun-browned and strong, warm on her bare skin. Anchoring her. God, he'd run a mile— *away* from her—if he knew what he was starting to mean to her.

That hand, impossibly tender, urged her to turn around. "I need to see that you're okay, baby." His other hand came up, his thumb stroking a little pattern over the hollow of her shoulder as he carefully pulled her back against him.

So she just let herself go. Turning around, she buried her face against his chest and let all the tears come out. And Jack's arms just held on tightly, wrapping her up in his strength as he waited for her to cry it all out. She'd known, when he came home, that they had unfinished business. Her memories of that night were slow and sweet, but the years had changed Jack. He was all man now, and ten years of fighting enemy soldiers and wildland fires had made a hero out of the boy she'd once held. He'd changed, as she had, but some things had stayed the same.

She still wanted him.

And he still wanted to keep her safe.

"You ready to tell me what this is all about?" He didn't remove his arm, just tucked her more firmly against him and settled down with his back against a convenient tree, pulling her into his lap.

"All right." Maybe she should have protested the seating arrangements, but, God, he felt so solid. So real in a world that was slowly turning into a nightmare. She just leaned her head back against his shoulder. It was easier that way.

Because giving up control, letting him in, was the hardest thing she'd ever done. Harder even than watching him walk away ten years ago, because, this time, she'd handed the control over to him.

"I'm waiting, baby." His husky growl in her ear warned her that the years hadn't taught him patience. Not when it came to answers.

"I should have told you everything about what happened, back in San Francisco. I thought the bare bones would be enough." She shrugged. "I figured you didn't need any more than that.

"Details always matter." There was no mistaking the intensity in his voice or the way his arms tightened around her. "So why don't you tell me now?"

She swiped at her wet eyelashes. She wasn't usually a crier. She didn't come apart when a man asked what the hell was wrong. So why was she doing it now?

"This isn't your problem to fix, Jack. You're a smoke jumper, and this is no wildland fire. We might have seen each other a time or two in high school, but that was years ago. I didn't need or want you to come riding to the rescue. And I didn't want you thinking about what happened, every time you looked at me."

"I have plenty to think about already when I look at you." She didn't miss the sexual tension in his body. "I've thought about what we had every single night, Lily. I might not have known what to do about it, but I thought about it. I thought about you. If you'd told me you were in trouble, I would have been here for you. I'd have come home."

He hadn't come home in ten years.

"You did come home," she pointed out.

"Nonna asked." He shrugged. "So I came."

"You weren't expecting to see me."

"No." Those arms of his shifted, wrapping around her waist and pulling her closer. "But I'm still here, Lily, and that's going to count for something. This time I'm staying put, and I'm ready to do something about us. First, though, I need to know what your deal is. Tell me why these fires scare the hell out of you—tell me what you haven't told me yet."

She inhaled slowly. "I was living in San Francisco, running marketing for a high-end bath-products line. Dream job, right? I had interesting work, great friends, a little condo out in Ocean Beach where I could run on the sand every morning. Picture perfect."

"And then what happened?" His voice was flat, but she didn't miss the tension in those arms.

"Little things at first. A trash can fire at the end of the street, not too far from my carport. The kind of fire that happens when you live in a city and someone tosses a cigarette too carelessly. No big deal."

"You didn't move here because some asshole couldn't be bothered to put out his butt," he said inexorably.

"There were more fires." She was twisting her fingers, she realized, when his large hands covered hers. Not stopping her, just reminding her that he was there. With her. She inhaled slowly. "Some old newspaper in the recycling bin caught fire. A little smoke, and I needed a new bin, but it was out quickly, thanks to a neighbor. I'd just gone out for a run, so I was safe, right? But there were so many of these little fires, Jack. I started thinking they couldn't all be coincidence."

There had been more than a dozen small, easily dismissed fires. Nothing too personal. Nothing too close. She'd been torn between staying in and going out. Wondering if these were just the normal hazards of living in a big city, if she was being paranoid. The nightmares had started soon after, vivid dreams of being trapped inside the town house while it went up in flames. Because, if she was honest, that was what happened when you didn't or couldn't put out a fire. It just got bigger, and those flames devoured whatever they could.

"You reported the fires."

"I did, or one of my neighbors did. The police thought maybe we had a local kid or a homeless firebug. But they still thought it was all pretty harmless."

"Something scared you, though. You knew those fires weren't harmless."

"Not at first. But, yes, when I really thought about it, I realized the fires didn't happen to anyone else. And then the things that burned changed." His hand came up, rubbing away the tension in the back of her neck. The farm's sign was a white shadow in the growing dusk. "He started burning *my* things, Jack. Not trash, not whatever he happened to find. I used to love reading. I'd bring home stacks of novels, crawl into the tub, and just read the night away."

She felt rather than saw his smile. "Bet that was a great sight."

"Then, one day," she continued, "there was another little fire near my house. He'd burned some of my books, Jack. Somehow he'd gotten into my house and taken a stack of paperbacks from my bathroom. That wasn't an accident. I'm not stupid. That's when I knew what was happening was personal. After that, it was all personal. My carport. The books he burned in my kitchen."

Too close, too fast. She'd bolted.

"I woke up, and *my house was on fire,* Jack. All my favorite books were piled up in the sink and on fire, and the cabinets were catching flame. I tried to open the door, but the knob was too hot. I turned around and ran, and I got out onto the fire escape. I thought: just let me get to the alley, and I'll be safe. It will all be over." This was the part she hadn't wanted to share, the part she'd glossed over every time she'd been forced to relive that night. "There was someone there, Jack. There was a man standing in the alley. He was masturbating while he stared up at my kitchen window. He got off, watching my place burn."

"Why didn't you tell the cops this?" He looked as if she was describing the weather, except there was no mistaking the tension in his jaw. He didn't like what she had to say. Which was fine with her. She didn't like having those memories, either.

"What was I supposed to tell them? They'd already suggested I was either making things up or paranoid or even setting the fires myself."

He was silent for a long moment, and then he shook his head. "Did he touch you?"

When she didn't answer right away, he asked again. "Goddamn it, Lily. I need to know. Did he touch you?"

"No," she said sharply. "The fire escape stopped a good twelve feet above the ground, and I saw him, and I screamed, okay? I just lost it, and I stood there, screaming, until the fire department sent someone around to check out the noise. Afterward, I left," she continued. "I packed up and I came here and I bought the farm. For a while, I thought I'd left all that behind me."

"And then the fires started again."

"Yes." She grimaced. She'd begun to fear weeks ago that *he* was watching her, choosing what to take away from her this time. He'd get into her house just like before, touching her things. "Just like before. Little things. Coincidences at first. And then he starts adding a personal touch, like it's a message he wants to send."

"You should have told me."

"I'm telling you now, because I have no choice. But I don't need a relationship with you to complicate my life any further. You fight fire, Jack." She could hear the weary acceptance in her own voice. Knew there was no way he could deny the truth. "Every day, you're willing to pull hose or jump out of a damn plane and right into the heart of a damned inferno. But me—I don't want to have anything to do with fire."

She'd grown up in Strong and had been happy enough to leave for college and a shot at a career in San Francisco. She hadn't realized what she was leaving behind until her new life had gone up in flames. Literally. Familiar and safe and as solid as its name, Strong was a place where you came home. A place where you put down roots and built yourself a future, one lavender plug at a time. Strong held more than happy childhood memories—it held her future.

She was going to be safe—and Jack Donovan was anything *but* safe.

She didn't want complications.

Jack grimaced. Damned if that didn't put him in his place. What she wanted, however, didn't matter when it came to her safety. Someone was after her. Watching her. Deliberately choosing personal items of hers to burn. And the man had to be a local.

Jack had spent years learning to read burn scenes for their clues. The what and where, the why of whatever blaze had eaten up charred acres. He just needed to find the pattern of the fires set by Lily's stalker. Too bad Strong wasn't a big city—there was a singular lack of security cameras in town. He needed to get Rio to run the names of local men. Whoever he was, he'd been in San Francisco at the same time as Lily.

"I didn't recognize the arsonist." He frowned. "But he'd covered his face."

"Why do you think you'd recognize him?"

"Even though the problem began in San Francisco, I'm almost sure your stalker has known you for some time," he explained, then went on before she could react. "You said there was more than one fire while you were living in San Francisco. Give me a window—a week? Two months? How long did this go on?"

She looked up. "Six, seven months. It's all in the police reports, Jack."

"Humor me," he growled. "Six months, maybe seven. Then you came here, bought the farm—and the fires started again."

"Not right away."

"What if he knew where to find you? What if he's from Strong—just like you?"

"And like you. So if I know him, you know him," she

mused aloud. "Everyone knows everyone here. That's the joy of small-town living for you."

"Lots of things to enjoy in a small town," he drawled. Kissing her simply seemed like the right thing to do. He was desperate to make her feel better, and the dampness of her tears in his T-shirt reminded him he hadn't found a way yet.

"Hell, baby, don't cry anymore," he ordered gruffly, nudging her chin up with his fingers. Another day, when she had her strength back and she wasn't confronting the evidence of a very nasty, very personal arson, she'd knock his hand into the middle of next week. Right now, though, she was letting him take care of her. Like he needed to do. The surge of fierce protectiveness was unfamiliar—but it felt right.

Damned right.

He looked down at her familiar face, those too-wide eyes of hers, and knew this was right. *They* were right. He wasn't ever walking away from her again. Somehow he was going to convince her of that truth. He didn't know what was going to happen when summer was over. He'd never stuck around to see summer wind down, never been around to see what could happen next.

"I'm here," he promised. Later, he'd explain that promise to her. Right now, though, he had his arms full of Lily Cortez.

"Kiss me, Jack," she ordered as if it had been her idea.

And maybe it had been. She twisted him into knots, so that he didn't know if he was coming or going. All he knew was that the woman he held in his arms was special, and she was hurting.

That, he knew, wasn't okay.

So he'd make it better.

Kiss her better.

He had her pressed up against him already. All he'd have

to do was pick her up, so that her legs—those long, lovely, too bare legs of hers—were wrapped around his waist as if they were already in her bed and he inside of her. His erection jerked, loving the fantasy. God. He'd thought she was trouble.

He'd had no idea.

Sliding his hands into her hair, he held her still, lowering his head to hers.

No time for subtle, not now. Just the raw, hard kiss he'd been saving for her all these years. Marking her. Branding her as his.

His lips tasted hers, ate the sweet, hot taste of her as his tongue stroked over her closed lips and pressed on inside. Drinking in her sweet whimper like a cool drink on a summer afternoon. She pressed closer, her softness cradling his hard heat. Urging him in. Warning him not to pull away. His Lily had her mind made up, and that was the sexiest thing a man could ever want.

So he kissed his way across her lips, nipping the soft curves. Opening her wide so he could taste her all the way. Every hidden place. Like he'd do with the rest of her just as soon as he had her back in the house. He could feel how hot she was where those wicked little denim shorts of hers rubbed against him. Rocking slowly against him in silent demand.

She was killing him.

Chapter Twelve

Jack took the stairs two a time, Lily cradled in his arms. When he hit the top, he hesitated but only for a moment. Her room. Not the guest room. He wanted everything she had to offer, and he wasn't going to let her push him into a convenient little box. He wasn't a guest. Damned if he knew what he *was,* but this feeling he had for Lily wasn't a temporary thing.

He'd dreamed of this night forever, wondering what he'd missed all those years ago. If he was lucky, he'd find out tonight. He'd been rootless, always roaming, since he'd left Strong. He'd gone from one summer to the next, never settling. So he wasn't going to hesitate now, when she was lying sweet and relaxed in his arms. Her eyes were watching again, but this time those baby browns were as hungry as his were.

Lily Cortez wanted him.

Damned if that didn't twist up his insides even as it sent the blood shooting to his erection. He wouldn't last long at the rate he was going, and that wasn't the way he wanted this evening to end. Tonight was for Lily. Sweeping aside the patchwork quilt with one hand, he laid her on the lace-trimmed sheets and followed her down. The hunger hit as soon as he touched the mattress, sinking into its yielding softness.

He finally had Lily Cortez in his arms, in a bed. And it was one hell of a bed, too. Despite the too-feminine sheets, the headboard was all iron curlicues. He could play out a dozen dark fantasies in this bed. Another night, perhaps he'd tie her to the bed, playing a delicious little game with the woman he held. He could take her a dozen different ways, show her the path to pleasure over and over. Tonight, though, deserved something special, a slow, sweet loving.

"You going to look all night?" Her voice was pure, husky invitation. "Or do you want to do something else, Jack?"

Lily. An old-fashioned name for an old-fashioned kind of a girl. She was classy. He'd recognized that truth back when they'd still been in high school and he'd been flirting with the impossible idea of making her his sweetheart. Good girls like her didn't fall for bad boys like him. Not for forever.

But maybe that was just one more rule he could break.

"Yeah, baby. Let's see if we can figure out what feels good for you." He hooked a thumb beneath the thin strap of her white tank top, stroking along the wicked edge of lace tracing those delicious curves. She was so damned fine.

"All right, Jack." She watched him with liquid promise as he drew the straps of the bra cupping her breasts down her arms. "Maybe we'll find something you like, as well."

"No worries there, baby," he growled. "You're the prettiest thing I've ever laid eyes on." Her breasts were sweet, pale mounds cupped in his sun-darkened hands, the nipples flushed with her arousal. And the scent of her— Christ, he could have lain down beside her and just looked and inhaled all night. He gave in to the urge to taste her, licking a path down her neck, exploring. Long before he'd reached those pretty little nipples, she was flushed.

"I like these." He sucked a nipple into his mouth, swirled his tongue around her as her hands pulled at him. Demanding more. When his lips let go, she clung to him. Savage satisfaction filled him. Yes, he'd been waiting and dreaming all these years, but Lily Cortez had clearly been entertaining her own fantasies.

"Undress," she demanded. "Now, Jack. I want to see what you've been keeping from me all this time." The sexy demand had him hardening impossibly, so he pulled the T-shirt over his head and dropped it to the floor.

"I'm all yours, baby," he drawled. Had been since he'd first laid eyes on her.

Jack Donovan was a delicious present she couldn't wait to unwrap. Big and sun-bronzed, his hard body filled her bed. He wasn't gentle. Wasn't patient. So the contrast of his masculine strength with her lace-trimmed sheets was overwhelming. Unforgettable.

Reaching up an arm, she drew him down and closer so she could feel the heated expanse of his bare skin against her breasts. Bare skin scored with small burns and scars.

She pressed a small kiss against one white pucker of skin. "What happened, Jack?"

"Firefighting." Those broad shoulders shrugged casually as he settled himself above her. "Price of admission, baby."

"It must have hurt." *God.* He tasted wild and smoky, and she couldn't get enough of him. Couldn't get close enough as she licked a little circle around one male nipple. The sweet, hot scent of summer poured in the open window, wrapping them both in twilight and warmth. The curtains framing the window barely stirred as the sleepy, heated air slipped in, thick with the scent of fresh-cut grass and lavender. She'd never smell summer again without thinking of Jack.

For the moment, he was all hers—and they had unfinished business.

"Just feel, baby." He opened his arms, and she wanted the safety he represented, even if it was only an illusion. *Just for tonight,* she promised herself. Or maybe even the summer. Afterward, she could go back to being strong. Being alone.

He was a large, warm presence, waiting for her to choose. The mattress dipped beneath his weight as he shifted, and her body slid instinctively toward him, into that seductive hollow.

"Yes," she decided, reaching for him. She slid her hands along his shoulders, and he felt so damned good, so sleekly muscled. So alive. She was choosing—choosing now—to live her life. To seize life with both hands.

Seize Jack.

"Yes."

His fingers reached for the snap of her shorts. "Lift up." When she did, he slid the denim down her legs. When she was wearing just her panties, she decided it was his turn to finish stripping.

Her turn to stare. God, Jack was gorgeous, all sleek and hot as she ran her hands over him, traced the heavy weight straining against the denim of his jeans until he bucked against her fingers. She couldn't wait to see him naked.

"Definitely your turn," she whispered. Reaching for him, she slid open the buttons of his fly, her breath catching as the soft material parted. He was every bit as glorious as her fantasies had painted him, his thick shaft making her clench and bite her lip with the sudden throb of pleasure deep within. She'd waited so long for this.

The summer breeze playing with the curtains picked up, bringing a whisper of smoke. *Fire.* Instinctively, she tensed, unwanted memories sliding through her head.

"Don't think about him," Jack growled. "He won't be back tonight. Think about this."

Her stalker wouldn't be coming back, not tonight, but she was frightened, when he wanted her melting for him. So Jack did what he did best. Distracted. Coaxed. And laid a counterfire.

Carefully he stroked a finger over the flimsy little ribbon fastening the two sides of her string-bikini panties. Traced the rounded curve of her hips, savoring her feminine gasp. He'd wanted her for so long, and now he had her in his arms. No way he would rush this night. No way he would ever forget the woman he held.

She needed to forget, though, forget the fire that had driven her into his arms. So he'd kiss her again, until there was no room in this bed for more than the two of them. Threading one hand through her long hair, he held her gently in place for his kiss. Let his mouth glide lightly over hers, in a slow, decadent press of skin against skin. When a small, breathy moan rewarded his efforts, he gave in to temptation and let his other hand slide slowly down, giving her one last chance to stop him.

She didn't, and he realized she wouldn't. Lily Cortez wanted him. She made him feel like more of a man than he ever had before. Made him feel like a goddamned hero. Special.

Loved.

Desperate for her, he softly touched her, brushing the tips of his fingers over her panties. Watching. This had to be good for her. Better than good. He wanted this to be perfect.

The heat of her against his fingers was unimaginable. The sweetest, hottest fire he'd ever experienced.

At his touch, she stilled. Unsure and curious but drinking in that simple contact between them. And Jack knew he'd never see a more erotic sight in his life than this, his fingers against the white cotton, her fingers wrapping around his wrist. Even as he feared she might reach out to stop him, she wrapped her fingers around his wrist, guiding him deeper. Slower. Her moan filling the heated air between them.

Abandoning restraint, Jack tore her panties from her, tossing the scrap of fabric onto the floor, and slid his fingers into her heat. Liquid welcome surrounded him. "You're killing me, baby," he groaned. "God, you feel so good."

"So do you," she whimpered, wrapping her legs around him in feminine demand, pressing up against his thick erection.

"Are you sure?" His dark gaze held hers. One last chance.

"Yeah." She'd been sure yesterday and the day before but had spun out the delicious anticipation. "I'm tired of running, Jack. Tired of putting my life on hold. I want to live."

"Good," he rumbled. "You're so damned good, Lily-bell. You have any idea what that does to a man like me? A man like me just might insist on licking you from head to toe, baby."

She couldn't hold back the shiver that rocked her. "God, please," she whimpered. He'd made her wait ten years for this moment. He could damn well stop teasing her.

"You real sure, baby?" That wicked mouth slid down her neck again, tasting her skin. Tasting her. As that big, strong body followed, heat tore through her. She couldn't hold in the little noises of pleasure, couldn't keep the husky whimper silent as his tongue teased the curve of her belly, his hands sliding down to cup her hips. Her head fell back onto the pillow, her hands gripping his shoulders.

"Kiss me," she demanded.

"Oh, yeah," he growled.

His shoulders parted her legs as he gently opened her with his fingers. No escaping the rush of heated pleasure, of knowing she was open to him and there were no more secrets between them. He'd seen her, held her. Now he was going to know every inch of her.

She was open for him. Wet and aching for him.

He exhaled sharply, and the sensual shock of that tiny puff of air against her wet, heated folds sent her pleasure spiraling impossibly higher. The whole world was slowing down. Waiting. For him.

"A little good-night kiss," he promised. "You'd like that, wouldn't you, Lilybell? A man should always kiss his date good night."

"If it's been a good night." White-hot sensation tore through her, stoking the anticipation.

"It will be. And you're a good girl, Lily." Wicked promise filled his voice, echoed in the gentle stroke of his fingertips just tracing the edge of those swollen folds.

"Maybe," she whimpered. "You're teasing me, Jack."

"That's not nice of me." Dark promise filled his voice. "I'll kiss you better. All better, Lily. Tonight's for you."

His first, gentle kiss on her pussy was sweet. Light. The wicked bolt of pleasure had her crying out. "You're so sweet here," he groaned. "I don't deserve you, Lilybell."

Then that wicked mouth was exploring her, tasting her. Licking every last inch. Just as he'd promised. When he found her swollen clit and sucked, she arched up, losing herself to the pleasure. To Jack.

"Jack—" He slid up her body even as the keening cry broke from her lips and that terrifying fire burned through her. But he had her.

"Right here, baby," he whispered against her lips.

Pulling away from her for just a moment, he took care of protection, rolling a condom down over his erection as he eased her back down into the sheets. The wind was picking up outside. "You let me in now, sweetheart. Please."

His fingers eased through her wet folds, parting her. "God, you're so wet." His harsh breathing made her clench in a primitive response to his desire. He pushed slowly inside, thick and hard. "I want you so damned bad."

Braced above her, he was a powerful shadow in the night. Fighting the need to take her hard and fast when he knew she needed slow and gentle.

"I'm all yours, Jack. We've got the whole summer." She moaned as he pressed forward, sliding impossibly deeper. Slowly retreated and moved again. She'd imagined a night spent in Jack Donovan's arms, but nothing could have prepared her for the reality. For the man so intently focused on her. The girl she'd been had wanted him, but the woman she'd become welcomed him. Outside, thunder rumbled, echoing the building tension inside.

Reaching up, she captured his mouth with hers, their fingers tangling together by her head. Fire burned through both of them, an impossible storm of pleasure. His hips moving, taking, pushed her higher and higher as she arched up and into his hot weight. Then he was tearing his mouth from hers, burying his face in her neck. Driving faster and harder, and it didn't matter anymore why he'd left. Why he hadn't come home sooner. The only thing that mattered was the man cradled in her arms and the husky growl ripped from his throat as he finally gave them both what they needed.

The hunger trembled through her, expanded and grew, until she shattered, the bright pleasure sparking, taking her higher. White-hot sensation exploded through her as she cried out his name into the lightning-charged night air.

He arched, pushing deeper, harder, then stilled. Muttered words tore from his throat as he buried his hands in her hair, stroking, gentling her, as he lost himself in her.

Her last thought before sleep claimed her was that Jack Donovan was worth every minute of her ten-year wait.

Chapter Thirteen

Like all mornings after, this one was a bitch. First thing he noticed as he came awake was the too-soft mattress. He dug an elbow in, fighting not to sink into the sea of softness as he dragged himself the rest of the way awake. Next thing to hit him was the now-familiar, dusky scent of lavender—and Lily. *Christ*. He'd spent the night. Inside. In Lily's bed.

He didn't sleep with anyone, and he sure didn't sleep inside, not when there were other choices. Sure enough, as soon as he got his eyelids open, there were the walls, pressing right in on him, the room getting smaller with each quick breath he took. In another moment he'd be sucking air like a winded runner. *Fuck*. He should have outgrown this.

Should have, could have, he mocked, forcing himself to breathe slowly and deeply. He fought fires that could clear a room of oxygen faster than a man could blink. He knew what breathless really was, so four simple walls shouldn't hit him this hard.

But when Lily shifted beside him, he jackknifed up in the bed.

"Damn it," he muttered, shoving his hands through his hair. "Get a grip, Jack."

Living in Strong had been almost impossible for him—

he'd always felt trapped, suffocated, wanting desperately to lash out at the adults forcing him to stay—until he'd discovered firefighting. Fighting fires was an acceptable outlet to channel the rage and desperation, so he'd spent summers and weekends—hell, weekdays, too, when the fire was bad and Ben Cortez was too shorthanded to mind—battling blazes. He'd lost himself in those battles. Tired, sweat-soaked, and smoky, he'd been too exhausted, when he'd finally tumbled into sleep and oblivion, to care much that he was surrounded by four walls and expectations he'd never live up to.

His cell vibrated again, a soft rasp of sound in the jeans he'd dropped on the floor. The untidy pile of clothes was another reminder he didn't want. He hadn't wanted to wait. Now he didn't want to remember just how badly he'd wanted this woman. Or how much he still did.

Lily was a sweet, hot weight cuddled up by his side. She might be demanding space between them during the daylight hours, but, right now, her body was as close as she could get. Her soft breathing tickled his skin, mingling with the cooler air from the open window. At least she'd left the window open. *God.* He turned his face toward the fresh air.

Still really early, he realized. The light was gray, one step removed from pitch-black. Shadows-and-secrets light. The crickets were still singing outside, but it was already hot and still. Perfect thunderstorm weather. And he had a call. He needed to get out of here.

Slowly, he started untangling himself. As he slipped away from the soft, warm curl of her body, the sheet followed, baring the curve of an arm. The rounded mound of a breast and the darker shadow of her nipple. Pure candy, those nipples were. The cool, early-morning air had them pebbling into delicious little nubs. He'd feasted on them last night like a starving man, and yet he still wanted to lean down, suck those tempting nipples right into his mouth, and tease her into wakefulness.

His cell vibrated again. No one would call him now unless there was an emergency. He needed to take the call. Relief pounded through him as he shot off the bed. Away from temptation.

"What is it, Jack?" Her sleepy voice reached out for him, her weight rolling toward him as she came half awake.

"Go back to sleep, baby." Her voice was all drowsy with promise and dreams, and suddenly he wanted nothing more than to ignore his call and sink back into the bed. Into her. Soft and sweet and warm, she was an impossible lure. But he didn't do mornings after. And he had to go.

Bending down, he swiped the cell from the floor. The numbers were the expected ones. Evan. His brother would just keep on calling until he got the answer he needed, so there was no real point in waiting.

He got his feet moving and out the door, ignoring the rustling of cotton as Lily pushed up on an elbow, watching him go. She had that impossibly feminine sheet pressed against the sweet, hot length of her now, cupping her breasts the way his hands itched to do.

He couldn't stay, so he pulled the door shut between them and took his call. "What's up?" It was still dark out, although the sky was lightening up over on the horizon. Fire at night was a damned good indication the cause was arson.

"Spotter called in a series of fires. They came up real quick, because our man had just scanned that area." This particular spotter was parked in an old fire tower just outside of Strong. He'd have a ringside seat if a wildland fire kicked up. "Right now we've got four fires. Popped up one right after the other. You know what that means."

"Arson. You think that's our boy?"

"You had that little fire out at Lily's yesterday. You said the bastard was watching, but you ran him off." Evan paused, trying to avoid a whole lot of awkward.

Jack filled in the blanks for his brother. "So he probably got a real good eyeful of me and Lily." He didn't mention what had been happening before that fire, or after, but Evan was proficient at filling in the blanks.

"Might not be any connection," Evan said slowly. "It's not impossible these four are just leftovers from last night's storm."

"It's possible," Jack growled. "But don't you of all people tell me it's probable. He's going to burn down the entire goddamned town."

They both knew what could happen to sleeper fires in the dry summer weather. "You want to put the plane up?"

There was a pause on the other end. He could almost hear Evan running numbers, pitting the cost of fuel against getting an easy peek at their possible hot spots. "Let's put her up," he said finally. "Get a good look from the air. If it's really arson, there may be more than four. "

Perfect. "I'll be there in ten. Round up the crew. We need to put those fires out."

That pause repeated itself on the other end of line, as Evan did some figuring of a different sort. Then he said, "Thought you were otherwise occupied."

"You called," he pointed out, ignoring the question in his brother's voice. "Have I ever missed a fire?"

"No." Again there was a pregnant pause. Hell, he hadn't known Evan had that much tact in him. Someone had been teaching his younger brother manners. "You've always come through, always gone up with the jump team. Just thought today might have been different, that's all."

Right. He wasn't touching that one. "There's nothing different about today." The words were harder to say than he'd imagined. "Whenever we get a fire, I'm there."

"Right." His brother's husky chuckle sounded relieved. "Of course I'm not putting up our plane without letting you know first, you bastard."

"True." Snapping the phone shut, he shifted into high gear. Four minutes to get the truck from the farm to the hangar; that left him six minutes to get his clothes on and his ass down the stairs.

Moving silently, he slipped back inside the room and reached for last night's clothes. A neat stack should have been within arm's reach of where he'd slept. Man didn't fight fires without learning to sleep light and to dress on the run. Instead, he'd dropped his clothes on the floor in his hurry to get into bed with his Lilybell. He had a feeling that change wouldn't be the only one he'd be making if he stuck around.

Definitely time to hit the road.

And yet he couldn't ignore his arousal. He still had the taste of her on his mouth, the sweet scent of her on his skin sending the blood rushing to an erection that was already hard and thick, demanding he crawl right back into the bed with her and make love to her all over again.

So, the question really was, was he running to the fire—or from the woman in the bed? Hell if he knew.

"You're going out?" Her sleepy voice reached out from the shadowy cocoon of the bed. He had to go. *Needed* to go. So why his feet were taking him toward her and not the door was a damned mystery.

"Fire call, baby." His knees hit the side of the bed before he could stop himself, before he could keep himself from curling the fingers of one hand around her wrist. Her skin was baby-soft there.

"So you're just leaving." Her words weren't anything more than a statement of the facts, but it didn't take much to interpret the flat tone of her voice. Yeah, he didn't need four-foot neon lights to know what the sheet shoved beneath her arms meant. He'd erased the intimacy of last night the instant he'd taken that call.

He'd always known the job came first, and, until now, he'd never had any regrets. Fires were just another iron-clad excuse to slip away when the nighttime hours were finished.

"This is what I do, Lily." Bending down, he brushed a kiss against the side of her jaw, the edge of her ear. Her stoic silence had him biting back an impatient growl. She'd known the rules. Known what he had to offer—and what he couldn't give her.

So why did this time feel so different? He told himself that what they'd shared the night before was just sex, even if having his Lilybell had been the hottest, most mind-blowing sex of his life. But he had a niggling suspicion— no, a deep-rooted conviction—that the attraction between them was more than sex. Long, slow, and sweet. That's how he wanted to love her. If he wasn't careful, she just might be more than a summertime romance for him.

She'd been kicked, and she was sure as hell down. But Lily was smart. When the San Francisco police couldn't ID her stalker, she hadn't stuck around for him to finish whatever sadistic game he was playing with her. And yet, despite all the lemons life had handed her, she'd been de-termined to get right on up again. He admired that. He admired *her*.

But the walls were still closing in on him, and the fires were a gift-wrapped present with his name on the label. He needed to get his ass in gear. Plane wouldn't wait—not long. He'd never backed down from a call, and he wasn't starting now.

Stepping away from the bed, he pulled his shirt over his head. Lily just sat there and watched him. Maybe that was a good thing, that silence of hers. Maybe she wouldn't make him say the things he didn't want to say. A man could hope.

"You're running away, Jack." She slid off the bed, taking the sheet and the silence with her. Wrapped the sheet around those curves he'd explored last night and shot his peace of mind all to hell.

"This is a fire call, Lily." He was explaining, and he didn't do explanations.

"No," she said, walking toward him. Damned if he was going to back up. He held his ground like he'd hold a fire line. Time was slipping away from him. He had to leave. "This isn't about some fire up on some mountain somewhere. This is about us. About you. If you don't want this to be any more than a one-night stand, Jack Donovan, that's fine. I didn't ask you for more than that. You go right on out that door."

The explanations just kept on coming. "I'll be back."

Her chin came up, and her face was pure stubbornness. "Don't bother," she said, all sweetness, as if he'd offered to bring in her groceries or do a little fetch-and-carry for her. "I've done just fine without you, Jack, so here's a news flash for you. The world is going to keep right on turning when you head on out that door. I'm not going to collapse in a tearful heap because you've decided now is a good time to leave. Last night was fun." She shrugged. "I admit I was curious."

"Curious?" His voice was a rough growl.

"Curious," she repeated sweetly. "And, now that you've answered all my questions so nicely, we're good." She nodded. "Good and done. So lock up when you hit my porch, and don't let the door hit your ass on the way out, Jack."

Damned if she didn't head right for the bathroom. She couldn't even be bothered to see him down the stairs.

He might not want to stay, but he wasn't letting her slip through his fingers like this. Not again. His hand shot out and shackled her wrist gently before he could think things through. "You call last night whatever you want, baby, but we're not *good* and done. Not by a long shot." He knew she heard the heated promise in his voice, because she stopped and gave him a look that would have done Nonna proud. It was the look that said she saw his bullshit and raised him, too.

She didn't scare, his Lily. Not easily. No, instead of running, she just turned and stepped into him. The heat and scent of her flooded his senses, making him hard again. Which was a bitch, because she'd kept that sheet between them, and he still needed to leave. "You want to leave," she accused quietly.

He did. He didn't. Jumping out of a plane at fifteen hundred feet didn't scare him, but this one woman did. She was getting under his skin. No one else ever had, and, even though she wasn't asking him to stay, he wanted to.

"Fine, Jack. You go. I don't want you to stay."

The anger and possessiveness drowning him came as an unpleasant shock. She was his. He didn't know where the primitive sensations came from, but damned if he didn't embrace them. She'd wanted him to change, so she was going to have to deal with that man he was becoming.

"I'm going to be late," he warned, his voice a low, throaty growl.

"What?" Those brown eyes mocked him. "You've got two minutes, Jack, before you blow your schedule. You can't take care of business here in two minutes?"

Turning away from him, she dropped the sheet without so much as a give-a-damn, reaching for her own clothes. Her body was pale and sexy in the gray dawn light, and his mouth went dry. Yeah, he hadn't had him enough of her. Even now, as she grabbed the clothes he'd turned inside out as he'd stripped her helter-skelter, he wanted to take her straight back to that bed and make her moan some more. Instead, he just watched as she tidied up. Her panties were tangled in the legs of her cut-offs, and the lace strap of her bra dangled from her fingertips as she turned and dropped the lot into a wicker hamper. Disposing of the memories.

Like hell. "Don't push me," he growled.

"I wouldn't dream of it, Jack," she said tightly. Turning her back on him, she stepped into a fresh pair of lacy white panties, and he swore he felt his control snap. Lily was playing with fire, and she was about to get burned. Before she could so much as squeak, he had her backed up against the wall of her bedroom. He was bigger, stronger. And she had him far too hot and bothered. Slapping one hand on the wall beside her head, he reached down and captured her chin with his other hand.

Those eyes of hers were pure challenge mixed with a healthy dose of anger. She didn't like being intimidated, but she wasn't running. Lily wouldn't run again. He knew that. And he couldn't ignore the sensual attractiveness of that bedrock strength in her.

He should have warned her, should have given her a chance to demand he get the hell out of her house, but he wasn't feeling nice. Hell, he was angry.

And possessive.

He didn't particularly like himself right now, but he wanted Lily Cortez, and he wouldn't hide that truth. So he lowered his mouth, not taking his gaze from her face. Those damned brown eyes of her eyes didn't flinch. Her angry look matched his, reading the reaction to her he couldn't hide. Whatever she saw there on his face, she must have liked the message, because she gave a little hum of excitement and melted into him.

Damn her.

His mouth slanted over hers, tasting, teasing, and he was so damned lost, he wondered if he'd ever find himself again. Her mouth was sheer, raw heat. She was wet and needy, so boldly honest in the sensual excitement she felt that his entire world had narrowed to her and the shadowy bedroom where he'd wrapped her up in his arms.

"Open up," he growled, swallowing her little gasp of feminine excitement. He brushed his lips against hers, stroking between their plumpness with his tongue. Drove inside her. No excuses. No hiding. Just raw sensation overwhelming him like a brush fire jumping the line and sucking all the oxygen out of his lungs. Drowning in the liquid heat of her.

Her tongue tangled with his. Exploring. Her mouth met his in a sensual throw-down. He'd kissed her at least a dozen times now, taken her mouth almost every way he could imagine last night. He should have recognized the taste of her, the intimate shape of that mouth. And yet this kiss was pure discovery and unexpected pleasure. He was never going to get enough of her.

She moaned something into his mouth. Maybe his name. Hell, she could have been uttering heartfelt profanity or reciting bad poetry. He didn't care. All he could do was thread his hands through her hair and hang on to this impossible, fabulous woman wrapped in his arms. Let his mouth devour hers, using his lips and tongue and teeth to stoke the furious blaze in her. With a wordless cry, she arched up into him, riding his jeans-clad thigh as the hot, wet heat of her silently demanded he scoop her up and carry her back to the bed she'd abandoned.

Their bed.

Instead, his cell buzzed, jolting him into awareness.

"I guess it's official. You're late, baby," she drawled.

His whole body jerked. Thick and hard, his dick rose to meet that feminine challenge. So he gave her back her challenge, gave her one of his own with each hot stroke of his hands. Possessive. Raw. He wasn't letting her forget what they'd just shared—or letting her dismiss him that easily. He thrived on challenges, and she'd just thrown down.

She eyed him like she hadn't been devouring his mouth. "Good-bye, Jack."

"I'm coming back, Lily," he growled. "Make no mistake about it. I'll be right back here, in your bed, tonight."

With that, he left.

Chapter Fourteen

Spotted Dick leveled the plane out, bringing her nose around for a final check. He was the best damned pilot Jack had ever flown with. Too profane and too ornery for commercial airline work, but he knew his way around a plane. Or a chopper. If the bird had wings, Spotted Dick could fly her. He had nerves of steel, as well, and no landing zone was too small or too short. Any landing he could walk away from was a good landing in Dick's book.

The crew was comprised of eight men. Jack had pulled military tours in the deserts of the Middle East, fighting his way through oil rig fires and gun battles. He'd learned more than he wanted about hot and dry and exposed. His third tour had taken him to South America. That tour was all about the drug wars and covert ops. The entire jump team was ex-military, ex-Marine, men he'd fought beside during those three tours. He knew them. Knew precisely what they were capable of. Fighting fires was simply one more battlefield, and they'd checked gear as soon as Spotted Dick put the plane into the air, because you never fucked with your gear. Gear was survival, plain and simple.

Beside him, Evan re-strapped his blade, whistling silently.

When Jack signaled to huddle up, they pulled in. Seven hard faces turned toward his. His jumpers were big, strong men. Fighters. Stubborn as mules. And damned uncivilized. They'd have fit just fine into Strong when the town had been a lawless mining camp. Hell, he wasn't sure all of them had gotten the memo that they were inhabiting the twenty-first century.

"I need to call in a favor," he said, "when we're done on this job. I need eyes and ears on Lily Cortez."

Even over the roar and throb of the plane's engines, he heard the low whistle from one of the jumpers at the back. "Setting the bar real high for the rest of us, Jack."

The other jumpers chimed in with cheerful obscenities, and Jack knew that this was simply playful banter. Should have been just another line in the game they all played. Enjoy life, enjoy the summer. Take what was offered because tomorrow there was always another fire. Another chance to jump. Another chance they weren't all coming back, because shit happened on the fire lines, and no one had ever pretended otherwise.

"She's off-limits," he said, because he couldn't pretend, and the catcalls cut right off. He didn't know what was written on his puss, but clearly the boys had gotten the message. Loud and clear. "Some son-of-a-bitch is stalking her. She cuts a damned flower out there, I want to know about it. As a favor to me. This is off the books. Give me your hours, and I'll take care of you, but this is personal."

They'd all known someone—a mother, a sister, hell, even a girlfriend of their own—who'd been given a raw deal by some bum. They'd fought covert wars, holding the invisible lines separating good guys from bad. They were damned good because they'd had two choices. Get real good, real fast—or die. Lily wouldn't know they were there, not unless they wanted her to know.

The plane banked smoothly, coming around. Jump site was coming up fast.

The four fires weren't that far away from Strong, but

they were in a location that was pretty inaccessible. Just the one main road in and then a handful of service roads. Problem here was water. Or, more precisely, the lack of water. You drove it in or you flew it in, but you weren't hooking up to a hydrant. Their job was to jump in and cut line until the fires burned themselves out.

Dropping a team made sense. Up in the air, the team had a big-picture view that teams on the ground wouldn't have. And, once you'd dropped, that same team became eyes and ears on the ground. He needed those eyes and ears.

Both here and on Lavender Creek.

He said the words that sealed the deal, guaranteeing that none of his jumpers would let Lily's stalker walk easy. "He's a serial arsonist."

This time, the curses weren't good-natured. A man who set fires was a danger. A walking, ticking time bomb threatening to take a team of good men with him, because they'd be the ones jumping into the heart of the blaze to clean up his shit. Now he'd dragged Lily into the mix, and none of them liked that.

"She down with this?" Sprawled on the floor of the plane, shouting to be heard over the engines' vibrations, Zay should have looked ridiculous. He'd rolled up the sleeves of his jumpsuit, exposing ink from a half dozen tours of duty across most of Asia.

He gave Zay the truth. "She won't know you're there. I don't want her to hear you or see you."

"Straight up?" Joey shifted, his head coming up from the gear bag he was organizing. "That's how you want to play it?"

"You ever met Lily Cortez?" Joey's silent head shake said it all. "Let me be real clear. She doesn't believe there's really a problem. She thinks she can handle on her own a man who'd set a forest fire just to scare the piss out of her. You and I—we both know what kind of a man sets wildland fires."

They'd read the profiles, even met some of the assholes who'd done that kind of thing. Almost all of their wildland arsonists were male. Looking for a little fame and glory or out for revenge or an adrenaline rush. A man like that was no one Lily Cortez should have to handle on her own.

"So we watch Lavender Creek," Zay drawled. "We stick to your Lily like a stamp to an envelope. Got that part. Then, say this little bastard decides to pay Lily a visit out at her farm—tell me how this next part unfolds. We return the favor?"

From the cockpit, Spotted Dick bawled a heads-up and an altitude. The first jump site was coming up fast. Jack had no illusions about his team. Hell, he had no illusions about himself. If the only way to stop the arsonist required lethal force, he'd do it. Any one of them would. Part of him wanted to give in to the primal urge to hurt as Lily had been hurt. Strong, California, wasn't a battlefield, however. Not yet.

"We take it to law enforcement first," he said, looking each man in the eye. "We give them the chance to deal with him." He knew each of them heard the unspoken agreement: if the law failed to take care of business, Jack's team would. If only for this summer, Lily Cortez and Strong were all his. His base. His territory. Whoever this arsonist was, his power trip was over as of this minute.

The spotter moved to the door. Three thousand feet below, the local fire crew's early responders had parked their trucks end-to-end along the roadside, turning the remote-access area into a parking lot worthy of a shopping mall on a Saturday. The road hugged the edge of a particularly virgin stretch of forest, where giant ponderosa pines punched their green tops up into the smoky sky. Usually a jump team wouldn't have been called out for what was essentially a ground fight, but Strong was shorthanded this season, and right now they had a chance to dig a scratch line to hold the small fires before they chewed up the neighborhood.

The fire's head here was a hot run of flame burning up the slope where a thick cloud of white-gray smoke billowed up into the bright blue. Flames were clearing fifteen feet, so there was plenty of fuel. The line crew had made an initial attack, but, on the other side of the line, maybe a quarter mile back, were houses. If the wind had shifted the other way, there'd be nothing but ash there. Could still go that way, from what Jack saw.

The situation report said the weather was only going to get worse, hotter and drier, so stopping these small fires now was key.

Unfortunately, the trees in this area were big-ass, well over one hundred feet tall. That meant their first jump spot for today was a narrow sliver of space he could barely see through the thick carpet of the treetops.

Next to him, the spotter cursed. "You're going to have to jump right through there." He jerked a thumb at the handful of openings in the canopy. "That's going to be a bitch to steer through."

Where the trees ended, a steep slope began and ended in a small patch of clearing.

As Spotted Dick brought the plane around, the spotter hooked his harness onto a restraining line tethered to the plane. If he fell out, the rest of the team shared the responsibility of hauling his ass back in. "Door's opening," he bellowed.

Jack threw an arm over his reserve chute, because if the chute caught a blast of air from the door and blew your ass out, zero to sixty, it wouldn't be pretty when you hit. Up ahead, the spotter grabbed the handles and pulled. The door slid free, fresh air exploding into the plane.

The drift streamers flew out the door and down. Jack caught a flash of sky like a giant bruise through the open hatch, the bright blue of the California summer streaked with black smoke. Even as he watched, the red, yellow and blue streamers snapped open, weighted down to mimic the weight of a jumper. That was one hell of a party down there, however. No cake-and-candles affair.

The spotter nodded and spoke into his headset. "Got us some drift. Two hundred yards."

Spotted Dick adjusted the plane, making a second pass as the spotter tossed out the streamers again, two hundred yards upwind of the jump spot. Dead-on hit. Good. The plane climbed higher to hit jump altitude.

As soon as they hit three thousand feet, the spotter was barking out orders. "Get into the doorway, boys."

They'd jump two at a time today because there were four nearby fires to contain. First out the door were Joey and Zay, Joey jumping with his customary war whoop, while Zay dove silently beside him.

The wind had either shifted on Joey as he cleared the plane or he'd a hit a downdraft, because he'd hung up maybe thirty feet from the ground. He flashed the plane the bird and then cut himself free. The next pair jumped better, and then it was Jack's turn to go with Evan.

Dropping into the open doorway, he hung his legs over the edge. He checked his release and lines, making sure the cutaway clutch was in plain sight. First man out had needed that clutch.

"Ready," the spotter roared. Jack sucked in air, coming up onto his feet. Arms and legs braced in the door. When the spotter's hand smacked his shoulder, he launched himself into all that open, empty sky. Counting off the seconds as his body rolled through the air, fighting gravity and the gusts battering at him. He pulled the handle on the four-count.

Over on his right, Evan whooped. Jack grabbed the steering toggles and banked, making for a small clearing below.

The ground rushed up beneath his booted feet as he punched down through a hole in the canopy, the sides of his chute grazing the thick, leafy cover. He didn't hang up, though, so he sent up a small prayer. *Take that.* Pulling hard on the toggle, he narrowly avoided one of the ponderosa's smaller cousins, and then the ground was barreling toward him. Twenty feet. Ten. His feet hit hard, the shock of the impact sending him running forward as he fought to keep himself upright.

Hell if he was ass-planting now.

Twelve hours to cut line. Another hour to hike back down the ridge and join up with the local boys who'd come out to do a little firefighting themselves. Evening was coming on fast, and the shift in the humidity might just save all their asses. This was familiar ground: he was right at home with the whine of the chain saw and cheerful obscenities. Swiping a bottle of water from a box set out on the tailgate of a pickup, he moved in, assessing. "What have we got?"

The four original fires had become one, and this close to the line, the furnace blast eating up the ponderosas had him sweating even though he wasn't close enough yet to spot what else was on fire. A thick, smoky tang blanketed the air, coating his throat and skin. He'd smell like bad barbecue by the time he was done here. The heat and dust were already almost impossible. Should have been the end

to another pretty summer day, and, from the looks of the
sky, maybe it was somewhere. Most of the horizon was the
kind of impossible blue and sunset reds that sent folks running on outside. To the north, however, was the familiar
gray haze and the smoke that promised fire.

After a second phone consult with Evan, he'd decided
against sending his boys up in the plane again. That was
overkill. They'd dug their line over the ridge, but there
was still plenty of hard, dirty work down here on the
ground, and he lost himself in it.

Swinging the Pulaski, he drove its sharp claw end into
the iron-hard dirt. Each blow reverberated through his
body, ripping through the muscles in his arms and shoulders in a familiar rhythm. Up. Down. Through.

This was where he belonged. Right here, right now, on
this line with his team, carving a strip of safety out of the
forest. No question about it. In town, he got that itch between his shoulders that signaled he needed to get the hell
out of there, but Strong hadn't been all bad. Not this time
around. Maybe it was that little light his Nonna got in her
eyes when she was going on about her plans for the place,
or maybe it was Lily's cussed stubbornness in hanging on
to a lavender farm she didn't know the first damned thing
about running, but he hadn't been bored.

He'd felt welcome. Needed.

And being needed for more than his back and a willing-
ness to launch himself out of a cockpit and dead center
into a fire zone was something altogether new. He'd sort
it all out later, he decided. Not now. Not when he had
work to do.

His Pulaski broke the earth's crusty surface and turned
over rich, black soil. When he and the other men were
finished, nothing would burn through the line here.
Strong could keep right on going, reinventing itself as a

tourist destination or whatever crazy scheme his Nonna had come up with this week. He wouldn't, he reminded himself, be here to see that makeover project through to its conclusion.

He'd spent longer in other places, strange places, during the five-odd fire seasons since he'd left his military days behind him. But leaving was always part of the drill, and Strong was just another tour of duty when you got down to it. Sure, he'd managed all right so far—hell, things had gone better than all right. Lily was a delicious challenge, and she sure made Strong a whole lot more interesting than other places. He'd make his two months, no problem.

"We know who spotted this sleeper's smoke?" Rio loped up to him, looking like he'd just rolled out of bed and not spent the day cutting line up on that ridge with the rest of the team. His hair was ruffled as if he'd shoved a hand through it. *Data points*—that's what Rio called their fires, plotting their sources of origin in his laptop. Jack didn't know what Rio did with all those numbers, but he sure as shit enjoyed collecting them.

Lifting a shoulder, he swiped his forehead on the soot-streaked cotton. "Flagger called it." Man was about to get a grilling worthy of the IRS. Poor bastard wouldn't know what hit him when Rio got his hands on him.

Usually, spotting secondary fires was monotonous but important work. You sent a handful of guys to flag a route into a recent flare-up, taking a compass reading and then picking an object in their sight line. Once they had that lock, they made for it, checking over their shoulders for the last flag. Flag the new site. Rinse and repeat. The work wasn't glamorous, but they'd find those sleeper fires fast, before they had a chance to grow into something bigger. Only other way to find them was to put a plane up and just keep on flying until you saw smoke.

The access road that would take them to the ridge above the fire was rutted and muddy. Worse yet, the way was blocked by fallen trees the team would have to clear. The team was already breaking up the fallen trees with hand axes and firing up the chain saw. Evan was on lead; he might prefer jumping, but that man knew the chain saw better than any of them and could make it sing in his hands as it chewed through old wood.

Mentally Jack marked snags. He'd send a team back later to clean up the hazardous trees on the side of the road— if they needed to use the fire road again, it would be clear. In one spot, the bole of a collapsed tree blocked the road and had the team limbing the fallen tree with a chain saw.

"Town like this," Jack muttered, "there shouldn't be all that much to burn."

"Just Ma's." Rio flashed him a grin, his face streaked with soot and sweat. "Lose her place, and you can kiss your pool table good-bye for the rest of the summer."

"Not to mention any hope of a cold beer," Evan grumbled.

Rio's good-natured curse was lost in a series of catcalls from a group of local firefighters. "You going to get your ass in gear, flyboy?" one of the ground crew called. "Because we're putting this fire out single-handedly over here."

Grinning fiercely through the mask of soot and ash and sweat painting his face, Evan headed toward the new flare-up, driving his Pulaski into the ground. Some of the boys here would be in it for the money, the chance to score big and get out, spend big and play the rest of the year. Build up a nice nest egg that bought a man some freedom to live a little. Most men couldn't do that with nine-to-five and a desk. Plus, this thrill of danger was the closest a man came to the battlefield without re-enlisting.

On the other side of the access road was a slice of

canyon—and a little development of ritzy homes. Most of them were summer places kept by the superwealthy who sometimes came up to Strong to play in the mountains. Fortunately, the houses were mostly empty right now. Jack's mind ran the logistics while his hands kept right on shoveling. A few of those houses would belong to locals. That meant people living there. People who weren't going to like an order to evac.

He hotfooted it up to the ridge. The fire hadn't climbed to the top yet, and another team was back-digging like mad, churning up the dirt to stop the fire's slow creep.

Clearing the top of the ridge, he got his first eyeful of what lay on the other side.

Hell. A few of the homeowners had done the prudent thing and cleared back the brush. House nearest the ridge, however, was just the prettiest little disaster-in-waiting he'd laid eyes on recently. Mother Nature had decorated the roof with a thick layer of dry pine needles, and then the happy homeowner had made matters worse by planting a real nice border of flowering shrubs around the place. Maybe if the damned plants had gotten their daily dose of water, it wouldn't have been so bad, but those bushes had dried up to a handful of brown twigs just begging to spark.

One hundred percent pure tinder. The few sprinklers belatedly wheezing and spitting water onto the front lawn weren't going to help much, either. Man of the house had now hauled himself up onto the rooftop, vigorously wielding a bright green garden hose. The anemic stream of water wet the roof and rained down on the dust-dry yard. The bright yellow plastic slide tucked up against the side of the house meant children inside.

This wasn't going to end well. "We need to evac the residents."

Rio nodded, doing a 180 on his work boot. "I'll get the sheriff on the radio."

There wasn't time for that. "They need to leave. Now." There was a minivan parked in the driveway. He figured they could toss a few essentials inside and hightail it down to the town. If they were lucky, they'd come back to a house. *Hell.* He hated working on the ground. He needed to be up in the air, where he could see the big picture and get right to the heart of the fire.

Ben already had his feet moving. "I'll go down there. Let them know what's up."

"You think they're going to listen to you?" Ben didn't have an evac order. No way he could force the homeowners to pick up and go.

"They will," Ben said grimly. "Folks around here still remember the last fire to hop that ridgeline. There's a reason these homes don't have more than twenty years on them. I'll just point out the similarities and let them know there's plenty of room for them down in Strong."

Jack nodded as Ben scrambled down the slope. If Ben said he could do it, he'd give the older man the benefit of the doubt.

There was one other house, higher up and perched smack on the edge of the canyon. Probably had one hell of a view. Searching his memory, he came up with a name. That mansion-in-training was the Haverley place. Old man Haverley had made piles of money building some Silicon Valley company from the ground up. He'd retired early, then come on up here to sit and stare at the mountains. Jack had gone to school with the grandson.

Wildfire didn't respect your bank account any. "Haverley at home?"

Rio shot him a surprised look. "Old man Haverley? He dropped dead maybe three years back. We all thought he'd go on forever, but we were wrong. His grandson has the place now. Edward."

Eddie Haverley had inherited himself a real nice place. He'd also clearly taken Fire Prevention 101, because he'd done all the right things to get that mansion ready for the dry season. The front yard was a nice piece of xeriscaping—all white gravel and drought-resistant plants. Brush was cleared and the trees cut right back around the edge of the property. The slope was clear, and there were well-positioned stone walls and a swimming pool, all ready to cut off a fire's advance. Hell, even the trendy fire pit was ringed with slate. Downright professional. His eyes narrowed. That preparation could just be money talking, as Eddie Haverley clearly could afford to hire the best.

Or not.

Was fire season a little more personal for Eddie?

Down below, people started hurrying out of the other house. A dog barked, and the minivan roared to life.

"You think they'll come back to a house?"

Fire was always impossible to predict. The wind could shift or the fire find a hidden source of fuel. All it took was one good dry patch.

"Let's get a plane up," he decided. "I want a load of re-tardant dumped here. Here. And here." He jabbed a thumb into the map.

"Not going to be cheap," Rio warned. "You want to burn the cash for two homes? That one"—he jerked a thumb at Haverley's place—"is sitting pretty sweet. He'll probably ride out these flames with just a little scorching."

Jack followed the pointing finger, looking down at the home tucked at the bottom of the slope. He should let them take their chances. It was just one house. The fire line should give the structure a fighting chance, and Ben had cleared out the owners. Even as he watched, Ben began trudging back on up the slope as the minivan disappeared down the road.

Those folks would be heartbroken if they couldn't come back home.

Hell. He'd be lucky to make it home tonight himself.

Chapter Fifteen

Lily should have been planning the next steps for her farm. She'd thought about hosting a pick-your-own lavender weekend, despite the crazy-making potential of inviting hundreds of people to tramp around her fields. Opening her farm up to the public wasn't something she was ready to do yet. Even though she knew it wasn't fair to blame Jack Donovan for the fire tearing up the nearby ridge, she wasn't feeling fair. No, what she was feeling was downright mean.

When she looked north, she saw the smoke, a thick gray-black column rising up into the sky. That fire was damned big, and Jack was out there.

Happy to be out there.

Well, she was happy to be where she was, too. Drying lavender took about a week, and today she'd taken the first step, hanging the fresh-cut stems with paper clips to wire lines strung up inside the drying shed, where the warm darkness cocooned the flowers and kept the color from fading. Another year, and she'd add roses and hydrangeas, see if she couldn't expand her line some. Only the dark blues and purples dried well. She'd planted Hidcote and Dutch lavenders, Royal Velvet and Provence. Scent clung fiercely to those stalks and to every inch of her skin. A dozen showers weren't enough to wash away the thick, rich aroma, and she wouldn't have had it any other way.

She'd just dropped the latest load of lavender at her shipper, and those flowers would be in Seattle florist shops by morning. Now her arms felt empty without their usual load. She needed something to keep her mind off the man battling on the ridge. He could be getting himself killed up there.

While she was strolling down Strong's main street, pretending there was nothing wrong. No one missing.

"Shipment's off?" Nonna called from her front porch.

Lily didn't want to stop and talk, but there was nothing casual about Nonna's question, and she had too much respect for the older woman to simply drop her a handful of words and keep on going. Plus, Uncle Ben would kick her ass two ways to Sunday if she took that approach. "Sure is."

Those dark eyes examined her face. "So you've got a little extra time on your hands."

Like hell she did. She cursed again, because just she'd borrowed Jack's favorite set of cusswords. What she had was a working lavender farm—there *was* no free time in that job description. "If I keep at it," she said, avoiding the question because she wasn't stupid enough to walk *straight* into Nonna's little trap, "I'll clear just enough to make things right with the bank this month."

Nonna took a ladylike sip from the iced glass set by her elbow. "So you have some time." The rocker creaked as Nonna got up and poured another glass of lemonade. "Sit with me."

Reluctantly Lily took the offered lemonade, perching on the edge of the porch. This was a command performance.

"You need to slow down some," Nonna said. "Take a

few minutes. Ben checked in a little while ago. Our boys won't be back for a while yet. They've got that fire on the run now, but there's still work up there for them to do."

She decided to give in with good grace. Jack Donovan wasn't hers, would never belong to just one woman. She'd share him with Nonna—and likely with at least a dozen more.

"Uncle Ben is used to fighting fires," she said cautiously.

Nonna just smiled, which meant Lily wasn't putting one over on the older woman. Not today. "But we both know I'm not worried about him, don't we?"

She threw caution to the wind. "I don't want to talk about Jack."

Nonna smiled. "Jack's never been an easy one. He's worth the effort, though, Lily. If you make that effort, I don't think you'll regret it."

She didn't need Jack. Well, maybe for sex—because sex with Jack Donovan had exceeded every fantasy she'd dreamed up on her own—but she wasn't stupid enough to confuse sex with anything else. That morning he couldn't wait to get the hell out of her bed, out of her house. To go fight a fire that could kill him. She stared at Nonna and wondered if she knew what her son was up to, if she worried herself sick whenever her boys rode out of town to chase a fire.

"It gets easier," Nonna said quietly. "And harder, too. Jack's real good at what he does, Lily. He doesn't take chances he doesn't need to take. The job he's doing is an important one."

"I know that." She did, too. She just wanted to be *as* important to him, and that needy part of her made her angry. She knew Strong needed him, but she needed him, too. Wanted him to need her, as well. If he thought he was sleeping with her tonight, he could damn well think again.

He'd be lucky if she let him stay on the porch. "He's a damned hero. I know that."

"Strong needs a man like that on its side." Nonna sighed. "But you've got your reasons to dislike fires, haven't you? What happened back in San Francisco isn't something easily forgotten. If you want to talk about it, I'm here. Or, if you want to forget it ever happened, that's your choice, too." Nonna's eyes promised sympathy. Warmth. A shoulder to cry on if she needed it. As if the older woman understood exactly what it meant to come home one day and realize that home wasn't a safe place.

"I want to forget." She swallowed. "I do. I'm tired of being afraid, of looking over my shoulder. I don't know if I can stop, though." Those memories of the flames were right there, waiting for her, when she closed her eyes. "Strong was supposed to be safe. How do I know this fire is just another summer fire? How do I know *he* didn't set it? And that, this time, he won't take everything I care about away?"

"We don't know." Lily didn't miss Nonna's deliberate choice of pronouns. "It seems pretty clear to me that this town needs saving in more ways than one." Ice cubes clinked, hitting the sides of the glass as Nonna thought over what she'd said. "Fire season is never kind, but jobs went away a long time ago. Strong needs all the help it can get."

It was true enough that many of the people she'd grown up with, gone to school with, were flat-out gone now. You wanted an education or a choice in jobs, you left. It was as simple as that. Some of them, though, well, some of them came on back, didn't they?

She had.

"We've got ourselves an ice cream place, a few antiques shops," Nonna continued comfortably. "Couple of places where visitors can lay their heads. The winery. But what else are folks going to do around here? We need more places like your farm, Lily. That farm of yours, it's going to bring in money and visitors."

"You're saying lavender is sexy?"

Nonna snorted. "Guess I am."

Nonna looked at Lily, took another sip of lemonade, and made up her mind. "He's a good man." Lily just froze, and that was all the confirmation Nonna needed. She hadn't missed the interest in Lily's eyes, not ten years ago and not now. She'd give Lily what she could. Not too much, because it was Jack's story, after all, but she was his mother, damn it, and that gave her some license to interfere. Just a little.

"You're talking about Jack." Lily gave a little half laugh that wouldn't convince anyone. She was fighting her feelings, just like Jack was. Lily had always been cautious. She wasn't outright denying the attraction, though, and that was good. Just maybe Jack wouldn't be so alone after this summer ended. "Why?"

"Why wouldn't I?" She headed on into her kitchen, leaving Lily no choice but to follow her or risk outright rudeness. She loved the vintage tile. Jack had done the whole kitchen over for her right before the boys finished high school, bringing the Craftsman home back to its former glory. Even then her boy had been good with his hands. She'd thought, for just a little while, that he'd choose a different path than the military, but there was no arguing that the service had made a man out of her boy. "You were always watching Jack, even when the two of you were too young to know what you were getting yourselves into." If she wasn't mistaken, that was chagrin she saw on Lily's face. "He's my son, Lily. Of course I saw what the two of you were getting up to. I had my hopes, too."

"What did you think was going to happen between us?" Challenge replaced chagrin. What Lily's voice didn't make clear, the stubborn set of her chin did. Jack wasn't going to have an easy summer of it, but that wasn't a bad thing. If he wanted this woman standing here in her kitchen, he'd have to fight for her.

Jack had always loved a good fight.

She started pulling sandwich fixings from the large refrigerator. "I've lived a pretty good life of my own. I've been kissed a time or two. Done my share of whispering and talking and hand-holding." There was amusement in her voice when she thought of those memories. And a touch of sadness. Sometimes it seemed as if she only talked in the past tense, about people and places long gone. Memories were good, but there was no holding on to them. They were over and done with. "I think I had a pretty good idea of what you kids got up to down at the swimming hole.

"Maybe." A smile creased Lily's face, lighting up those beautiful eyes of hers. "We got up to plenty of mischief, Nonna, but that was all. We weren't too outrageous."

"Did you want to be?" She added mustard to the first stack of ham sandwiches. Rio would want his plain, so she laid out more bread.

Lily, bless her, grabbed the plastic wrap and started in on the sandwiches. "It wouldn't have mattered, Nonna. Jack was never going to be any less than a gentleman." The mental picture she got, thinking of Jack as a gentleman, had her snorting. Jack was a fighter and a protector. Raw. Hard. Lily had seen sides of Jack he wouldn't share with a mother. He was no gentleman. Jack had never held back a day in his life. Except maybe that one.

"He kissed you." The knife sawed effortlessly through the thick bread. "Back in the day," she clarified, because she had a pretty good idea what had happened since Jack's return to Strong.

"Yes." Lily's voice was cool, but Nonna didn't miss the hint of nostalgia. "He was damn good at it," she admitted, laughter coloring her voice. "I'd be lying if I said he wasn't. I wasn't his first."

"But do you want to be his last?" Nonna started loading up the cooler. Not too heavy, she decided, or she and Lily would never get the blasted thing into Lily's car to take to the boys.

"Jack's not the settling–down type."

"Not the settling type, that's for certain. I ever tell you how he came to me?" Lily's mute shake of her head was carefully nonchalant, but there was no missing the interest in her eyes or the way those capable hands stilled on the sandwiches. She had Lily hooked.

"Jack," she continued, "well, he was always first out of a room, first to end a conversation. Not to be rude, you understand, and not because he didn't care, but because he needed to be the one who ended it. He'd already had too many people walk out on him, and he was only ten. He was all wiry muscles and scrapes, just plunging in and letting me know, even then, that he'd be staying put just as long as he felt like it and not a minute longer. He made me realize that the dreams I'd had about being a foster parent were just that. Dreams. He made me work for his trust every day. He'd already been in three, maybe four different houses by then. He figured mine would be just another stop on the road." She shook her head. "Turns out, I'm even more stubborn than he is. That had to have been a shock for him, but, somehow, we all survived."

"What were his birth parents like?"

"Not much for hanging around, so Jack didn't get a chance to know them, but you'd understand all about that." Lily's mother had left her with her uncle and hit the road, never to return. "You had Ben, though. Jack—well, he didn't have anyone at first."

"When did he meet Evan and Rio?"

"They're quite a trio, aren't they?" She treasured those memories of raising a pack of wild boys. She'd been like Wendy with the Lost Boys, even though she'd never been the sweet and nurturing type. She'd given them all of herself, and that, it turned out, had been just enough. They were every inch her sons. "They met as runaways, down on the beach. Accidental doesn't mean they weren't family, though. You couldn't separate those boys. Caseworker made it clear she wasn't responsible if I tried. Previous foster mom only wanted to keep one. The lot of them took right off."

"They ran away?" It wasn't hard to imagine what could—and would—happen to a ten-year-old boy out on his own. Nothing good. Nothing she wanted to imagine happening to Jack.

"Tried." Nonna shut the lid on the cooler and started pulling cold cans of soda out of the fridge. "Course, being not quite ten, those boys didn't get all that far. They'd made their point, though."

"You took all three."

"Of course I did. They were a package deal—the boys had made that clear. Folks around here thought I was just plain crazy. Maybe I was, but I wouldn't have traded those boys for anything. There I was, looking forty closer in the eye than I liked, and I had this big house. Together, we made it a home. Three years after they came to me, the state of California finally let me make it legal and adopt them. Since then we've had our ups and our downs, but we've got each other's backs, and no one lies to anyone in this house. They've never let me down."

She shouldered open the screen door. "Give me a hand with this, will you?" She took one end of the fully loaded cooler, waiting until Lily grabbed the other, and then she marched toward that little import Lily loved so much. "Don't have much trunk space in this thing, do you?"

"There's enough to suit me," Lily grumbled, too preoccupied to notice just what Nonna was up to. She was trying to imagine Jack Donovan as a scared, rebellious, ten-year-old boy. They'd grown up together, in the same town, but she hadn't paid him much attention until she was older. Until high school, when every new hormone in her body had sat up and taken note of him. She'd just bet he'd been every bit the heartbreaker then that he was now—but that was dangerous curiosity she didn't need, any more than she needed or wanted the unexpectedly sweet tug on her emotions brought by Nonna's tale. Jack had landed with Nonna, and he'd found a happily-ever-after too many kids in the foster care system never got.

"Pop the trunk." Nonna set her end of the cooler down, leaving Lily no choice but to follow. The weight of the loaded cooler wasn't inconsequential. "You take this on up to the camp for me," Nonna suggested. "They'll be hungry now they've got that fire under control."

Lily opened her mouth to refuse, but Nonna wasn't the kind of woman you said no to. Not once she'd put her mind to something. She'd clearly decided to throw the pair of them together and see what happened.

Getting into the car to head up to the fire camp, Lily knew her decision to be a good girl and do as she was asked was only part of the story. Because part of her—the shameless, pleasure-loving part of her—wanted every minute Jack Donovan would give her.

Chapter Sixteen

Granddad's place was light and airy, a well-designed mansion carefully placed to take advantage of the stunning mountain views. The back of the house was built straight into a canyon, so that the lower floors flowed seamlessly into the rich earth. More than one design magazine had sent a photographer through the place, gushing over the floor-to-ceiling windows and the architecture that blended outdoors with indoors.

Eddie hated the place.

Hated everything it stood for.

If he could have, he would have burned the house right to the ground. But he wasn't that stupid. Fire that big would draw more attention than he wanted right now. Insurance claim would have investigators crawling all over the property. This morning's wildfire had done fuck-all as far as razing the place went. He'd had hopes there, but Jack Donovan had put up a chopper and dumped an obscene amount of fire retardant on their happy little gully. He'd saved the neighborhood, and Strong would have given the man a hero's welcome if he'd wanted it.

Still, he couldn't go cold turkey, could he? And he needed to work out the finer details of the little messages he was crafting for Lily.

The fire pit was his own personal touch on the place. A man really could learn everything he didn't know from the DIY network. A little show-me-please and some vigorous use of the black AmEx card, and he had himself a safety zone where he could let off a little steam.

The sun was still riding high in the sky because dark came far too slowly in the summer months, but he dragged the wooden Adirondack chair right up to his little theater anyhow. Fire-resistant slate surrounded the bronze fire pit. Pit looked like a funeral urn, which he figured was appropriate. After Granddad had died, he'd tossed the old man's ashes right on in there. Now every fire he set there further reduced his nemesis to a messy black smear.

He liked that.

The subject of today's little bonfire wasn't quite as satisfying. Now that his Lily had come home, she spent all her time working on that farm of hers. Not much he could pick up from her trash there, so he'd hacked up a handful of lavender plants. Dash of lighter fluid and a few matches later, and he had a ringside seat to the best-smelling barbecue in all of Strong.

Eventually she'd notice what had happened to her plants.

He was counting on it.

Maybe he'd bring her the remnants, just in case she proved slow on the uptake.

That was another happy thought, so, while the flames got themselves going, he eased his zipper down, nice and slow.

Fire licked right on up the wood like a living mouth on a cock.

That was real good, too. Wrapping his hand around his dick, he stroked in time to the rhythm of the flames. Sucking in the heady scent of lavender, the sweet smell of Lily and fire, with each hard stroke.

★ ★ ★

The sun was just starting its slow, heated dip-and-slide behind the mountains when Jack finally got the chance to shower the fire off himself. The fire crew had set up a portable shower rig, and the cheerful sounds of the fire camp around the hangar almost drowned out the welcome splatter of lukewarm water hitting his skin. Guys hollered and music played, and every breath he took smelled of pine-scented soap and fresh-cut grass from somewhere close by where someone had taken the lawn mower out for a little spin.

The telltale signs of the day's work headed right on down the drain. After he'd done his cleanup number, he shut off the water and moved on out. Nodded a greeting to the next man in line.

Pulling on a faded pair of jeans, he draped his towel around his neck and shoved a hand through his hair. Solar-heated shower, his ass. There was something to be said for heading back to Lily's farm tonight as he'd planned.

"Those fires were no accident." Damned if Ben Cortez wasn't lying in wait for him. Given the intense look in the other man's eyes, he was surprised he'd been allowed to finish his shower before the interrogation and debrief took place.

Maybe Ben was right. Maybe he was dead wrong. That was what made fire such a challenging bitch. "Could have been," he allowed.

There were too many variables during summer season to be dead sure without bringing in an arson team. If you didn't find a man with a gas can and a lit match, you called in a team before you let the accusations fly. Especially when you weren't sure what name to hang the blame on. He needed to play it real cautious until he had the information he needed.

"What the hell do you mean?" Ben hooked a hand onto

his hip. Glaring. Jack recognized the look in the old man's eyes. Fire had his back up, and he wasn't letting go of what they both suspected was the truth.

Stalling for time, he ran the towel over his head. "Fire likes to eat up the evidence, Ben."

Ben shook his head, stubborn to the bone. "You feel it just like I do, Jack. We both know it. Those fires were set."

"This another one of those moments where your bones are talking to you, Ben?" He'd never discounted any of the older man's hunches, not when his instincts were screaming, too, but he couldn't take instinct to the sheriff. It was real hard to write an arrest warrant for a nameless guy on a dirt bike.

"No." Ben slammed his hand down on the card table that was doing double duty as command central. "But when I get the boys out there, we both know they're going to find something."

"Walk me through it, Ben." He needed to hear that the other man had sensed the same pattern he had. "Lightning is the likeliest cause of any wildfire. So why isn't this Mother Nature setting a few hot ones underneath our asses?"

He'd seen enough of the burn pattern from the plane. He'd damned sure seen the speed and the height of the fames. What else had Ben noticed?

"Fire likely started near those homes on the ridge, either right by Haverley's or by the road. Besides the spotter, several neighbors called the fire in—but they all saw a different set of flames. That kind of pop-pop-pop—one little fire next to another—doesn't happen accidentally."

"So what's in it for our boy?"

"He's getting something out of it," Ben said grimly. "Not insurance money. We didn't lose any structures today."

"But it didn't look good there for a while."

He shrugged in acknowledgment. "Could also be crew, looking to pick up some overtime, but I'll vouch for my team."

Ben nodded. "So it's not money our boy wants. He's getting off on this some other way."

"Pleasure. He likes setting things on fire. Likes watching them burn. He lights one or two or three, he's going to want to light another." Lily had said her stalker had been masturbating while he watched her kitchen go up in flames. He'd been aroused.

"Serial."

"Yeah. Or he's going to get fucking inspired by the fire a lightning strike kicks up, and he'll set one of his own. But one won't be enough."

"How many fires did Lily have before she came home?" Ben asked.

Too many. "If he followed her on back, he's not going to stop with one fire. Hell, is there any number that would be enough?"

Ben eyed him grimly. "I don't think so, Jack. I think he's going to keep coming back and back, until he makes a mistake or he's got what he wants."

"Bastard's going to come for her."

"So you've got someone watching, Jack." The chief didn't take his eyes off Jack. "Because she's a fine woman, just like Nonna. I'd hate to see either of them hurt."

"I'll keep her safe, Ben."

"You do that." Ben paused, and, sure enough, he couldn't leave well enough alone. "You partner up with a woman like that, Jack, and you won't have regrets."

"When are you gonna make Nonna an honest woman?" Offense was the best defense, right?

Ben just glared at him. "We're not talking about me here, boy. This is all about you and Lily."

Jack shoved away from the table. "Hell, Ben. This is none of your business." He already had half a town breathing down his neck. He didn't need Ben on his case, as well.

"Speak of the devil," Evan called, a small smile playing across his lips, as if he had himself a little secret he was enjoying. "Or maybe we've got us a visiting angel."

Jack knew Lily was no angel, even if she was spun-sugar on the outside. Inside she was hiding a bad girl who wanted nothing more than to come out and play. All he had to do was convince her to play with him.

Although he was going to have to do something about the car. He winced. That car of hers might have been an expensive little import once upon a time. Jack guessed that motor was still pure fun, despite the piss-poor paint job and the battered leather seats. A lavender wand dangled from the rearview mirror, the braided strands of dried flowers bouncing up and down with each rut she hit. Hell, he was surprised she hadn't painted the damned car purple.

Lily was a slow, deliberate driver, meticulously trying to steer her car around each pothole.

"Going to take her all afternoon," Rio observed cheerfully. He was camped out with half the jump team. Taking care of the housekeeping that went with jumping. After the day's jump, they were going through the chutes. Rio was drawing a needle in and out of the fabric with the same precision he'd used at the firing range during their tours of duty. Chute was just a different weapon, and you didn't go back into battle without giving your weapons all the TLC they needed. They'd all darned chutes when they had to. Sure as hell, you didn't trust your chute to anyone off the team.

Once the car was parked carefully, Jack rose to his feet.

He'd never brought Lily here, and he found himself wondering what she thought about the base camp, the beat-up plane parked out on the short runway and the men and equipment scattered around the hangar. No air-traffic control or bags of peanuts here. The car door opened, and she slid out, deliciously feminine in his masculine world.

Yeah, he'd enjoy playing with her.

"Couldn't wait until tonight?" he drawled, enjoying the outrage blossoming in her eyes. She'd wanted to play—so he'd play. Adrenaline rushed through him.

Jack was big and wet, pulling a white T-shirt over his head. Jeans hugged powerful thighs, and those booted feet of his moved with sheer determination. *God*. She shouldn't find him so damned sexy. He was six feet of trouble. She should have tossed his damned supper at him and left. Instead, damned if she didn't take a step closer.

"Nonna sent me," she said, giving him an artificial smile. "Sacrificial lamb and all that." When his eyes narrowed, she added, "I brought food."

He took a step toward her, that familiar smile curling his lips. "We both know food wasn't what Nonna had in mind." That was true enough, and there was no missing the good-natured, masculine chuckle of agreement from one of his brothers. He loved his Nonna, but he wasn't above grabbing this bull by the horns. "She wants me to keep you, plain and simple."

"There's nothing simple about this," she growled, grabbing the cooler wedged inside her trunk. He slid in front of her before she could do more than get her fingers wrapped around the plastic handles, lifting the cooler out effortlessly and carrying it over to the picnic table. Nonna could plan for the future all she wanted. No matter how attractive that fantasy of happily-ever-after was, Lily had to be practical. Right now all she could think about was the short term. Sure, maybe she'd dreamed about Jack—a time or two—when she'd been younger, but that had been years ago.

Now she was all grown up.

She knew better.

She'd known she'd take as many nights as she could get in his arms. Jack Donovan was a weakness, six feet of sexy demand she couldn't—and didn't want to—resist. She'd thought she could enjoy what he was offering. She'd planned to seduce him if that was what it took. His determination to go after her stalker was something else altogether.

Something she hadn't calculated on or planned for.

Why would he play the white knight for her?

"Eat with us," he coaxed. His fingers curling around her wrist sent her catapulting right back to that night at the pond. Some things hadn't changed. The little grin tugging at the corners of his mouth was still pure mischief.

"I'm not hungry," she grumbled, but she sat. Awkward silence reigned at first, but she filled that by passing out Nonna's bounty. She'd never met a man who'd pass up a free meal, and Nonna was a great chef.

"It always this hot?" One of the newer men on Jack's team volunteered this little conversational nugget. Jack sat back to see how she would respond. Weather up here in the jump camp was more than just polite small talk, she knew, and, sure enough, all heads at the table swiveled, watching her.

"It's summertime." She shrugged. "Hot and dry. Always that way up here. Maybe we get a few showers, but most of us will be irrigating heavily before the month is up." She knew all about watching the sky and praying for rain clouds. When the water dried up, the drought stressed her lavender. Stressed plants meant less oil—and less fragrance. Water was more valuable than gold out here, but too much could be just as much a threat as too little. Each day was a careful balancing act between too much and too little. She was dependent on the grudging rainfall; when it rained, everything came alive, and her dreams survived one more day.

"The farm have its own water?" Jack was a dark, brooding presence beside her. His muscled thigh pressed against hers. She scooted away, but that leg followed. He took up all the space. All the air.

"Some," she acknowledged. The jump team sprawled around them, some laid out on the ground, others parked in white plastic lawn chairs. They'd spent the whole day cutting line. Fighting back the fires threatening Strong.

Yeah, they really did want to talk about the weather. "Lavender Creek has its own well," she explained, "but not enough for much more than drinking and bathing."

"No creek?" Rio teased, laughing when she shook her head.

"That namesake is a trickle now. You couldn't get much more than your feet wet. All the irrigation water is pumped in." Lavender Creek wasn't in the difficult, dry situation of Central Valley farmers, who had to pump their water out of the reservoirs and canals crisscrossing the state's sun-baked middle. All those cars zipping past on the freeway saw only orchards and fields. Green and brown. Not the daily life-and-death struggle to get the water where it needed to go.

"You think we've got rain in our future?"

Rio answered, shaking his head. "Not from the forecasts I've seen. Maybe we'll catch an unexpected break, but the next couple of weeks are looking to be hot and dry."

"Damn," she said feelingly. "That's not going to make things any easier."

"No," Jack said quietly. "We're going to have sleeper fires."

There wasn't much to say to that kind of conversation stopper, so she hunkered down and paid quality attention to her lunch. The next twenty minutes provided a companionable silence as the jump team settled down to the serious business of eating, the rustle of paper and the pop of plastic lids replacing conversation. Nonna hadn't stopped at ham sandwiches. No, she'd added fried chicken. Coleslaw. Biscuits. Clearly she hadn't gotten the latest message from the Surgeon General about restricting fat intake.

"You don't do anything without your brothers," she said, when the picnic table finally cleared out some and most of the team had wandered away in pursuit of showers and rest.

Jack heard the note of accusation in Lily's voice when she mentioned his brothers. She wasn't the first woman to complain about Rio and Evan's constant presence, but he'd tell her what he'd told the others.

That he was a package deal.

He cut her a slice of the peach pie she'd been craving, because Nonna made the best pie this side of Sacramento, and he waited until she'd dug her fork in before he answered her unspoken question.

"We're family." It was that simple, but she wanted the words, so he tried to find a handful of sentences that explained a relationship he didn't completely understand but valued more than anything. "Before we came up here to Strong, before Nonna adopted us, I was pretty much on my own." He told her about life on the streets of San

Francisco. He left out the uglier parts, but he knew she'd fill in those gaps. She'd lived in the city herself, and, even though she'd seen it through different eyes, she'd know precisely how rough things could get for a boy on his own. Instead, he told her about the beach where he and Rio and Evan first met and about the sight of the Pacific Ocean battering the San Francisco coastline.

That ocean had been all wild power. Damp, too, but he'd been young enough not to mind. Young enough to love the way the salt spray whipped off the waves beating against the shore and delivered a load of wet on top of his sleeping bag. They'd lived off hot dogs coaxed or earned from the vendors at the nearby zoo, slipping down onto the sand after dark, once the police had made the first of their nightly sweeps.

He'd been big enough to be mistaken for an adult, so to the authorities he was just another homeless guy looking for a place to lay his head. It hadn't been entirely legal to use the beach as his own personal hotel, but those same cops had had more to worry about than a couple of harmless sleepers. As long he'd kept his nose clean and minded his own business, it'd been all good. And he'd had himself an ocean view and a bit of peace and quiet.

"None of you had any family?" She asked the question lightly, but he knew that absence worried her.

"Evan didn't." He cut her another piece of pie because the first was gone and he'd never forgotten her sweet tooth. "Rio, on the other hand, he needed to put some space between himself and a father who used him as a punching bag. It was easier to just go down to the beach and cop a spot there. No one bothered us. There was plenty of space for everyone."

No one, on the beach or off it, asked too many questions. The three of them had had each other's backs, and together they'd made their own family. Hell, they'd even picked their own last name. The original Donovan had been a local guy who ran construction and gave them odd jobs. Donovan and Sons—that's what they'd called themselves.

It had been Rio's idea that they needed to get themselves an education. Never mind that getting that education meant going right back into a system they all hated.

"We'll stick together," Rio had argued, "and it's just for a few years." When foster care tried to split them up, they'd run away; after the third time, the adults in charge had accepted the truth. No one split up the Donovan brothers.

Strong wasn't the ocean. It sure as hell wasn't the beach. Parts of it, though, were just as wild and unfettered as all that water had been. If a man paid attention to a handful of unwritten laws, well, everything else was negotiable. And some things he had every intention of *taking*.

"I'll see you tonight, baby," he growled, brushing a thumb over her lips. "You count on that."

She stepped backward, sliding away from his touch. The look on her face was no invitation. "You've got a bed here at base camp with your brothers. Sounds to me like you want to be staying in it tonight."

She headed back to her car as if they'd settled matters between them.

He'd straighten out that little misapprehension of hers later tonight, all right.

One way or another, this particular wildland fire season could burn up their town. Strong couldn't take another economic hit. Nonna knew that. Over time, entire families had packed up and moved away, chasing jobs. Chasing dreams that required a bigger stage than Strong had to offer. She'd recognized years ago when she'd decided she was going to rebuild her town, put it back on the map, that the job wouldn't be easy.

"How bad was it?" She turned her head and looked over at Ben. Neither of them was young anymore. Those added years, she figured, meant she had a little more experience to throw at the problem, but time didn't make it any easier to get the work done. Now she was like an old cat who wanted nothing more than to curl up where the summer sun spilled through the window. Not because she had to, but because she'd learned the value of slowing down. Taking the time to soak in those heated, sleepy moments, because those were firefly moments—here today, gone tomorrow. Someday soon, she promised herself. Just as soon as Strong—and her boys—were good and settled.

Ben stretched his legs out in front of him, his boot heels hitting her porch with a familiar thud. "Couple of brush fires," he acknowledged. "Nothing we couldn't handle, but those fires burned faster and longer than they should have. Trees weren't cut back from that ridge up behind Haverley's place, and the flames got up into the deadwood there. Burned real hot for a while."

She closed her eyes, the map of town as clear as day in her mind's eye. Jack had offered to take her up in that plane of his, fly her over the town, but she didn't need wings to see the place—it was all mapped out in her head. "That ridge borders Lily's lavender farm."

"Fire didn't jump," Ben offered.

"But it could have." Nonna set her glass down. "If there'd been wind, Ben, we'd all have been in trouble. That fire just needed a little more fuel, and it would have been knocking on Lily's front door."

"And that's why we called Jack," he reminded her. "To stop that from happening."

Making a decision, Ben reached over and took Nonna's

hand in his. Real casual-like. Could have been just two old friends reaching out to each other for a little comfort.

Could have been.

Life, he thought, was too damned full of *could have beens*.

Chapter Seventeen

Lily stared at the man standing in her doorway and knew she shouldn't have been surprised. Jack Donovan had never backed down from a challenge in his life, and her suggestion that he spend the night at base camp—rather than beneath her roof and in her bed—had been pure challenge. Now that he was here, she wasn't sure what she wanted. Looking at his familiar face, those broad shoulders filling up her doorway while a sensual grin tilted that wicked mouth of his, well, she recognized the now-familiar hum of desire low and warm in her belly. Some things didn't change, no matter what other feelings were piling up between them.

Just because she wanted him, however, didn't mean she had to lie down and let him tromp those boots of his all over her. Give him an inch, and that man would take a mile. "You shouldn't be here, Jack. I told you you should stay with your brothers tonight."

She wasn't sure what was making her so prickly, but, placing her hand on his chest, she gave him a little shove.

He didn't move, just looked down at her. "I'm not leaving. Not unless that's truly what you want, Lilybell. You give me those words. You tell me to go." When she didn't say anything, just stood there watching him, he came toward her, stepping inside, and she moved out of his way.

He didn't misread that little feminine retreat as he grabbed a chair. He leaned back lazily, watching her with those sex-sleepy eyes of his. "Then, I'll go. Not until then. But you have to say the words, Lily."

She couldn't say those words. Not to him. She hadn't been able to say them in high school—and she couldn't say them now. Frustrated, she banged the screen door shut and followed it up with the outside door for good measure. Her fingers hesitated over the lock. In or out. Once again, it was time to choose.

"You're sure this is where you want to be, Jack?" She had to ask.

"I came over here, Lily. No one forced my feet through those doors. Why the hell wouldn't this be where I want to be?" That sexy growl of his had her wanting to believe him.

"Word gets around." Her back hit the door, and she realized she didn't really want to get away from Jack. *Hell.* More like she was locking him away for her very own. Pure fantasy, she knew, but sometimes dreams were a really good thing. "I know all about your high school girlfriends. Hell, I heard more than enough about the women you met in the service. This town isn't good at keeping secrets."

His growl of irritation did things to her, made her body sit up and take notice. Irritated, Jack Donovan was magnificent. "Those women are my past, Lily. Only people here right now are you and me. I haven't asked you about your old boyfriends."

Her sudden snort of laughter broke the tension. "You wouldn't have to. Five dollars says someone in Strong already filled you in."

His reluctant smile told her she was right before he gave her the words. "Twice. First day I was here."

He eyed the closed door, and she wondered for a moment if he'd turn around and leave.

Part of her knew that would be the wise thing, but that ache in her belly had her figuring out a way to hang on to him. "You don't like being shut up inside." She took a step toward him. Nonna had made it plenty clear that he couldn't stand the sensation of walls closing in on him.

"Bad memories," he growled, "and, yeah, I know I should get the hell past them."

"It doesn't matter," she said, meaning every word. So she took a deep breath. "We can go out onto the sunporch." Could make love on the daybed there.

He stilled, not missing the promise in her voice. "You real sure, baby?" He was big and tough and more than a little rough around the edges—but she wanted him. Wanted him to stay as long as he would. If she was lucky, she'd have a summer with him. One long, lazy, heat-filled summer. Those memories would have to be enough.

"Stay with me, Jack." She held out a hand, her feet already moving toward the sunporch.

"I'll stay," he agreed. "But I'm thinking we need to have us a conversation about what you might—or might not—have heard about my past."

"Not tonight." Tonight she just wanted his hands on her. She wanted to explore all that sun-kissed skin of his. If they tried to figure out what Jack could commit to, they wouldn't make it to his bed or hers. She didn't want to pick that fight tonight. She didn't think he really did, either, but he hadn't budged. Just kept on watching her with those dark, knowing eyes of his. "You going to come over here and kiss me, Jack?"

Jack never backed down, not from a challenge like that. He and those brothers of his, they lived for a challenge, and, sure enough, he leaned forward.

"Just remember, you're not in charge here," she said, purposely baiting him, knowing his hot button.

His slow, sensual smile should have warned her. "You think not, baby?" He was all alpha male as he came out of his chair and stalked across the floor toward her until he had one powerful arm braced over her head. "Because I'm pretty damn sure I am."

Memories of that high school night all came flooding back, the young man and his truck. She hadn't been ready for him or his potent brand of sensuality then, and they'd both known it. He'd backed off because, she realized, Jack Donovan was honorable to the bone, even if he didn't advertise it.

"I won't push you," he said quietly, "if you don't want me to. But I think you do, baby. I think you're not sure just what you want, other than pleasure."

"And you are?" Obviously, he hadn't missed the feminine challenge in her voice. He leaned right into her, trapping her between the wall and that hard, lean body she'd explored last night. *God.* The memories. Part of her wanted to melt right into him, while the rest of her wanted to make him work for what he wanted. Work for her. Making love with Jack Donovan was impossibly good.

Making love. Was that what she was doing? A flash of panic had her stiffening in his arms.

"Just a little game," he whispered, mistaking her apprehension. "Just a little fun between you and me, baby. If you don't want to play, we'll stop right now."

This wasn't love. It couldn't be. No, *this* was fire and heat, setting sensitive nerve endings aflame until she shifted restlessly. Wanting more.

Wanting Jack.

He didn't move, just reached out and drew the back of his hand down her cheek. Those hands made her shiver.

Callused and strong, Jack's hands were impossibly gentle. Firm.

"You want to play this game, baby, you know what you need to do for me." His head lowered. "You tell me what you want from me, let me know just how I'm going to be touching you tonight."

Silently she shook her head.

"You will, baby," he promised. Heat burned through her in a sensual reaction, and her skin was on fire, flushed and damp like the sensitive folds of her sex. She was wet for him, and she needed more. So much more. "I made you a promise last night, a promise I'm keeping now. I'm going to make you hungrier than you've ever been."

"You can try," she breathed.

"Is that another dare?" His mouth moved closer to hers, just a whisper away. God, she wanted him to shut up and kiss her.

"If you want it to be." She loved his demands, loved that he wasn't going to let her hide from the sensations building between them. That he wouldn't hide, either. With Jack, what you saw was what you got.

And his harsh groan told her a lot.

This man holding her, her Jack, wanted her.

He lowered his mouth to hers, and that first meeting of their lips was almost innocent. His lips rested gently against her mouth, his eyes holding her gaze. Watching her. She closed her eyes, and sensation exploded through her. One of his hands slid around the back of her neck, cupping her, urging her closer. Those strong fingers coaxed the tense muscles of her neck to relax, while his other hand drifted down to her hips. Despite the gentle pressure bringing her closer to him, there was no missing the thick press of his erection.

Almost innocent.

Definitely wicked.

The next teasing brush of his lips was too gentle. Too light. With a little moan of frustration, she rose up on tiptoe to chase that teasing mouth of his.

Instead of giving her what she wanted, he pulled back, putting a whisper of space between them as he stripped off her tank top. "You want more, you have to tell me, baby."

She arched up against him, desperate for more contact, the fiery brush of his skin against hers. "Don't you tease me, Jack."

"What kind of a kiss do you want?" he asked relentlessly. "Harder? Softer? You want to open that sweet little mouth of yours so I can come right on in?"

"God, yes." She couldn't contain the little shiver of pleasure. Even that small ripple of sensation was almost too much. "I want it all."

"You don't want everything, Lilybell. You don't know the fantasies I've had." The dark promise in his voice made her want to demand more. Demand everything from him. "You know what men think about up at base camp during fire season, baby?"

Mutely she shook her head as he rested his mouth next to her ear. She was going to come, just from his words and his kisses, and that wasn't the way she wanted this to end. She wanted all of Jack, not just the tease and the promise of him. So she tightened her arms around him, pulling his body against her in silent demand.

"We work hard, we play hard, Lily," he whispered harshly. "We're out there, keeping your sweet little ass safe, so when we get ourselves back to base and we're hot and sweaty and bone-tired from it all, we fantasize about a little appreciation." A finger stroked down the curve of her breast, pushed down her bra, circled the cherry-red tip. She felt the sweet, sharp tug all the way to her sex. "Like, maybe, when I came home, you'd take me deep into that luscious mouth of yours. You know what just the thought of all that wet heat surrounding me, sucking me in, does to me?"

He sucked her nipple into his mouth, giving her a taste of his fantasy. She threaded her fingers through his hair, melting, desperate. His tongue ruthlessly flayed the sensitive nerve endings, drawing an erotic path around the little tip. God, she was going to come.

"Jack," she whimpered.

"Not yet, Lily," he warned, hearing her unspoken message. He led her to the porch daybed, then spread her out on it. "You don't come yet. Not until you've heard every one of the fantasies I've been tormented with, up at camp. Maybe," he whispered, his husky growl sending goose bumps shivering across her skin, "I'll tell you just how lonely those camps get sometimes. Just us boys, baby, and no women to kiss or to cuddle. Any women there are off-limits, co-workers. Just one of the boys. It gets real lonely up there. Sets a man to thinking . . ."

He stared down at her, then pressed a hard kiss against her mouth. Those hands of his didn't stop their sensual exploration, sliding, stroking knowingly. Learning the soft curve of her waist, the gentle mound of her tummy. That soft brush of skin on skin could have been an innocent caress. That wicked touch wasn't. He was teasing her, and she was fighting a losing battle. Shifting restlessly against him, her legs slid apart, her hips moving against his. Welcoming him.

"You ever have a naughty dream, Lilybell? Ever wonder what it would be like to have a man kiss every inch of you?"

His thumb traced a little pattern over her hip bones. "Every inch, baby," he growled.

She'd been waiting, wondering, for years. Those were midnight fantasies, dark and sexy and tantalizing. Now this man was claiming her.

"You tell me, baby," he groaned, resting his mouth against hers, "and I'll give you what you want."

She was on fire, her mind pleasure-hazed. Thinking past the heated pleasure weakening her, leaving her wet and aching and wanting, wasn't going to happen. She'd lost control of these sensations, and all she could do was hang on, let the pleasure and the man take her. Knowing she was driving him every bit as wild as he was driving her.

"Kiss me," she begged, and he did. His kiss was hard and deep, demanding the response she couldn't hide from him as his mouth took hers. And yet she felt safer than she ever had. Wrapped in Jack's arms, surrounded by the primal heat of him, she felt safe. Cherished.

"I'm going to taste you. Every inch of you, Lily. Take these off." That sexy growl and the tug of his fingers in the little bows decorating the sides of her panties had her dampening.

He drew her shorts and panties down her legs. The erotic tug of the damp cotton against her sensitized skin sent bright sparks of pleasure shooting through her. She was so close to something, some bright, hot pleasure she hadn't known was possible. His dark eyes watched her, dipping down to where she was wet and slick for him. She felt powerful, feminine, as his breath caught hoarsely. He watched her as if she was the center of his universe.

His hands caught her shoulders, anchoring her. "You know how beautiful you are, Lily? I've wanted to see you, touch you, for as long as I can remember. Standing there on your porch, all I could think about was kissing you. Here." His mouth trailed a heated path along her breasts. When he drew a nipple into his mouth and suckled, sensation rocketed straight to her clit. Lost in the pleasure, she knew he was still whispering praise. His pleasure. She didn't know what he was saying anymore, but the way he said it made her feel cherished. Beautiful.

Her panties fell to the floor, the tiny scrap of cotton and lace a white flag of surrender on top of his clothes. She was just as hungry for him as she'd been when they first made love. She'd waited years for this. For this man. Now she was going to claim every inch of *him* as *hers*.

Her hands slid down the hard muscles of his back, reaching underneath his tee. So much bare skin. So much Jack. Strong and sure, his shoulders filled her vision as he came over her. Her breath caught as his hand moved lower while he cradled her head, angling her mouth for his kiss.

His fingers slid into the sensitive folds of her pussy, and he stilled for an endless second. A male sound of satisfaction tore from his throat, and then he was kissing her harder, deeper. Those fingers stroked. Parted her and traced an electric path straight up to her clit. She couldn't think, couldn't breathe. Her world was only this man, this bed. One finger pressed into her. Slowly. A delicious tease that promised fullness. Tearing her mouth from his, she buried her face against his throat and just drank in the pleasure as she tasted the salt of him against her tongue.

"Come for me, baby," he urged throatily. "Let me give you more." A second finger joined the first, stretching her. Those fingers curled deeper inside her and sent a shock of pleasure searing through her as he pressed. Stroked. She had to come now, had to find that release.

Wordlessly, she arched up against him, taking him, riding him. Her flesh milked him, tightening. The tension built as the little pulses of pleasure gathered and grew, and then she was flying, coming apart in his arms as she cried his name.

Chapter Eighteen

Jack slid his fingers reluctantly away from Lily.

Lily didn't hide what she felt for him, all that heat and lust in her eyes just for him. Did she understand the electrifying effect that honesty had on him? He was hard, had been since he took the steps to her porch and stood in her doorway. Every inch of him had known he shouldn't be there, shouldn't have picked up the challenge she'd thrown down. She hadn't understood just how hot a tease those words were, and yet there was no stopping his breath from catching at the sight of her waiting for him, all pink and gold, on the daybed.

"Undress for me," she whispered throatily. He hadn't thought he could get harder, but damned if he didn't, the pleasure slamming through him.

"I thought I'd be able to change your mind." The words spilled from him in a harsh groan. Pulling his shirt over his head, he tossed it behind him. Her eyes drifted downward from his face, a feline smile of satisfaction curling her lips.

"You look good for an old man, Jack. Real good." She reached out, and her fingertips traced a line of fire down his chest. Sensation slammed into him. "Take the rest of it off."

His fingers tugged buttons free, pushing the worn denim

down his thighs. The sexy little catch of her breath as he stood there before her had him hardening still further.

Her hands tugged him closer, and he went. He wasn't about to refuse her anything, not when she got that sexy little crease between her eyes as she stared hungrily at his dick. She wanted him, and that interest made him feel like the biggest man of them all. King of the world.

"Careful, baby," he groaned. "I'm not made of stone here."

"Parts of you clearly are," she teased.

Her hands closed over his hips, pulling him nearer. As her head lowered, her hair spilled around him, and the erotic tease of those silky strands sliding over his erection had him fighting for control. Slowly, so very slowly, she moved downward, and all he could do was hang on, threading his hands through her beautiful hair, lost in the fiery sensations lashing him.

"All mine," she whispered, pressing a light kiss against the very tip of him, a tiny butterfly caress of a kiss that sent sensation scorching through his veins.

"Lily," he groaned. "You're killing me."

"Good," she whispered, pulling back. He wanted to drag her closer, fought the primal urge to guide his dick deep into her mouth and fuck her until there was no telling where one of them ended and the other began.

Her tongue licked a naughty path around the head of his dick. Tasting. Exploring. When she finally sucked him deep inside that hot, wet heaven, he wanted to beg for more. His own groan shocked him, hoarse and guttural. Her touch was too good, too much.

Her lips parted around him, and, God help him, he thought he was dying as her mouth slid down his shaft. He'd never been so hard, so desperate, as she took him.

"God, just like that."

She wrapped a hand around his thick flesh, and there was nothing hesitant about her. She was all woman. Knowing. Sure. Her other hand cupped his balls, her mouth moving over him. The delicious tug of her hand up and down his erection almost sent him over the edge right then and there.

When she pulled back, blowing on the damp head, bright pleasure exploded through him. "Christ. That feels so good."

His hands tangled in her hair. Guiding her. Holding on to her because the world had narrowed to her and him and this bed.

And still her mouth worked on him. Tasting him. Learning him with each naughty stroke. He fought not to drive himself into her mouth. Fought the need to come, to fill her with himself.

"You have to stop, baby," he groaned finally. Reluctantly pulling himself away, he briefly reached over to snag a condom from the pocket of his jeans before he lowered her down onto the bed and covered her with himself.

"Tell me you're ready, Lily." He slid between her legs, and she opened for him willingly, pulling him deeper into the cradle of her hips, up against the sweet, wet heat of her. He couldn't wait, couldn't hold back another minute because he knew—just knew—nothing would be better than this connection between them, and he wanted all that feeling now.

"I want you, Jack." Her arms came up to hold him closer, and then he was sliding in, sliding home. Moving to take his place between her thighs. She took him. Cradled him inch by heated inch as he pressed inside, stretching that tight, silken sheath until she was wrapped around him like a sweet, hidden glove.

"You feel so perfect," he whispered harshly. "So goddamned perfect, baby. Yes, move just like that," he groaned as she wrapped her legs on either side of his hips. Moving with him. He laid his face against the side of hers, and every breath he took pushed him deeper inside her, dragged her scent deeper.

"That's so good, Jack," she whimpered, her eyes drifting closed. "I need more."

She pulled him impossibly closer, wrapping her legs fiercely around his waist, and held on. He stroked in. Out. His hands reaching beneath her to cup her ass and hold her closer as he fought for control. Fought to make sure she found what she needed before he let go.

"Just like that," he praised. Bracing a hand beside her head, he kept his full weight off her. His whole body was tightening, his cock desperately hard. Christ, she was killing him, her body milking his. Tiny spasms rippled through her, each small pulse sending an answering spike of pleasure through him.

He tensed, then moved faster, harder as her hands clutched at his back. Guiding. Demanding. "Now, Jack."

"Baby, you can have whatever you want." He slid deeper, losing himself in her sweet, wet heat. Stroked in and out of that sweet, hot pussy as he drank in her little groans of pleasure. Her nails dug into the tense muscles of his shoulders as he took them both to the edge. Pleasure tore through his body in a fiery shock of sensation, his whole world narrowing to this woman and where the two of them were joined. Her eyes watched him take her, widening with the helpless, fiery pleasure of it all.

"Come for me, baby." He dropped a hand between them, finding her. His back arching, he drove them both over the edge, and his body tightened, pressed tightly against sensitive nerve endings as she dissolved around him and he shuddered out his pleasure in her arms.

* ★ ★

Lily came awake, her neck protesting its unfortunate angle. Sometime during the night she'd sprawled over Jack's bare chest. With each breath she inhaled the clean, spicy scent of him. He hadn't left, and he hadn't taken a fire call. Maybe that was a victory. Maybe it was because they'd slept on the daybed on the screened-in porch. Either way, she knew things would never be the same between them again. Last night had made their relationship more than a one-night stand.

Jack, of course, was still Jack, and he'd still be leaving at the end of the summer. No matter how naughty or hot the sex had been, some things hadn't changed. Jack was still a temporary kind of a man, a ride-in-ride-out cowboy.

She still wasn't sure she was ready for a summertime romance, but it sure looked like she'd gotten herself one. So she'd enjoy Jack Donovan, take everything he had to offer. When summer was over and his job here was done, she'd finally have her memories of him. After the last two nights, she knew she wasn't going to be prudent. Wasn't going to send him on his way any sooner than she had to.

She wasn't hiding anymore. She'd live her life, see where it took her.

For years, she'd fantasized. Now she had the real deal, all six foot plus of him. It was still early, the sun barely creeping above the horizon. The light in the yard was watery and pale, the crickets still singing their drowsy summer song. There was just enough light to make out every delicious inch of Jack asleep on her sunporch. Long and lean and sexy, he sprawled on the cotton sheets. One hand was over his face, while the other tangled in the orange fur of the barn cat. The cat had snuck in and was curled up now against Jack's side, trusting the bed's larger occupants not to roll.

Yeah. One summer was better than nothing. Jack's bare

chest was peaceful. Beautiful. With the windows all open and his face turned toward them, he seemed to drink in the cool morning air. It would be hotter than hell in a matter of hours, but right now the morning was still cool and pleasant against her skin.

The sheer sexiness of the man had that lazy heat building in her again. The cat cracked an eye when she slipped off the mattress and padded across the floor, but the man didn't stir.

Question was, how had this man become what she really wanted? When she'd come home, she'd sure thought she knew exactly what she wanted. To be safe. To *not* get burned. Jack was the antithesis of everything she'd believed should be on her wish list. She wanted roots and a home of her own. She wanted a place where people looked out for one another and greeted each other by name. Knew each other's stories, even when that was enough to drive you crazy because those stories always followed you. That curiosity meant that folks were interested, plain and simple. You were part of the fabric of the town, for better or worse, and gossip certainly wasn't the worst thing that had ever happened to her.

From all accounts, her mother had loathed the unabashedly small-town feeling of Strong. She'd always been looking for an exit ticket, but instead she'd found a series of failed businesses. Yellow-pages advertising, time-shares, even a wine-of-the-month club—she'd tried them all before Lily was five—and failed—until she'd decided the best business decision was dropping her daughter on Ben's porch and hightailing it out of Strong for greener, more urban pastures.

Jack had hightailed it, too, and he'd made it perfectly clear that Strong was merely a stop on his tour of duty. So how did she deal with the inescapable fact that she wanted to nudge the cat aside and crawl back onto the daybed with Jack, spoon up against him? Lose herself there. Shaking her head, she backed out of the sunporch, flinching at the soft whisper of sound as the latch clicked into place. The cat's ears flicked, but Jack Donovan slept the sleep of the dead.

From the kitchen window, she eyed the fields surrounding the house. Right now, as summer got under way, those fields were an intense blanket of color. This early in the morning, the scent was powerful, almost suffocating in its sweetness. The incessant drone of the bees getting a jump start on their own day was a familiar chorus.

A good day to harvest.

Pouring coffee into her favorite mug from the pot she'd set on auto-timer, she added cream and a heaping spoonful of sugar. Sweet and strong, the coffee was perfect. Wandering out onto the front porch, she plotted her plan of attack.

Growing good lavender required two things. Sun and water. People were more complex.

On impulse, she liberated one of Jack's T-shirts from the duffel he'd dropped inside the door to the porch. She'd take a little piece of him out to cut lavender. Sliding her feet into her flip-flops, she shoved her hair into an elastic tie and hit the door.

Harvesting lavender was hot, satisfying work. With each new breath she took, the heady perfume threatened to overwhelm her senses. Armed with a pair of small hand shears, she carefully cut the spikes from each plant, just as they were opening. Usually she'd have waited until the late-morning sun had dried off the dew, but since these were for grower's bouquets for the florist, she could cut early. Methodically she cut long stems for the bouquets, bunching and tying each handful with rubber bands.

When Jack had come charging on up her driveway, a knight errant she hadn't asked for, he'd brought other, hidden dreams back to her. She'd carved out a good life for herself, and she would, she acknowledged to herself, fight tooth and nail to keep it. More than money, the farm represented the future she was trying so hard to achieve. Each plant she set into the ground was a promise.

Maybe there were promises she and Jack could make each other. Maybe not. The last two nights had been some sort of a start, though.

Jack smelled of smoke and man and something spicy Lily couldn't name. If summer had a scent, that scent would be Jack Donovan. He'd come home. Bronzed and muscled from the work he'd done firefighting, her Jack was determined as hell to keep her safe. Yet all she could do was remember the fear.

Every time he smelled like smoke, she remembered.

She was afraid. She could admit that to herself now. She'd been afraid when the first fires started, but they'd been little. Easily dismissed by everyone, so she'd ignored her instincts. Instincts that screamed: *run*. She should have listened to those instincts. What had happened had been far more than a trash can fire or a carelessly tossed cigarette. Now just the smell of smoke was enough to make her breath catch and her heart race. A hundred-plus miles and there still wasn't enough space between herself and San Francisco. Wasn't enough to make her forget the heart-stopping moment when she'd woken up.

The room was too warm. Maybe the AC had gone out, but some instinct told her no. This heat was different, a suffocating blanket weighing down the thick air. No light came through the curtains covering her bedroom window. All she heard was a rapid-fire crackle, a sound almost like sticks clattering together or water running. The sound was all wrong. That sound didn't belong in her home, any more than the high-pitched, regular ping of the fire alarm did. Oh, God.

Dropping out of bed, she staggered to the kitchen and saw that the door was impassable. And then the horrifying sight of her books burning in the sink, the flames spreading throughout the kitchen. Back in the bedroom, she crawled helplessly to the window and the fire escape. For a long moment the window stuck, resisting her shaking hands, and then the sash shot up, and she tumbled out into the smoke-filled night air.

The red-and-blue pulse of police lights strobed through the night sky, the heavy rumble of the fire trucks greeting her. Help was coming. Clinging to the fire escape that ended twelve feet above the alley, she scrubbed her eyes with her hands, distantly startled to realize she was crying. It could have been the smoke making her eyes tear. Her hair and her skin, her clothes—the sharp, gunpowder tang of smoke permeated her to the very bone. This smoke wasn't the familiar scent of a just-struck match or the flicker of just-doused candlelight. Everything was unfamiliar. Acrid. She had to get away.

And then, the man down there, down in the alley behind her town house, made a noise. A harsh little noise of indescribable pleasure, and she looked. She couldn't see his face, concealed by the shadows, just the thick, jutting threat of his cock. He'd unzipped his chinos and stood there, legs spread, one hand on his cock and the other massaging his balls as he watched the fire eat up her home. Above them both, glass blew out of her kitchen window and rained down on the dark, flame-lit space.

She sucked air into her lungs, and she didn't know what to do. He was between her and the alley's exit. The fire was above her, and no one was coming. Then his head turned, really slowly, and he looked at her.

"Your fire's absolutely lovely, Lily," he said, his voice a harsh, damaged creak of sound. His hand moved faster, slapping against his skin as he strained. "Don't you like my little present?"

He took a step toward her, the semen spurting from the end of that cock in a thick stream, and she found her voice and screamed and screamed.

★ ★ ★

Afterward, she'd come back to the place to walk through the damage with the insurance adjuster. The adjuster had been professional but sympathetic, commiserating with her on her loss and assuring her that she was in good hands. He'd had no idea. These were more than just things. This was her home.

Had been her home. Now *he'd* taken that home away from her.

The fire's heat had blistered the cabinets, scorching a deadly calling card on the wall separating the kitchen from her bedroom. There were holes where flame-heated nails had burst free, and everything still recognizable was wet and smoke-singed. Curling and blackened. The heat had warped the window frames, rendering them as molten as well-used candles, and all the glass had blown right out. The fire, the adjuster noted clinically, had been fast and hard.

But here she was. Alive. The adjuster promised to cut a check so she could get on with her life, rebuild when she was ready.

How could she ever be ready?

The fire had destroyed the kitchen—and so much more. She'd lost dishes and towels, pots and pans. It wasn't as if she was sentimental about the appliances, but Ben had given her the blue glassware vase that had belonged to his mother. "Something blue," he'd teased in a parody of the wedding tradition when he'd handed her the vase to take with her to her new home. A little piece of Strong for her very own, because he didn't want to wait until the day she married to share their family pieces with her. The blue glassware was gone, consumed by the fire or overrun by the firefighters. It was silly to cry over something so minor, but those were *her* memories, damn it.

And that vase had been a reminder. She'd looked at the

colored blue glass every morning, and she'd remembered the loving uncle she had, the place she'd come from.

When she'd paused, stricken, in the doorway, the insurance adjuster had simply assured her the smell would come out. Take it down to the studs and rebuild, he promised. Give the place new Sheetrock, electric, cabinets, and paint. Dry it all out. The fire would be a memory in three months. No one would ever know a terrible thing had happened here.

She, on the other hand, knew she'd never forget.

Least of all the man fisting his cock as he watched her home burning.

This fire hadn't been an accident. The most terrifying confirmation of that came long before the police report had identified the source as suspicious. She'd been staying with friends, but she'd received a package. An anonymous cardboard box with no return address that held her favorite coffee mug—a mug that had been sitting on the draining rack in her kitchen. The oversize pink ceramic cup with its cheerful kittens was kitschy. Fun. She'd had it since her college days, and it had held the four cups of coffee she made every morning.

I thought you'd want this, the note had said.

What she'd *wanted* was to toss the box, the note, and the mug into the trash and pretend none of this had happened. Instead, she'd dutifully taken the mug and the box to the police station. She hadn't even liked having the package in her car. Her mind raced, creating end-of-the-world scenarios. And, after leaving the box at the station, she'd just kept on driving. Kept on driving until she hit Strong and realized she'd come home.

She'd used the adjuster's check for a down payment on her farm and cleaned out her 401K for the rest. The nightmares had dwindled, but they never disappeared. Just as she never quite managed to forget the scent of burned wood. Burned dreams.

Now here Jack was, stirring things up. Making her remember.

She let the thoughts and worries go, losing herself in the soothing rhythm of cutting and binding the fragrant stalks. She wasn't going to figure Jack Donovan out in a morning—or even a night or two.

He was summer romance, as sweet as the flowers surrounding her. She'd enjoy every moment, soak in the heat and splendor. When fall came and he went away, she'd put those memories away and move on with her life.

Chapter Nineteen

Buying the old firehouse was the craziest thing Jack had ever done. He had no idea what had gotten into him.

"You sure you want to do this, boy?" Ben was watching him like he was committing the error of the millennium. That disbelieving gaze didn't help his nerves any, but this made sense. Felt right.

"Yeah. I do." Before he could chicken out, he signed his name at the bottom of the stack of papers. And then again and again, initialing each page in the stack. Disclosures. Addendums. Dire warnings that the old firehouse wasn't the soundest structure in Strong.

Hell. He probably should just set the place on fire and let the boys use it for practice.

One hundred forty thousand dollars. He could afford it, but this was more than money. He'd bought property before, but never in Strong. Never as more than an investment.

And no one—no one in his right mind—would consider the old firehouse an investment. Not unless there were oil wells gushing underneath the crumbling foundation or a streak of gold ore a mile wide. Which—he examined the last page—he apparently hadn't purchased the rights to anyhow. Anything valuable belowground belonged to the town, free and clear.

Hell.

He didn't know why he was doing this, but the Realtor was already gathering up the papers. "The title will be recorded this afternoon." The Realtor hesitated, then stuck out his right hand. "Congratulations."

"Best of luck, you mean," Ben grumbled behind him. "This place will take a shitload of sweat equity. Any moment you're not fighting fire is gonna be spent right here, wrestling drywall and termites."

The Realtor dropped the key into his hand. "No reason you can't move on in right now. She'll be yours as soon as I get back to the office." Which was five buildings down the street.

Tilting his head back, he let his head rest against the peeling paint of the firehouse's porch as the Realtor scampered down the sagging steps with the check and the paperwork. "You think I'm not pressing you into service, Ben, you thought wrong."

Ben snorted. "I figure I owe you that much, since I'm the reason you're here."

Nonna had made the call on Ben's behalf, sure enough, but coming back hadn't been just for him. Or her. Sure, he'd wanted to help out an old friend and mentor, but he'd had business here. Personal business. He hadn't known it, but he wasn't hiding from the truth anymore.

"Part of the reason anyhow," Jack said.

"Right." Ben tested the wood of the balcony, and the paint flaked off in his hands. "Plenty to do here."

Shoving away from the wall, Jack opened the door. The lock stuck and took a little finessing before the door finally opened up and let him in. An unexpected sense of possession filled him. He had himself his own little piece of Strong now.

A piece that smelled strongly of mildew.

The floors inside creaked with each step. The place

wasn't so big that he didn't know where to head. He passed the two bays for fire trucks and skipped the upstairs loft for off-duty firemen. He poked his head into store-rooms and a dressing room. Pegs for the guys to hang their jackets and drop their boots. In front of him was the old firehouse office. On a hunch, he realized there was some-thing he wanted to check out. He'd bet no one had wanted to be the guy stuck behind the rusting metal desk that greeted him when he forced that warped door open. He'd have wanted to be out where the action was, first on the scene.

When he went inside, Ben was right on his heels. He beelined it to the metal filing cabinets rusting away against the back wall.

"What are you after?" Ben asked.

"Shut up," he said, "and start looking, old man." His own fingers were walking double-time through the near-est cabinet, myriad old fire calls condensed into reams of ancient logbooks that had been left behind, no longer con-sidered useful. "Lily's stalker likes fire. He has to be a lo-cal. How much you want to bet he's set fires here before?"

Hell, Jack himself had been one of a handful of boys who'd loved the ride-along. Nothing unusual in getting a thrill from riding up on the fire truck, being first on the scene. It would have been more unusual if any of them *hadn't* gotten a thrill from riding out on the engine. They'd all come running when Ben had fired up the siren and gone to work. Maybe a half dozen other boys, besides him and Rio and Evan. What he wanted were those names.

Ben's gaze swept over the pages of call records. "What, exactly, are we looking for?"

"Names. Patterns." He hadn't expected to spend hours combing through dusty old paper, but his gut told him it was important. This old firehouse held answers, and he was going to find them.

Lily was Ben's niece. Now she was Jack's lover.

Maybe he should have left her alone.

But he'd already walked away from her once, all those years ago. He'd regretted what he'd missed; somehow even then he'd known that Lily was a once-in-a-lifetime woman.

He knew he wasn't the kind of man she deserved. He'd known that from the moment they met. He was hard, and he was ruthless. He knew these things. On the streets, these were good things to be. The strong survived, and he'd never regretted or second-guessed his choices. Until now.

Lily was strong, too, but a different kind of strong— quiet, with the kind of backbone that was pure steel. You didn't notice until you pushed her, and damned if she didn't push right back. She didn't have to be loud to get her point across or to demand respect.

The pages of the logbooks were neat and tidy. Ben's handwriting reflected the man. Pages and pages of orderly entries marching up and down the columns in clear black and white.

"You always wrote our names down," he said. "To make us feel special, I'm betting, but every time we rode out with you or we showed up at a scene to lend a hand, you gave us a line in the book. You treated us like we were real firefighters, even though we were just wannabe kids."

"Whether you helped with handing out equipment or slung hose, you were helping to fight fires," Ben said quietly. "Sure, you didn't have professional experience and I wasn't letting you too close to those flames, but you were all fighters, Jack. Hell, I don't think you or your brothers knew how *not* to fight. Every day, every fire was a new battle, and you'd charge on in. Head down, fists out. You were taking us all on. There's a lot to respect right there. You earned your place in that logbook."

Each name brought the flash of a childhood memory. The truck. The adrenaline rush and the sense of danger. That moment when the truck pulled up to whatever fire needed fighting and he got his first eyeful of what they were facing. There'd been a sense of belonging riding that truck he hadn't found anywhere else. He'd always been bigger, taller, stronger than the other boys. It hadn't been long before he'd been slinging dirt and hauling hose with the adult members of the team. On the job, they were all part of that same team, joining forces because together they were far more than the sum of their parts. All that mattered was getting those flames put out.

There were more than a dozen names in the logs from those long-ago summers. Some of the boys were long gone, but some were still right here in Strong. He was on to something, and he knew it.

Grabbing a dusty pad of paper, he started listing names as he found them. "I'm ruling the three of us out," he said tightly. "I know my brothers. They didn't do this thing."

Ben gave a short nod. "Didn't think any of you did."

Jack couldn't help thinking of Lily's vulnerability, his memory providing a detailed image of the way she'd looked in his arms. In his temporary bed. She'd been sweet and trusting and so damned hot. He wanted to taste her again, see what it would take to make those soft little cries for him fall from her lips once more.

Christ, he needed to leave her alone.

"This particular summer," he said, stabbing his pen at a logbook and holding it out for Ben to see, because the hell of it was, he was standing shoulder-to-shoulder with Lily's uncle, and no way did he want the other man to guess the thoughts running through his head. Ben wasn't stupid. He knew what Jack had gotten up to the last couple of nights, but he wouldn't want the details. "You had a series of grass fires. Trash can fires, too."

Beside him, Ben was nodding. "Garage fires, as well. I thought at the time it could be some kid up to mischief. We didn't find anything at the scenes, but maybe there were too many little fires for them all to be accidental."

"What if whoever is going after Lily rode along on those calls? You think he'd want to see the effect of his handiwork? Maybe, just maybe, he'd have gotten off on setting those fires and then putting them out himself."

"Or making us all run around." Ben was nodding slowly again. "Like his own personal cleanup crew."

"He likes power." Jack pushed down his rage. Anger wasn't going to help Lily, not right now. He didn't like or understand these new emotions tearing him apart. He had never been possessive. Not about women. "With fire, he could be the one in charge. Starting things."

"So who had that kind of itch all bottled up inside him?" Ben wondered aloud.

"A dead man," Jack said grimly. Scanning the list, he marked a handful of names with pencil. Damning ticks. He needed Rio and his software know-how.

"We're all concerned about Lily," Ben said.

"True." He hadn't said otherwise, had he?

"So you don't have to do this all by yourself." Ben looked at him pointedly. "You think I'm going to sit back and let whoever this is come after her? Hell, no. He's going through me first."

"Fine," Jack said tightly. Flipping the page, he made more marks. Seven of them, including his brothers, had gone out on calls that summer. Isaiah, Ethan, Eddie, Charlie Joe.

"Just how involved are you getting with Lily?"

"Don't push, Ben." Charlie Joe—C.J.—Jack remembered, had left for a summer sleepaway camp after three weeks. And Isaiah had twisted his ankle at a fire and been out of commission for weeks.

"She's my niece," Ben said. His voice was calm, but older man wasn't budging. "If you're seeing her, you tell me straight up."

"Fine." There had been more than twenty calls in July. July was typically hot and dry, which meant grass fires weren't out of the ordinary—but they'd ridden out on a dozen of those calls in one particular week. And all of those fires had started without an obvious cause. "These belong to our boy," he decided.

"Are you seeing Lily?" Ben wasn't letting this one go. "Or did you sleep with her, Jack, and now you're moving on?" Maybe a deaf man would miss the unspoken warning in the other man's voice. If Jack hurt Lily, Ben would be coming after him.

That was good. He'd help the man himself. "Yes," he said tightly. Lily deserved better. Question was: could he give it to her?

"Which one is it?" Ben's hand came down, covering the printed pages. Apparently their investigation was at an impasse until Ben had some answers to his questions. "You going to hurt my little girl, Jack? Because I'm not going to be okay with that. She may be all grown up, but she doesn't need the heartache. She's lost enough."

"What do you want from me, Ben?" He never explained himself, but this was Ben. Lily's uncle. Ben had practically been a father to him, and he knew precisely how much Ben meant to Lily and vice versa. So he'd explain. As much as he could and no matter how uncomfortable it made him feel.

"I can't promise happily-ever-after and wedding bells," he said carefully. "And I don't think that's what Lily wants. Not from me. I'm not the kind of man you should want sticking around for your little girl anyhow." A tiger couldn't change its stripes, so he'd do what he'd always done, and he'd leave when summer was over. In the meantime, he'd see Lily, and he'd fix up the firehouse and turn it back over to the town.

He didn't want anything more from Lily Cortez, did he? So why did the thought of another man taking her into his arms, settling down with her in a little house in Strong, make him see red?

"Don't sell yourself short, Jack." Ben shook his head. "You say those things long enough, maybe you'll start believing them."

He'd spent a lifetime moving from one place to another, never stopping for long. That was who he was, part of what made him a damned fine firefighter. He'd never had a problem coming—or going. When that call came in, he just picked up and moved on to where he was needed. The urge to stay put—stay with this one particular woman—scared the hell out of him. He'd fought his battles, held the line in one firefight after another, but he'd never *cared* about whether or not the fire took more than Jack kept away from it.

He couldn't afford to care now. "*You* never married," he pointed out.

"And I'm not asking you to," Ben said quietly. "Just asking you to treat her right. And I know you'll do that, but she's like a daughter to me, Jack, so I have to ask. Someday you'll have a daughter of your own, and you'll understand how I feel."

Lily was a damned special woman. No matter how bad Jack was at holding up his end of this conversation, there was no question about that. Lily mattered. Maybe he already knew how Ben felt. Not exactly, because there was nothing paternal about the attraction blazing between Lily and him. But he understood Ben's need to protect Lily.

Drawing his finger down the page, he forced his mind back to the business at hand. Two other boys had gone out consistently with the engine, riding along to the summer's fires. Eddie Haverley and Ethan McBride. Both of them were still right here in town. Ethan owned a ranch, while Eddie had some sort of consulting business. Not that Eddie, who faced the world armed with a trust fund, had to work to pay the bills.

He looked down at the page again to confirm the pattern coming together in his head. Not just little grass fires. There had been a series of fires on Haverley land as well.

He tapped the page to get Ben's attention. "Take a look at this, and tell me what you think," he said. "What do you know about Eddie Haverley?"

Nonna walked into the firehouse as Jack and Ben were closing up the logbooks, slipping through the door in that quiet way she had. "You took the plunge," she observed, giving Jack her usual kiss. "This place has been empty a real long time now."

Yeah, he'd fix the old place up some and move his boys into it. He didn't like walls, never had, preferred sleeping out at the hangar or on Nonna's sunporch. When he was younger he'd often slept there, where he could open the windows and pretend the walls weren't closing in on him.

"This is temporary," he warned. He wasn't filling up whatever kind of empty she meant. And, with Nonna, every conversation had more damned layers than a cake.

Nonna, of course, just looked at him. "Uh-huh," she said. The Adirondack chair Ben had brought over earlier as a "housewarming" gift creaked as she settled back into it, folding her legs beneath her. Jack bet Ben had known precisely who would be sitting in that chair.

"I don't stay put," he repeated. He needed her to remember that.

"I know, baby." Curled up in the chair, she looked smaller than he remembered. And just a little bit sadder. There was a shadow to her eyes he didn't remember. "You never did stay put. Not once."

Chapter Twenty

Friday night was free concert night in Strong. Sprawled on the grass, listening to a local band belting out a nearly unrecognizable rendition of bluegrass, Jack figured the concerts were free because no one in his right mind would pony up cash for this kind of noise. Still, Main Street was lit up real pretty, the beer was cold, and there were worse places to lie in wait for a woman. It looked as if the entire town had come out to park their asses in lawn chairs and eat dinner out of red plastic coolers. Plenty of barbecue and laughter.

His team was making themselves right at home. Joey was whooping it up with a curvy brunette who might or might not have been in Jack's high school biology class. Either way, she had her fingers wrapped up real tight in Joey's T-shirt, standing on tiptoe to whisper something into his ear as they improvised a set of moves Jack was fairly certain wouldn't win any dance competitions. An appreciative grin lit up Joey's face, though, so his friend was clearly enjoying his dance. A second tug on his shirt had him following the brunette off the improvised dance floor and into the shadows. His hand on the girl's shoulder flashed a quick signal, and Zay melted away into the edges of the small crowd.

Eddie Haverley hadn't showed his face yet, but Jack wouldn't miss him if he did.

Where was Lily? She should have been here by now. His intel said she'd left her farm and headed down the road. All he could think about was kissing her. Running his hands over her hair, down that curvy little body of hers. Pulling her just as close as she could get. He wanted to go on holding her for the next fifty years or so.

Hell, he hadn't known he possessed a side like that—and it scared the ever-loving shit out of him. Men who had families didn't jump out of planes at three thousand feet, because that wasn't the responsible thing to do. Those men kept their feet firmly planted on the ground and punched a nine-to-five somewhere.

Ben came up beside him, and he turned to the older man as if to a lifeline.

"How do you know?" This wasn't the kind of shit he usually discussed, but Ben knew Lily, and he probably knew way more about relationships than Jack did. *Because,* he mocked himself, *you run like hell just as soon as there's any chance of things sticking.* Now he needed to understand what long-term really meant.

Needed to understand this woman he feared was holding his heart in the palm of one small hand. "How can you be sure you've met that one woman you can settle down with?"

Ben took a careful sip of his beer. "You want to hear about all the times I've fucked up?" He shook his head. "It's instinct, Jack. You've just got to trust those instincts of yours. How do you know a fire isn't going to flash back over you? You just know, Jack. You've been doing it long enough. You know what the land and what your gut is telling you, and, at some point, you trust your instincts, and you jump."

"You ever done that?" From the other side of the street, Evan flashed him a signal, and Jack forced all the unwelcome emotional back-and-forth to a far corner of his mind. Lily was walking up the sidewalk. She'd come. He could just make her out, laughing with her friend Miriam. The one who ran the florist shop.

Ben snorted. "I'm standing here with you, aren't I? Told you I should be the last person you take advice from. All I know is, if you're asking the question, maybe you're on the right track here."

"Right." He wanted to move the conversation in another direction, but his brain shorted out, taking all reasonable thought with it as Lily strolled into view. God, she was so beautiful. She was wearing a wickedly short romper, a pretty little pink swoop of soft fabric that clung to her ass and her breasts and made him itch to run his hands down her sides. Tiny pink ribbons held up the bodice above the short shorts. And, God help him, there were little buttons marching down the front of the romper. He wanted to reach out and unbutton her, peel back that fabric, and taste every inch of her.

Down, boy. He needed to get to her. Fill her in on the Eddie Haverley situation. She was shooting blanks in the dark if she didn't know the name of her stalker.

Manning up, he stalked over to her, ignoring the raised eyebrow she sent his way. He didn't care if she objected to his possessive manner or not. She was stuck with him. "You're late enough," he said, "that I thought you weren't coming." *Real smooth, Jack.* Maybe he could just write sad love notes while he was at it. Rip out his heart and hand it on over.

"I wasn't aware we had a date," she said coolly. Was she a little pissed that he'd been so preoccupied lately and hadn't seen that much of her? She did a little side step when he reached for her arm, but he wasn't letting her get away, not now, so he captured her elbow and drew her up against his side.

"I need to talk to you." He steered her over to a wrought-iron bench. Looked harder than hell, but it was a pretty little spot in front of the window of a particularly cluttered antiques shop. That would cover their backs for the moment.

She shrugged. "What's so important?" she said. "You haven't seemed much into conversation with me lately."

Okay, so she was pissed, but he'd deal with that later. He got right down to what was important. "I think I know who our stalker is." That got her interest, all right. She turned toward him so fast, her hand slammed into his thigh. He put one hand over hers, trapping her fingers against his leg. Savoring the feel of her.

"Who?" she demanded.

"Eddie Haverley." Quickly he sketched out the reasons for believing Eddie was their man. "You ever date him in high school? Give him any reason to believe there was the possibility of a relationship between the two of you?"

"No." Her brow puckered as she thought it over, but at least she'd stopped trying to pull her fingers free, so he loosened the prison of his hand and stroked her palm softly. "Eddie's older than me," she pointed out. "By a couple of years. I can't have spoken more than a handful of words to him." She shrugged again, and he wrapped his hand around hers before she could pull free. "Not that I remember. He didn't ask me out. I didn't ask him."

"I think he believes you're his." He was sure of it. That sense of possession explained the fires. The need Lily's stalker had to hurt her.

"Then he's crazy." She looked sideways at him. "I don't belong to anyone."

"No, baby," he agreed quietly. "That's true."

Something flashed in her brown eyes, but he didn't stop

to try to figure out what it could have been. He needed her to understand what was at stake here. "But we think he's the one stalking you. So we're watching for him."

"Okay," she said, surprising him. He felt suddenly off balance, unsure of himself. Somehow, she was turning the tables on him, being unusually accommodating. "You want me to make a spectacle of us, draw his attention? Is that the reason you're here, Jack?"

"Lily—" He damned sure didn't have any words to give her. He didn't know how to explain to her that she'd up-ended his entire world, and he didn't know where he was or what to do.

"You smell good," she whispered, leaning closer to him. "No smoke."

He inhaled, too, and the familiar cherry and vanilla scent of her filled him. "You, too," he said.

When she breathed, this close, her breasts brushed his hands, hands aching to hold her. He almost cursed, because they were in public, but she was moving closer, leaving not an inch to spare between them.

She smiled up at him. "Dance with me, Jack."

As he had every evening for years, Ben walked over to her place, two lemonades in hand. Nonna couldn't remember the last time he'd missed a night. Rain or shine, there was Ben. Once he'd picked his course, he stuck to it. He dropped into the chair next to her. Familiar. Comforting. The porch was empty until he got there. He gave his usual little huff as he stretched, letting his body curve into the chair. There he was, on the wrong side of sixty, and he couldn't bring himself to rock the boat any more than she could.

But she wanted that change, she realized. She was lonely, and she was wondering if it wasn't finally time to nurture the seeds time had planted between her and Strong's fire chief all those years ago.

Every evening like clockwork he'd climbed the stairs to her porch and dropped into the seat beside her. It felt good to sit down in the evening and let the remainder of the day wash gently over her. Even better, she thought with sudden clarity, to be sitting there right beside Ben. God willing, he'd be sitting beside her for years to come.

He handed her the second beer and popped the top on his own can. "Our Jack and Lily, they're almost ready, Nonna."

"Don't," she said suddenly.

"Don't what?" Even he hadn't missed her interest in hooking that pair up. She'd thrown them together every opportunity she had. Horse had left that barn, so it was too late for her to start regretting and second-guessing now.

"Don't call me Nonna. That's not my name."

"You've been Nonna for years," he objected. "Just about ever since you brought those boys home to stay. Why would you mind the name now?"

"It's not my name," she said slowly, the words suddenly coming to her. "It's what I am. Some of the time."

"Fine," he groused. "You want I should call you Mary Ellen? I can do that."

She knew he could. Ben had always been capable of anything he set his mind to. "Mary Ellen will do just fine." The paint on her Adirondack chairs was starting to peel—she'd need to refinish them before too long. Maybe even choose a new color for them. Those chairs had been a pale lilac for longer than she could remember. "Chairs are getting worn out," she said out loud, running her fingers along a curl of paint.

"You let me know when you're ready to paint." He

looked over at her, hoisting his cold beer in a silent toast. As if he could read her mind. "I'll come over and help."

"Maybe next weekend." She thought for a moment. "A new coat of paint would be good."

"You thought of a color?" His eyes challenged hers.

She'd wanted something different, hadn't she? A slow smile creased her face. "Red," she decided. "Fire engine red."

"I'm touched." He took another swallow of his beer and settled back in the chair as if he belonged there.

Chapter Twenty-one

The open window brought her a burst of lavender with each breath she took. The scent of lavender and, beneath that, on her skin, on her tongue, the hot, wild scent of Jack. He was her warrior man, hard and strong. It was all too easy to imagine him on some battlefield, fighting for their country. Jack had always defended what was his.

Even a temporary, summertime lover.

While he effortlessly carried her up her stairs, she indulged in that little fantasy, drinking in the strength and the heat of him. She needed more of him, needed to touch those strong forearms, stroke the hard muscles beneath the faded cotton of his T-shirt. Each subtle brush of his skin against hers as he carried her to her bed set nerve endings on fire, had her sinking into sensual bliss. The darkened house was slowly filling with moonlight, starlight from her farm. As her eyes adjusted, the dense darkness outside faded, resolving into familiar shapes: the greenhouse and the rows of lavender plants. His now-familiar face looked down at her, watching her and not the steps he mastered so easily. He was so strong and male, with dark stubble shadowing his jaw.

He was so damned sexy.

She wanted to reach up and touch that face, wanted to

turn over and find him lying beside her every morning. Forever.

Problem was, Jack wasn't a forever kind of man.

He was the heat and lightning of a summer storm, all thick tension. A dominating presence promising heat and power but no rain.

Heat unfurled low in her belly now as she watched him. She could enjoy the heat, though. Just for this one moment, this night in the string of nights he'd give her, she could enjoy Jack Donovan. She certainly wasn't going to fight the fire he woke in her.

He swept the white coverlet back, laying her down on her cotton sheets. If this was all she could have of Jack Donovan, this would be enough. She'd make it enough. "Take your shirt off."

She slid a hand up his arm, beneath the sleeve's frayed hem. The old cotton was soft with washing, the lack of color stark in the moonlight. "I want to see you, Jack." She wanted to take him as thoroughly as he'd taken her.

"Whatever you want, baby." He pulled the shirt over his head in one smooth movement, dropping it carelessly to the floor.

"You look good enough to eat." When her tongue traced her lips, his eyes followed, and heat jolted through her, a visceral, feminine response to the raw arousal in his eyes. "I'm going to taste every inch you can give me."

"Lily." His harsh groan told her clearly enough just how much he liked the notion. He leaned over her, threading a hand through her hair. "You're going to be the death of me, baby."

"Only the good kind, I hope," she teased. Her voice was husky, unfamiliar even to herself. When she stretched, his eyes followed the feline movement, and she loved how sexy she felt, imagining herself through his eyes. Seeing the pleasure he didn't hide from her. His other hand pulled open her top, baring her.

"You're not wearing a bra, Lily." Those strong, knowing fingers of his cupped a bare breast. Stroking. Learning her anew.

She hadn't bothered with a bra. She'd wanted that wicked freedom. Wanted to know that only the thin cotton of her romper top separated her from him. From the sweet, hot sensation unfurling inside her.

"I hoped you'd be coming home with me tonight," she whispered, drawing his scent deeper inside her with every breath she took.

His mouth raked the bare column of her throat. Hot and demanding, he began exploring each sensitive curve as she shivered in delight. Anticipation. That wicked mouth moved up, over her jaw, the curve of her face. Finding and capturing her mouth in a long, slow kiss that had her melting, reaching for more as she stroked her tongue deep into that wicked mouth. God, she loved the taste of him.

The low growl of thunder echoed across the hills, and his head half turned toward the open window. "We might have more sleeper fires," he whispered against her skin. His tongue licked a wicked path along her collarbone. "All that thunder. Lightning. But not tonight, I hope." He trailed his knuckles along her damp flesh. "Christ, not tonight."

"Good," she groaned.

Somewhere, somehow, she'd accepted the firefighting side of him. Soon, too soon, he'd be right back out there, fighting fires.

But tonight—tonight, Jack Donovan was all hers.

Jack lowered himself down onto Lily, giving in to the primal satisfaction of pinning her sweet body between his throbbing erection and the mattress of her bed. The approaching storm was making its presence known, the air thick with heat and tension, but the electric sensations streaking through him had nothing to do with the storm.

Had everything to do with the woman in his arms.

Staring down at that familiar face, he knew he was going to give in to the need. He wanted to be here, with Lily. He couldn't deny that truth any longer. She meant something—everything—to him. She'd woken some side of him he hadn't known existed, and now, plain and simple, he couldn't get enough of her.

He wanted to give her the words, tell her how she made him feel, but he'd never been good with words. She deserved a damned sonnet or an epic poem. Instead, he was speechless.

"Are you going to kiss me," she asked, "or just watch me?"

He could have watched her all night, just stayed there, braced on his elbows, his mouth a breath away from hers. Her legs wrapped around his waist, pulling him deeper into the sweet, heated cradle of her thighs.

"You're playing with fire, baby." She didn't like what he did for a living, who he was. But she wanted him. That was going to be enough, he decided. Had to be enough.

"I know," she whispered. "But you like that fire, Jack. You were born to fight fires." He didn't miss the sad acceptance in her eyes.

That sadness made him want to howl, but there was nothing he could do to change the truth. He was who he was, and some things weren't changing. Tomorrow— tonight, even, if that storm kept right on rolling over Strong—he'd be right back out there. Front and center in the firestorm. All he could do now was kiss her until she forgot the danger for a moment.

Threading his fingers through her dark hair, he spread

the lazy curls over the pillow. She looked like a fallen angel, with that pout to her lips and her honey-colored bedroom eyes. His angel.

Lowering his mouth to the delicate curve of her ear, he traced a hot, damp path. Slowly. He'd promised to taste every inch of her, and he kept his promises. "Lily . . ." His voice sounded harsh, even to his own ears. No way he could hide the truth from her. Every inch of him was hard and wanting. She'd take him straight to heaven—or send him straight to hell.

He slid his hands down the curve of her throat, his thumbs testing the bright little beat of her pulse. Stroking downward. Sure. Knowing. She went still beneath him, but that little betraying tremor gave her away. She wanted him, too. So he said the words out loud, because they were still an unbelievable gift.

"You want me, too." The curve of her breast fit his hand perfectly. Her skin was impossibly soft, and that pale, secret spot where her bikini top had covered her drove him crazy. He was dying for her, a starving man, and she was a lavish feast, so he cupped the delicious weight of her breasts, filling his hands with her while his thumbs teased her nipples. Slow and deliberate. Filling his senses with her.

Lightning flashed outside the window. The quick, hard burst lit up the room. Her eyes were still watching him. Just like she had in high school days. Those eyes had driven him crazy, had had his hands itching to touch her even then. Now those same brown eyes watched him again. Trusting him. He wouldn't screw this up. Whatever it took, he'd be the man she needed in her arms tonight.

He kissed her slowly, sinking into her. Savoring the unforgettable taste of her mouth as he pinned her against the mattress, his fingers seeking hers. Threading through hers as he lowered himself onto her. The soft, lush warmth of her body welcoming his was a sharp counterpoint to the sudden rush of air through the open window. The storm was almost on top of them. She tasted so good, so right, all he could do was keep on kissing her. This was what he'd been missing all those years he'd run from Strong.

Thunder sounded closer. If he looked, he'd see the bright spikes of light illuminating the hills. Those weren't the sorts of fireworks he wanted. Not tonight.

He slid a hand to the buttons on the front of her romper, where the soft pink fabric still hugged her hips and the round curve of her thighs. "Lift up," he growled.

She did. Slowly, languorously, she raised that sweet little ass of hers, her fingers tangling with his on the buttons. The heat in the room had her skin flushing. A bead of moisture streaked her skin, and he followed the errant drop with his tongue, tasting her. Drinking her in.

The soft, slow eroticism of the moment seduced him as thoroughly as the woman he held. Every touch was magnified. More intimate and close than he'd ever found in bed before. He didn't, he realized with a shock of awareness, want this fast and hard at all, just close. And yet, when he finally slipped the romper off her, he had to fight the urge to sink right into her. It was almost painful to stand up, leave her for the few moments it took to drag off his own jeans and roll on a condom, leaving the pants tangled with her clothes on the floor.

"Time's up," he promised. Stretching out beside her on the bed, he pressed her down into the mattress with his body.

Outside, the thunder was louder, growling irritably. The impossible summer heat prickled his skin even as her heat melted him. Melted ten years of reserve.

The too-soft mattress gave beneath his weight, sending him rolling into her. Onto her. Pinning her down. She laughed, and something gave inside him. Melted. Christ, he wasn't walking away from this. From her. He could feel the devilish grin tugging at his mouth and didn't even try to hide that smile from her. She was under his skin, a part of him, and he was okay with that.

"Think that's funny, do you?" Her eyes laughed up at him, as he lowered his head to devour her mouth. More than okay. He kissed her, hard and deep, pressing her down into the bed as they devoured each other. Her sensual response had him locked against her, lost in the hungers tearing through him.

When he finally tore his mouth from hers, his breath was a harsh gasp in the still air of the bedroom.

He wanted her. Wanted her so bad, he ached with it. "If I'd had any idea," he growled, "that you'd be so damned hot, baby, I'd never have let you go that night."

Her pique at that remark washed over him, sudden as the storm building outside their bedroom window. "You didn't let me go, Jack."

He had. But he wouldn't make that mistake again. She gasped as he captured a cherry-sweet nipple in his mouth and sucked, but the would-have-could-have memories tormented him. "I would have touched you here." His finger traced the curve of her breast. "Tasted you here." He curled a finger around her nipple, coaxing.

She arched in his arms, her sweet moan filling the air as her fingers curved against his skin, her nails marking him.

"Yes," he growled. "Like that."

"No," she said. "Like this." Taking charge, she pushed him back against the pillows, coming up over him.

"I'm feeling just a little bit naughty, Jack. Up for a little revenge." The hot, wet heat of her straddling his thigh was driving him crazy. He fought the need to pull her down, under him. When, finally, he reached for her, she teasingly pushed him back down, sliding between his legs.

He froze, a dozen wicked midnight fantasies running

through his head. "Just a little?" His voice sounded hoarse to his own ears.

"Mmm," she agreed. "It's time for that taste of you that I wanted." Her fingers trailed down his stomach, tickling his navel with a suggestive little circle. "Maybe you'd be okay with that."

"I'm thinking I would be." Hell, he was about to come up off the bed. His entire body was tightening, standing at attention. About to explode right out of his skin.

As her hands wrapped around him, the sweet, hot pressure rocked his world.

The teasing glint in those brown eyes warned him she wouldn't show him any more mercy than he'd shown her. She watched his face, the softly erotic tickle of her breath around his rigid erection making his fists tangle in the sheets. Whatever she saw on his face must have been the right answer, because she gave a little smile and lowered her head.

His whole world stood still as the dark curtain of her hair parted around him and her lips closed over him. Her little hum of delight sent shivers through his body. He had to fight not to arch off the bed, not to drive himself deep into her mouth.

Her hands wrapped around the base of his shaft, coaxing, guiding. Stroking as if she couldn't get enough of him, either.

"Christ, baby." Sliding his fingers through her hair, he held on. Fiery sensations streaked through him with each sensual, damp tug of her mouth. Pulling him in deeper. Opening up, trusting him not to drive too fast, too hard. She was killing him.

She touched him, the delicate, questing stroke exploring the long, hard length of him. "Lily," he groaned, and he wanted to say something. Needed to tell her how she made him feel, how he was so lost in her that he'd found something new. Something unexpected. But he couldn't hold on, couldn't hold the thought. Instead, his fingers were fisting in her hair, anchoring himself.

He moved in and out, fucking her mouth in an intimate echo of how he'd taken her before. Filling her. Faster, harder. There was nothing soft and dreamy now about how she was touching him, taking him. This was raw and wet and unbearably intimate.

She slid her mouth up the hard shaft, sucking hard at the engorged tip. *Christ.* He was going to come in her mouth. Forcing himself to pull away, he tugged her up and over him. He didn't want to come alone, to leave her behind him.

Her face was fierce as she came down on him, sheathing herself on his erection.

"Let me," he said, already reaching for her, his hands on her hips. One thumb slid forward, parting her lush folds to find her clit and stroke around and over in teasing circles. He wasn't leaving her behind. She melted around him, bucking against his hand as she rode him.

Taking him with her right over the edge. "Please," she said. And, "More."

He watched her, watched the pleasure light up her face as he lost himself in her. Felt the fiery heat consuming them both as he drove up into her and she took him deep, deep, seeking more of the sensations flaming between them. He took her even as she took him, and he didn't know where he ended and she began, just that they were there together, wrapped around each other in the bed, and he'd never felt more alive in his entire life.

She came, shuddering, holding on to his shoulders and crying out his name, and he let go, stroking deeply, burying himself in her as he pressed his lips against her shoulder. Tasting her. Drinking in the small contractions fluttering through her as her release washed over her and she relaxed against him.

He spilled himself deep inside her, gathering her up in his arms. Holding her tight because he wasn't letting go of her, he was letting go of himself. The pleasure was too hot, ripping him apart, and he'd never thought he'd die burning or welcome that fire. He could hear his own voice, hoarse and rough, muttering small words. Of praise. Pleasure. Intimacy.

Afterward, he collapsed beside her, tucking her into the curve of his arm. Outside their window, the summer storm was finally breaking, the dry lightning giving way to a cool sweep of rain rushing over the lavender fields and toward the farmhouse. The lacy curtains at the window rustled, stirred to life as the rain kept on coming, racing through the open window and washing over the room. Dampness dotted his skin, sank into the tangled sheets, and he laughed, pulling her tighter against him. Welcoming the cool wet against his heated skin.

Her breath caught on laughter as she turned into him, her hands coming up, seeking him.

"I love you." Her hands fisted tightly in his short hair as she pulled him toward her, words spilling out of her like rain from the clouds outside. "I love you."

Chapter Twenty-two

The words hung in the air between them, where she couldn't take them back. Too damned bad for Jack. He'd never liked talking about emotions, feelings. He'd been the original bad boy, loving the girls and leaving them. Hell, she'd watched him leave a trail of broken hearts behind him in Strong for years. He shouldn't have been at a loss for words, should he? He had enough experience for a dozen men, with women handing out their hearts while he ran the other way. Well, fuck him, she thought, blinking back frustrated tears. Some things just needed to be said, even if they were met with silence.

"Those words are a gift, Jack." She stood up, pushing back the rain-dampened sheets. "They're not a trap, and you don't have to say anything. I just needed to say them." She paused. "Wanted to say them. To you."

When he seemed to be struggling for a response, she laid a finger across his lips. "It's okay," she said. He nipped gently at her fingers, and for a moment she resented the soft thrill of pleasure that little touch gave her. She didn't want to make this about sex. Not right now. "You don't have to say anything, Jack."

For a long moment there was nothing but the sound of thunder echoing off the hills. No lightning, just sound that was all empty shake-rattle-and-roll. The worst part was, Jack didn't say anything. He just got more still than any man she'd seen, all leashed power, all wary male in her too-feminine bed.

She'd known better. She'd known the words would scare the hell out of him. Now he'd run from her. Because those words she'd given him were too big a clue. This wasn't just a summer romance. Not for her. His dark eyes were impossible to read, watching her while he searched for words he could give her, but maybe not the words she wanted to hear.

"You don't expect me to say anything." He said the words quietly, but her stomach pitched anyhow. What had she really expected him to say? To do? Had she secretly been having a fantasy in which he gave her back some loving words of his own? Jack Donovan had never promised happily-ever-after. He'd offered happily-right-now, and she'd—well, she'd taken him up on his offer, hadn't she?

"No." She stared back at him, wishing she could retract the words. Because, no matter how well her mind had known the truth, now that truth was breaking her heart.

"Not one word?" Disbelief crept into his voice as he sat up in the bed and glared at her. "You tell me you love me, and that's it? You're not expecting some sort of reaction from me?"

"Fine," she snapped. "Now that we've got my feelings clear, let's talk about yours if you're feeling so obliging."

"You want to talk?" He stared at her incredulously. "I don't know how to do permanent and happily-ever-after, Lily. I thought I'd made that perfectly clear. You know where I come from, Lily. I grew up in a series of foster homes. My parents were just names on a piece of paper, and they weren't passing out engraved invitations to come home and play family."

"You have a home and a family right here in Strong,"

she said, so quietly he had to duck his head to hear her. "You have Rio and Evan and Nonna. Don't tell me you're not family, or that the threads and years binding you all together aren't closer than any blood ties could be."

Jack shook his head at Lily's words. "We have each other's backs," he agreed. He remembered a little boy and his dirty, ragtag, loyal band of followers hiding beneath a freeway overpass because it was raining and they had nowhere else to go. They'd fought together, done their tours of duty together. Now they had their team of fire jumpers. Life was good.

Where he'd come from hadn't been.

Childhood had been a series of unfamiliar houses and unfamiliar beds. Places where he was just passing through and passing time. He'd lost count of the number of times he'd woken up in yet another room and not known where he was. No, the darkness would just press in on him, even as the walls threatened to swallow him up. So he'd shove the covers back, jump up, and pretend he didn't want to put his back to the mattress and pull those damned covers right on up over his head. Instead, he'd looked for—and found—the door.

He didn't like walls, and he always knew where his exit points were. It made him a hell of a jumper.

"Damn it, Lily." He shoved a hand through his hair. The powerful muscles of his shoulders flexed, and her eyes noticed. "I don't know. We're good in bed together. And I like spending time with you."

"Great. We're best of friends."

"Friends don't say 'I love you.' "

"Sure, they do." Angry-looking tears stung her eyes. "Friends can love each other."

He shook his head, pulling his clothes on. "Not like this. I don't want to be your friend, Lily."

More thunder rolled through the heavy air. The shower had been only a brief reprieve.

"Then tell me what you want to be, Jack!" she cried.

He couldn't bear the loneliness in her voice, but he didn't know what to say. His only response was the soft snick of the door latching behind him as he went.

The familiar pickup headed down the road. Jack, she knew, would do what he wanted to do. Which was leaving. Again. Maybe, he'd come back. She wasn't sure if that was even what she wanted. He'd made it perfectly clear that he wasn't the settling-down sort.

In San Francisco, she'd had a single pot of lavender on her deck. Her expensive, chrome-and-glass deck. She'd wanted more than a pot out of life. She'd wanted acres of deep, velvety wands of the purple stuff. She'd wanted space and freedom and the chance to dream. Now she wanted Jack.

Some dreams came true with sweat and tears and a hell of a lot of work.

Other dreams were never more than pipe dreams.

It didn't take a genius to figure out in which category Jack fell. She swiped away the angry tears with the back of her hand.

No. Dressing hurriedly despite the late hour, she stomped downstairs, then grabbed her pruning shears and a bucket and headed outside. She'd been a fool to let Jack Donovan into her heart—again—but she wasn't going to curl up in a little ball, either. Maybe he'd wake up and realize he was capable of more than he gave himself credit for.

The unexpected whiff of smoke startled her out of her thoughts. A little puff of smoke coming from the compost heap behind her potting shed. She looked down at the bucket in her hand. Five steps to the spigot. Maybe twenty to the shed. All she had to do was dump a little water.

When was the last time she'd turned the pile over? Usually she was so very careful—had she forgotten something this time?

Maybe this was an accident, but her feet weren't moving. Instead, the unwelcome reminder was hurtling her straight down memory lane.

Where was the door? She hadn't been able to find the door. Her bedroom had been so very, very dark, except for that orange seam of light luring her out toward the kitchen. If she opened the door, would she find an escape route—or would the fire on the other side of the door swallow up the air where she hid? She had to choose. Had to make a choice to open the door or find the window behind her.

The air was dense with smoke, and each breath she took filled her lungs with a little less oxygen and a little more smoke. There was a cough tickling her throat, but she knew that once she started, she wouldn't stop. Those coughs would tear her apart.

The fire behind her potting shed was just a little thing. There weren't even any flames.

The doorknob was hot. That was a bad thing. The window was behind her.

Her feet were frozen, glued to the ground. She needed to act, to *do* something.

Was that a little puff of cooler air on her back? Yes, she needed to go back. And out. Then this nightmare would be over, and she'd be free.

She turned, forcing her feet away from the smoldering pile. This wasn't right. Wasn't natural. She knew she hadn't been careless, so she was going to do exactly what she'd promised Jack she'd do. She'd call it in, and then she'd grab the hose and see what she could do before the boys rode up and did their Sir Galahad thing for her.

She tried to scan her environment. Tried to make out

any possible vulnerabilities. There was no obvious lurker, but to get to the compost heap, she'd have to go past the potting shed. Heading straight for her car wasn't an option—her cell phone and her purse with her keys were inside the farmhouse.

Behind her, the farmhouse's front door was closed. That was good. That was exactly how things were supposed to be. Making a decision, she quickly retraced her steps and went inside, locking the door behind her. She'd grab the purse and the phone and then take the car down the road before she called for help. If he was watching her, she wouldn't be sitting still, waiting for him. Jack had eyes on her farm, too, so all she needed to do was buy enough time.

She was reaching for her purse when she heard that familiar hoarse voice. Behind her. In her house. "Took you long enough."

She'd gone straight from one nightmare to another.

"Oh, God," she said, and she knew the words came out like a whimper. This man—this unexpected, unanticipated, *unwanted* threat—had just sucked all the oxygen from the room. Her heart pounded so loudly, she could hear each desperate knock. Adrenaline had her lunging for the door, her fingers scrabbling at the lock, but the man in her house had a gun—she could see it—and she had just a handful of seconds to think about whether she wanted to roll over and play dead or if she'd rather die reaching for the gun in her purse.

Eddie Haverley came out of her rocking chair, moving fast. Her fingers on the lock were almost faster, but he slapped the gun's barrel against her hand, and the world exploded. "You're not leaving me," he said. "Never again, Lily. You're mine."

She froze, her fingers pinned beneath the unforgiving metal. A bright shock of the pain tore through her, reminding her that, right now, she was helpless. He had the gun and the upper hand. Her purse was so close and yet impossibly far away. She had a phone in there. Pepper spray. A handgun. All she had to do was close the six feet—but that short distance could have been across Siberia.

"Why are you doing this?" she asked, because she had to do something to fill up the horrible silence. Understanding why he was here might give her something she could use. Instead of answering, however, he stepped closer, and she pressed herself against the door, not wanting to betray how much she loathed contact with him but not able to stand still. His skin smelled of smoke and metal and an unpleasant, damp heat. He wasn't a big man, but he was broad-shouldered.

Strong enough to hurt her.

Beneath a battered baseball cap, his hair was close-cut. That and his clothes—chinos and a flannel shirt—were perfectly nondescript. Camouflage. She could have walked past him a dozen times and never noticed him. He let her look, his fingers plucking the perfect pleats in his pants. Pinching the fabric up, smoothing it down.

"You shouldn't have let *him* in," he said finally. His fingers wrapped around hers, moving her hand away from the latch. Effortlessly, as if she was a small child, he snapped her wrists together and bound them. She hated this feeling of helplessness, hated the fear twisting her stomach into sick knots. "I don't like Jack Donovan," he said simply. "I never have. You were never going to belong to him."

Chapter Twenty-three

Eddie plucked again at the pleat in his pants, then smoothed the abused cotton down before he led her outside to his pickup. "I had to hide until he left. Your boyfriend's not too smart," he gloated.

He tossed her casually into his truck, her head slamming into the steering wheel, before sliding into the driver's seat. She levered herself up. Even if she could get her door open, he'd be all over her before she could even scream.

"You could try it," he said, all conversational, throwing the truck into drive. If she went through that door now, she'd eat the pavement—that was, if she managed to avoid the truck's tires.

The sticky dampness on the side of her head was plenty of hint that the dull ache would only get worse before it got better. Looking down, she saw blood speckling the expensive leather seats. He'd pistol-whipped her hard enough to get his point across. The door might be her best option. She let her eyes slide slowly to the side, looking for the handle.

"You go out that door," he promised, "and I'll just hurt you that much sooner."

He'd already hurt her. The gun resting in his lap was pointed right at her, too, another reminder that this was no friendly outing.

"Why are you doing this?"

His hand stroked the trigger, but his eyes didn't leave the road as he took the route up into the mountains. Fast, but not so fast that he'd draw attention. The truck's four-wheel drive ate up the distance. "You don't remember me," he accused flatly.

She stared at him, searching his profile for clues.

"We went to school together," he observed. "You'd think a couple of years together like that, you'd remember." An accusation.

Eddie had been a couple of years older than she, and he'd kept to himself. They'd gone to high school together for a short while, before his grandfather had plucked him out of the public school system and sent him to a private boarding school. She tried to remember if they'd shared anything more than a handful of brief conversations about mundane topics and couldn't think of anything.

"I've been watching you, Lily." His voice was harsher than she remembered. Damaged by smoke? "You thought you were so clever, picking up and running when I found you in San Francisco, but all you did was run straight back to me."

Eddie's free hand reached out and stroked the shiny pink patch of skin where she'd brushed her arm against something metal and hot before escaping her San Francisco home. The scar was now taking on an even much darker, more sinister meaning.

"Don't touch me." She tried to pull away because her stomach heaved when he touched her, and she didn't want his hands on her in any way. She had a feeling Eddie's fascination with her scar was just the tip of an iceberg she really, really didn't want to see. Unfortunately, he had a gun. And, as the cold metal pressure now against her neck warned her, his gun hand was rock steady.

"I gave you this," he continued, ignoring her attempts

to free herself. "A little love bite." His thumb wouldn't stop moving over her skin. *God*. She was going to be sick, and that wouldn't get her out of here. Get her away from him.

She wasn't going there. Didn't want to think about what he wanted from her.

"Your boyfriend's not coming for you," he said casually, and she couldn't hold back a flinch. He sounded so very certain. The gun slid against her skin again, reminding her that even the biggest, toughest man was no match for a well-aimed gun. Jack had suspected Eddie Haverley, but would he have seen this coming?

The truck swerved through the canyon roads, the dry landscape rushing past her. With each new turn Eddie took, she slid helplessly in the seat. Her head throbbed where he'd struck her, and within minutes it had smacked into the glass of the passenger side door twice more.

No one would find them out here. No one would even think to look out here.

God. She was going to be all on her own. She'd told Jack she could take care of herself, damn it, but she hadn't realized she'd be facing down a madman—without a weapon of her own.

"Why?" she asked, because she needed to know, and Eddie Haverley was clearly in a talkative mood. "Why are you doing this to me? What did I ever do to you?"

Finally, briefly, he took his eyes off the road. "This is for us." The look of heartfelt honesty in his eyes chilled her. Whatever Eddie Haverley was, he wasn't sane. Not completely. "I did this for us, to show you how good things could be between us, Lily. I thought you knew that." Hurt colored his voice. "I thought you knew what those fires meant."

She thought furiously. "You burned my things, Eddie.

Anything I cared about, you set it on fire. My books. My house. My *farm*."

"Those were messages," he said sadly. "You weren't listening to me, Lily. I had to get your attention."

"What kind of messages?" she asked carefully. They were slowing down. He turned the wheel sharply and sent the truck bouncing down a narrow, rutted track. She saw a small cabin up ahead. Rustic. She'd bet there was no running water. No electricity. Off the grid. Intended as a weekend getaway spot for campers or people who just wanted a little getting-back-to-nature. People who didn't want to be contacted and just wanted to lose themselves in the mountains ringing Strong.

Another time she might have admired the wooden shake roof. The little porch with its obligatory Adirondack chairs and red geraniums. Right now that porch was a neon sign spelling out: *end of the line*. She had to do something soon, or she'd be able do nothing at all. She wasn't stupid. Once a man had a woman alone in a confined space like that, that woman ran out of options, and biology triumphed. He was bigger. Stronger.

He just wasn't smarter, she reminded herself.

Slow anger started to burn inside her, burn away some of the fear. He'd turned her life upside down. He'd stalked her. Set her things on fire. Set her *home* on fire. If he'd lit a new blaze on her farm, she'd . . . she didn't know what she'd do. But it would be bad. Very bad for him.

He threw the truck into park, the expensive ride shuddering to a stop on the gravel parking strip. Turning in his seat, he stared at her. "You didn't understand my messages?"

Silently she shook her head, letting her gaze run over the surrounding forest. The cloudy sky. As if the U.S. Marines might drop out of the clouds and rescue her ass.

She'd take them. There were times when being independent and getting it done for yourself mattered. This wasn't one of them. Staying alive mattered most right now.

Those clouds looked like another storm was coming. Her breath caught. *Not clouds. Smoke.* A thick, deep, black bank of the stuff so damned close, it crept up over the tree line and blocked out the sky.

She must have blinked—stupid, stupid—because she didn't see him swing his fist, and then she was hitting the ground, hard. Her breath left her in a single, painful evacuation. Even though she knew it was only temporary—unless he used the gun on her—her mind couldn't convince her body to wait it out. To not panic at the sudden vacuum her lungs had just become. Score one for Eddie.

Choking, she rolled onto her knees. Shoved upward on her bound wrists. Her arms buckled, and she saw movement from the corner of her eye.

She was almost ready for the kick that sent her sprawling back into the dirt. He stood over her, straddling her. One foot pinned her wrists, and, fuck, that hurt. One minute, she had one long minute to stare stupidly at his choice in footwear—expensive men's loafers, a rich amber color. Those shoes were meant for striding around city streets and kicking back in high-powered boardroom meetings. They weren't mountain wear, as the red dust streaking the expensive leather announced.

"You should have listened better," he said reproachfully. "I loved you, and you were supposed to be mine. When you didn't listen, when you didn't pay any notice to me, I needed to get your attention. You weren't being the good girl I know you are."

He knelt over her, and now his knees pinned her wrists to the ground. Any more weight, and she'd hear bones cracking. That she didn't meant he was playing with her. If she'd had any energy left, his restraint might have pissed her off. As it was, she settled for lying there, desperately trying to inhale much-needed oxygen into her abused lungs.

Her skin crawled at the sexual tone of his voice. His thumb was once again exploring the healed burn on her forearm. He wasn't sane, and he had a gun against her throat. He wouldn't miss so close, and she didn't need to be a marksman to know what would happen when a bullet tore through her throat at this range.

"Instead," he continued, his fingers tightening on the gun, "you chose *him*. Jack Donovan. Just like in high school. I saw you that night, you know," he added conversationally. "You went swimming in the old pond, just like you always did at the end of the week. I'd watch you, and you never knew I was there."

The growing sound of roaring flames seemed to mix with the pulse of plane engines and the relentless beating inside her head. He'd knocked her head against the ground, she realized. Hard enough for her to see stars. And spots. Large, dark spots. And the smoke mushrooming inexorably over the nearby ridge. Not that Eddie seemed concerned.

Of course, he'd probably set the fire himself.

"That's not a nice thing to do," she said carefully, painfully. Maybe if she kept him talking long enough, those Marines would finally charge to the rescue. All she knew was that she couldn't let him get her inside that cabin.

He looked wounded. "You didn't want to look at me when we were in school, so I watched you when you were alone. I didn't hurt you. All I did was look."

"Some moments are meant to be private." She made a small, trial movement to escape him, and the gun bit into the skin of her throat, making her feel even dizzier and more nauseated.

"No," he said. "You wanted me to look. You loved me,

and just didn't know it yet. Then *he* showed up, and I knew I was going to have to do something. You wouldn't *stop* looking at Jack Donovan, and then he kissed you, and I knew I'd have to do something if you were going to be mine."

"But you didn't. Not then."

"No," he repeated, and his fingers tightened around her arms. Forcing her to her feet and toward the porch. "He went away. I thought that might be enough. I gave you a little time to get over him and realize you were really meant to be mine." His voice rose. "And then you left. You weren't supposed to leave, Lily. I was willing to let you have a little freedom," he continued. When his feet hit the porch, she gave up on subtlety and dug her heels in. "But you'd had enough time. I needed you to pay attention to me."

"So you followed me and started setting the fires."

"Of course." He stared at her. "I knew you'd understand. Fire is so beautiful, Lily. Just like you. You're scared," he added suddenly, surprise coloring his voice. "You don't have to be scared, Lily. I'm going to take good care of you."

"I . . . I don't want to go inside." She left off the *with you.*

"That's okay," he said, surprising her. Dropping into an Adirondack chair, he pulled her down into his lap. Through his chinos, she could feel the hard pressure of his erection.

"I want to leave."

"No." He gestured toward the ridge where the smoke bank was building. She could smell its acridness now. "Right now, we're waiting for Jack, Lily. We both know he'll come. That's a big fire, and he'll want to put it out." He nodded. Plucked at the abused pleat on his pants. "He's going to be coming right to us. We can watch my fire eat him up when he tries to rescue you. The big, bad hero needs to learn a little lesson. He doesn't get to choose you. *I* chose you first."

"What . . . what have you done?" she gasped.

"Forced him to choose," he said calmly. "You'll see, Lily. Jack would rather be fighting fires than holding you."

She fought back panic. Because she knew that if it was a choice between her and the fire, Jack had *already* chosen. He'd picked the firefighting. He might come up to that ridge, but he sure as hell wasn't going to be looking for her. No, he'd be jumping straight into hell, because he was a damned hero, and he fought fires.

So she was all alone, and there was no one to blame—or call on—but herself.

So, fine. She'd do.

Or she'd die.

Chapter Twenty-four

The lookout tower had begun life as a water tank for the railroad cutting through Strong. Later, some bright soul had gotten the idea to build a tiny cabin on top of the tank, so the town's spotters could park their asses forty feet in the air and watch for smoke. Now the wooden tower was damned old and jonesing for historical-site status. Most of the fire departments he'd worked with had abandoned towers—putting a plane up might be more expensive short-term, but nothing beat the view. The view from a tower usually wasn't all that great. Strong's tower had been built on fairly flat ground, so it provided just a little extra visibility.

Jack hadn't complained when his number came up for watch duty that early morning. The itty-bitty cabin at the top of the tower was just big enough to hold two men and a couple of armchairs—and how the hell his boys had hauled the armchairs up there, he didn't want to know. Rio had only said that, if he had to park his ass up there, he was damned well picking his seat. Good enough for Jack. And the perfect place to do a little quiet thinking on his own.

I love you. He never wanted to forget those words. And then she'd told him it was okay for him to not say it back.

Hell, she'd practically shoved him out the door. He should have been grateful. Instead, he was angry. And hurt, he admitted. Worse, he wasn't sure she was right to be so cynical about him. He was pretty damn sure he wasn't walking away from Lily Cortez. Ever. She was under his skin and inside his heart, and he was a fire burning way, way out of control when he thought about her.

He was getting set to climb on down and send some other poor ass up to do lookout duty, when he saw the smoke on the horizon. Without the tower, he wouldn't have spotted the cloud for another ten, maybe twenty minutes.

It was damned big smoke, too. The dark column punched up from the horizon, a boiling black screen that was far more than a couple of charred logs re-burning after a little time off to smolder. Too much, too fast. That was human carelessness or arson looking him in the eye— not a wildfire.

He radioed the smoke in, barking orders into his hands-free as he swung down the ladder from the lookout tower.

His cell vibrated even as he threw his truck into gear and pulled out.

On the other end of the line, Rio didn't waste time.

"Bastard's got her. I picked it up on the Web feed. I had me a ringside seat and couldn't do a thing. He had her in the truck before I hit the gas." Anger and disgust colored Rio's voice. Rio never had tolerated mistakes, from himself or anyone else. "He had a gun to her head." So Rio would have backed off because that was the best way to get the intended victim out in one piece. "He took off in a truck."

"You followed him."

"Yeah." Brief pause. "Hung back, though, because I didn't want him spotting me. Lost him up in the canyons.

He was driving too fast." Hotrodding it in those canyons was a death warrant. They'd lost a high school classmate to those roads. After that, they'd learned to respect those dangerous curves. "I got a real good look at his face. It was Eddie, all right."

Eddie Haverley had just signed his own death warrant. There was no excuse for what he'd done—what he'd tried to do—to Lily Cortez. Anger and fear tormented Jack at the thought of Lily being in that man's hands right now. She'd be scared. Angry. Would she trust him to come for her?

She believed he'd walked away.

"I want a plane ready to go up," he answered. "I'm two minutes from the hangar." The countryside blurred past the windows of his truck. God help anyone who got in his way now. "You have my plane gassed up. Loaded and ready to go."

"You magically got coordinates now?"

"You lost Eddie in the canyons. There are only a couple of ways out of there. I've got a big smoke suddenly out on the north ridge. I'm betting that's him. He's waving that fire in our face, Rio. So I'm going to pay him a house call."

The hangar came into sight, and he finally slowed down, because wrecking Betsey now wasn't going to help anyone. Lily. He couldn't stop the cold fear snaking through his gut.

He got out of the truck and hit the ground running. The plane was right out on runway where she should be. Evan was running hose from fuel tanks. Five minutes, and she'd be good to go. He'd grab gear and be out of there in under ten.

When he hit the tarmac, however, Ben was on an intercept course.

"Not now," Jack growled, throwing his gear into the plane. He'd suit up as soon as they were airborne.

Ben put a restraining hand on his arm. "You need to hear me out."

"Wrong," he snapped.

Rio was running command center from his laptop. Maps and coordinates flew across the screen as Jack geared up.

Ben shook his head. "That's a massive fire out there."

"I'm getting to Lily," Jack countered.

"Her, too." There was something in Ben's eyes. "But this isn't just about her." He held up a hand when Jack cursed low and hard. "Not just about her—she's where this all started, where I'm thinking it ends. Far as we can tell, Eddie Haverley set himself a nice little wildland fire. I don't know if he intended his fire to grow this quick or this big, but it has. Now we've got us a wildland fire eating up acres. So I need to know, Jack, what you're intending to do. I need a jump team in there. I need a goddamned fire line, and I needed it an hour ago."

Fuck. And that was Jack's job, wasn't it?

He was supposed to keep the entire goddamned town of Strong safe and sound. He'd signed up for that the day he'd brought the jump team here. Bail on them now, and there might not *be* a Strong tomorrow.

On the other hand, he was damned sure Eddie Haverley didn't plan on keeping Lily around much longer, either. Bastard had a whole lot of anger, and she was a convenient target.

"Put the plane up. Get the team," he snapped to Rio, and Rio tore off toward the hangar, bellowing orders. Around him, the base exploded into action as the ground crew ran for their trucks, throwing fire packs and hard hats into the truck beds and getting ready to roll out. The trucks would be slow. They'd have to stick to the access roads, cut their way through any new snags. It would be at least a half hour before they got close.

Spotted Dick clambered on board, and seconds later the engines roared to life as Rio pounded across the tarmac, followed by seven members of the jump team. Evan was close on his ass, tossing a gear bag to Jack as he jumped up into the plane.

"Jack." His name sounded more like a curse on Ben's lips. "I need words, Jack. Tell me where this is headed."

"I'm putting a jump team up, Ben. You want a line, you'll get a line. " He dragged on his jumpsuit and helmet. Four minutes to taxi and no time to double-check his gear. There was just enough time for a hope and a prayer. Any gear Evan gave him would be good.

The last man made it through the open door, and Jack swung up behind him, pulling the netting across the door, and then the plane was racing down the runway, jolting up as the pilot cleared the sandbags at the end and aimed for the brightening sky. The ten minutes it took to make the distance between base camp and the ridge were the longest ten minutes of his life.

The view from the plane wasn't helping, either. The fire ate up the forest beneath them, turning the too-dry underbrush into a crispy bed of red-hot embers that shot up the trees and exploded into new life in the canopy.

Rio tapped him on the shoulder, pointing to the coordinates on the laptop's screen where he'd lost Eddie's truck. Figured. That was the heart of the smoke. When the plane pulled in close, he moved to the open doorway and started scanning. Right there. A big black pickup parked in front of a small hunting cabin. There could have been someone on the porch, but the plane's angle made it hard to tell. Still, that was the truck, all right. And the road was a welcoming beacon of open space. Narrow and hemmed in by some killer ponderosa, but the wind wasn't bad right now, and a skilled jumper could bring it down there without hanging up.

The perfect welcome mat.

Just over the hill, a bright orange line of fire crawled slowly upward. She'd crest, and then she'd come barreling down, devouring the backside of that ridge in no time. If the team jumped on the other side, they'd have a good chance of containing it before it hit Strong. If the wildfire made the ridge, though, Strong would be right in its path.

"What do you want me to do?" Spotted Dick roared the question at him, holding the plane nice and steady. Left or right. Over the ridge toward the fire or keep on heading straight for Lily.

Christ. This wasn't a choice he wanted to make.

The jump team watched him, Evan and Rio's faces front and center in that crowd of concern. They'd stand behind him. Jump with him, too, wherever he told them to jump. He could drop the entire team onto Eddie Haverley's driveway, and they'd go, no questions asked. Which was why he needed to do the right thing here.

"Get ready to jump," he ordered. "We've got fire here and here." He stabbed a finger at the ridge's coordinates on the screen. "Hold the line here. We've got open space, so if we dig fast enough and the wind holds steady, we can keep the goddamned fire from jumping the canopy. There's a dip site four miles over, so radio Ben and tell him to get every chopper he's got up in the air. I want every load he can give us. Dick will drop us and go back for a load of retardant." His team nodded, staring him in the eye. "I'm not losing Strong today."

"You sure?" Evan stared at him, then out the door. "We all know that's got to be Lily down there. Don't know how much time she has or if she can wait until this fire is out."

Christ. He wanted Lily safe. He wanted to pull her into his arms and tell her all the things he'd kept back last night. This time, if she'd give him those words, if she told him she loved him, he'd give her those words back, with interest. He loved Lily Cortez. That was the truth, plain and simple. She had to be alive. Eddie Haverley wanted to fuck with the two of them, so he wouldn't have killed her. Not yet. His mind shied away from the truth. That Eddie wasn't sane. One burst of temper, and Lily could be no more.

"The team jumps here," he repeated. "That's Eddie's fire eating up that ridge. He's burned three acres, maybe four. He's sitting there in that cabin, waiting for us to come and stop him. He wants that challenge," he said confidently. "Because, for him, this is a game. After you jump, Spotted Dick will swing back around, and I'll go in for Lily."

Evan cursed. "I'll go with you."

"No." He shook his head. "We'll already be a man short, and I need every pair of hands we've got digging line. I'm doing this one alone."

A deadly game. He didn't like dropping his team into the heart of what was probably a lethal trap. Eddie Haverley didn't need to sit there with a sniper's scope to pick Jack's team off. First responders were always at risk, and the jumps killed more men than the fires ever did. That was what happened when a man went out the door of a plane fifteen hundred feet up, with only a nylon chute and some padded Kevlar between him and the ground below.

The ten minutes it took to drop the team over the jump site felt like an eternity. Looking out of the plane as his boys jumped away, chutes snapping open, he could only pray he'd be on the ground in time.

The plane banked hard, turning away from the jump site, and then the hunting cabin and the black pickup were front and center, and his ass was braced in the open doorway.

Showtime.

Chapter Twenty-five

Jack had done his buddy check with Rio before his brother had jumped at the last site, so he was ready. He held still in the open doorway, the wind tearing at his face as the flames down below ate up the forest, and it was all he could do to wait. Leaning out, he dropped the streamers, watching the red ribbons plummet and then snap open, marking the wind's direction.

The only clear jump site was the open road leading up to the cabin, and he'd deliberately dropped the streamers there. A little red-herring action for Eddie Haverley. Updraft and drift wouldn't be too different over the trees carpeting the sides of the road, and those tops would give him some cover as he came down. He had no intention of landing his ass on the road, dragging an open chute, while Eddie unloaded any gun he was packing.

Trick was coming down and deliberately hanging up in those branches without impaling himself. He'd sure as hell done it by accident on more than one jump, so he knew the theory of it. At the controls, the pilot bawled out the altitude and banked the plane back around.

"You got this, Jack?" The spotter's face was intent on the road unfolding beneath them, watching those red streamers settle. "She's not too bad. Road's clear."

"I'm not aiming for the road." The plane dropped

again, roaring in as low as the pilot could take her and still give Jack enough altitude to open the chute and ride it down to the ground.

"Shit, Jack." The floor vibrated beneath their feet, and a new plume of dark smoke shot up on the other side of the ridge. Had to be an accelerant over there. "Good luck."

Spotted Dick brought the plane over the road leading up to the cabin. A straight shot up the gravel road, the cabin's shake roof was mossy and half caved in, but there was no mistaking Eddie standing there on the porch, watching the wall of flames advance. Jack didn't know what the stupid bastard thought the plan was, but Eddie Haverley was about to star front-and-center in a barbecue. There was a motorbike by the side of porch, so perhaps Eddie planned to outrun the fire.

Good luck with that one.

Jack braced himself. The engine roared, and the spotter's hand slapped his shoulder hard. *Go.* He launched himself out the door, arms tucked in, legs straight. Cleared the plane and looked down.

He saw a flash of color behind Eddie. Lily. The barrel of Haverley's gun rose and fell, and Jack wanted to howl. The drag chute snapped out behind him, jerking him upward briefly before gravity reasserted her control and he started the downward haul toward the ground. He picked his spot, a nice, dense crown of pine, and steered toward it.

Jump thousand.

Look thousand.

Reach thousand. He got his hand on the rip cord and got ready to pull, because Lily's life depended on his getting this right.

Wait thousand. Five hundred feet. Four.

Pull thousand. Right on cue, the chute exploded open as he yanked the cord. The trees spun wildly beneath him, and he dragged hard on the toggles, steering for the patch of pine he'd picked out.

Check your canopy.

Sky was clear above him, the plane disappearing back over the ridge to make another pass and assess what the boys could do to catch the fire. When he looked down, the forest was rushing up to meet him. Deliberately, he steered for the canopy. The bristling tops of the ponderosas rushed up to meet him, and the chute tore loudly as the fabric caught and he crashed through the top layer of branches, feet out. He'd hang up, and then he'd need to cut himself free.

He was gambling on that. This close to the ridge, the smoke boiled up around him. Given the speed of the fire gobbling up the forest, Eddie must have used an accelerant, but he'd also picked his spot wisely. If, that was, his goal was really to set the entire goddamned ridge on fire. The forest here was heavy with old fuel, carpeted with endless summers' worth of dry debris. Nothing had been logged in decades, if ever.

He could hear the buzz of choppers in the distance, but that water wasn't getting here quick enough. He'd seen enough fires to know this particular mountainside was going to burn hotter than the flames of hell.

Branches tore past his face as he punched through the outer layer of the canopy. For a moment, he sank, ass-deep in branches, and then the chute caught. Held.

If he'd come down on that road, he might as well have handed over the gun he'd holstered on his thigh. If the gun wasn't enough, he had the knives in his boots. Two hands. More than enough to kill a man, he knew—if Eddie Haverley didn't use Lily as a shield. The only way to counter that threat was to get the drop on him. He'd have heard the plane coming in, but he'd be expecting Jack to drop into the clearing itself or along the road. The road would have been nice, but it was also a clear shot from the front porch of that little cabin.

So here he was, hanging like an ornament from a Christmas tree, while time ran out too quickly.

Pulling his hunting knife from its sheath on his arm, he cut himself free, the blade slicing through the nylon cords like butter. Two seconds to cover his head with his arms and let gravity do its thing, pulling his body down through the canopy to the forest floor. Five seconds later he was taking a hard landing on his steel-toed boots. Everywhere he looked, there was smoke and embers, small flames chewing at the groundcover. He hoped like hell his boys were digging line like madmen on the other side, because this fire was damned hungry.

He was crouched outside the bushes by the cabin in under two minutes.

The curtains were closed, but the front door was cracked open.

Bastard was watching for him.

He weighed his options as the wind sent embers skittering across the little clearing where the long-gone hunter had planted the cabin. Wind was picking up, and that was bad news. The cabin roof was already stressed, with small, hazy patches of smoke rising from the shingles. He could vent his way in, but then he'd lose any element of surprise. Window was too damned small. Which meant either he went in the front door—or he waited for Eddie to come on out.

He eyeballed the sky again. *Fuck*. The cabin was square in the path of the fire now. He could see the orange glow spreading down from the ridge a quarter mile up from where he stood. There was more than enough fuel between the cabin and that line, too. No way that fire was stopping, and the road wasn't wide enough to do much good as a fire break. No, the fire would hit the canopy and jump clear across.

He needed to get Lily the hell out. Now.

Her avenging angel—although Jack was, she admitted, more devil than angel—exploded through the cabin's only door. The precise report of the Beretta he'd palmed as his booted foot rearranged the cabin's door had her crying out in shock.

"Drop the gun," Jack barked. Eddie Haverley, she realized, was only getting one chance while he contemplated the Beretta trained on his forehead and the hole in his shoulder. The man would never use that arm again. Seven rounds left, and Jack's face warned he'd empty the rest of the clip if that's what it took.

"Bastard." Eddie had a gaze like black ice on a New England highway. Those cold eyes boring into Jack signaled he'd hit a death patch and was now spinning out of control. "You should have stayed out of this."

The smile curving Jack's mouth was cold and hard. All straight-up soldier. "Make me."

She knew Jack needed her to get the hell out of his way. She edged toward the door, but Eddie lunged.

She was still dizzy and slow. And that let Eddie get too close. Jack squeezed off new rounds as her own survival instincts kicked in.

Sure enough, even as Eddie's body jerked from the bullets' impact, his hand grabbed at Lily's ponytail, his bloody fingers threading through her hair. That hand pulled her head back, and he wrapped an arm around her throat, squeezing the air right out of her. Inhaling became a thing of the past.

"You can't have her." The raspy voice had her trying to

cry out in terror and fury. She wasn't *letting* him do this. Not again. Not without a fight.

"I'm not yours," she wheezed when he eased up on the throat pressure long enough for her to get the words out. Pressure came right back, though, so clearly her answer wasn't satisfactory.

Jack brought the gun barrel up and slammed it into the side of Eddie's jaw, the stainless-steel barrel meeting skin with satisfying impact.

Eddie cursed, swinging her around effortlessly, her body like so much putty in the face of his anger-enhanced strength. And she could feel the heat from the fire building outside. As he grabbed a hunting knife from his boot, she estimated she had only a handful of seconds left.

Kicking, she cursed. Her heel connected nicely, first with Eddie's shin and then his groin. The howl of pain said she'd hurt him where it counted.

But it still wasn't enough to stop the blade, so she brought up her forearm, blocking. Just as she thought the blade would surely slice her, Jack's next shot cut off Eddie's stream of obscenities, and then Eddie was falling away from her, toward Jack. This was the warrior she suspected only his fellow Marines had ever seen. Moving smoothly, he was pure, lethal predator. Striking the side of Eddie's head with his right arm, Jack hooked a leg around the other man's leg, immobilizing him. Eddie screamed, but Jack slammed his other hand up against his chin, forcing Eddie's head and body back. Not hard enough to kill, but enough to immobilize.

Eddie went down and stayed down.

"Move," he ordered Lily, wrapping the T-shirt he wore under his jacket around her face. The water from his canteen sloshed over her face, wetting the fabric and her hair. "Stay low. Go fast."

He hit the floor, pushing her in front of him, on hands and knees. Smoke was filling up the cabin. Too hot, too soon. The heat pressed them down onto the floorboards, leaving them no way to stand up. Fire was going to flash over. Jack didn't need his years of experience to tell him that. He needed to get her out of the burning cabin. Now.

Hunched over to keep as low to the ground as possible, he kicked open the front door with a booted foot and spotted the geraniums in their coffee cans. Little wisps of steam curled up from the battered cans. *Hell.* "We need to leave, Lily."

The clearing outside wasn't much better. Orange flames flickered all around, momentarily stymied by the strip of gravel parking. He'd bet money that, as soon as that gravel ended, the flames would circle around. There wasn't going to be any way out, even if he could get the truck running.

"Jack," she said hoarsely, tugging on his sleeve. When he followed her gaze, he spotted flames flickering along the ceiling, mixing with the smoke in on-and-off bursts of orange fire. If they were still inside that cabin when those flames finished what they were working up to, they weren't getting out.

"Go," he ordered. "Outside." Never mind that it was hotter than the furnaces of hell out there. Staying inside wasn't going to buy them any more time.

"Okay," she gasped. "Just point the way."

Behind them, Eddie cursed, rolling over. He pushed himself to his knees.

Fuck. Jack palmed his gun, ignoring the uncomfortable heat of the fire-heated metal. Hot enough to burn, but not too hot to fire. Not yet. He wasn't going to feed the bastard to the flames, but his first priority here was Lily. He had to get her out of here. Anything else was pure bonus.

One minute, Eddie was just there, swaying on his knees and cursing up a storm. Next minute, the fire blew outward. Fifteen hundred degrees of pure, agonizing hell came calling for Eddie, and that damned fire sucked the oxygen right out of his lungs and cut the scream short before it could even begin.

Jack was already rolling out the door.

He hit the porch hard, taking Lily with him. He tried to twist to take the brunt of their fall, but there wasn't time to worry whether she was under or over him. Getting the breath knocked out of her was going to be the least of her worries.

No, the problem was that a flashover like the one that had just incinerated Eddie Haverley wasn't the end point for a fire. All that sudden explosion of flames meant was that the fire had hit maximum intensity. Right now that blaze was lighting up the little cabin, twisting through its foundation and devouring its walls. Those bright orange flames just tore through the wooden shingles, and Jack knew that the burning building was about to turn the whole clearing into a bonfire.

Outside, it was raining small orange embers. Could have been a real pretty sight, like tiny shooting stars, except he was in the middle of a fucking hot zone, and he didn't have an evac route. He flicked on the radio but got only static.

"Where's the jump team, Jack?" Panic filled her voice. Yeah, she didn't need his kind of experience to know that things were getting real bad down here on the ground. "Can we take the truck?"

"I don't have the keys, Lily, and that road isn't clear." Slapping embers off her, he shoved her into his Nomex jacket while he scanned the clearing. The cabin. And the canyon. There. If they got inside that shallow depression, maybe they could wait this one out. "The boys jumped on the other side of the ridge. That's where they're holding line."

"We're on the wrong side of the fire line. God, Jack." She turned toward him, fighting panic and exhaustion. He wanted to pull her into his arms, wrap her in whatever reassurance he could give her, but the sound of the approaching fire beat at them in waves, the deafening crackle of flames devouring summer-dry brush. Every few seconds there was a sudden burst of sound when the flames found a particularly dense or dry spot. Plenty to feed the fire here.

The number of embers raining down from the smoky plume overhead was increasing. Too close, he thought. They were too damned close. Thousands of feet of black smoke punched defiantly into the sky overhead, dwarfing them, and now he could see the flames a good hundred feet above the forest crown. Jumping the road. Even if he could start the truck, they wouldn't be able to outrun this fire.

"We have to take cover." Making the decision, he dropped his pack, going for the paperback-sized canvas bag that held the shelter.

Lily stared at him. Ash streaked her incredulous face. "Are you crazy? You'd need a bomb shelter out here. We have to run."

Men had died running, and he knew a bad situation when he saw it. They'd make a hundred yards, and then the fire would jump the trees, and they'd be front and center in an inferno.

"Get the tent out," he snapped, dropping to his knees beside the depression he'd spotted and digging at the dirt with his Pulaski. The more space he bought her, the more air she'd have when the fire flashed over. "Now, Lily," he growled when she hesitated. "We've got maybe ten min-

utes, and then we're starring in a burnover. Get the fucking tent open. Otherwise, when that fire flashes over,
we're going to burn from the inside out. Lungs go first,
Lily, because God didn't intend for the human body to
suck down that kind of superheated air."

The crackle of plastic told him she was doing her part.
Good, because a quick glance over his shoulder warned
him they were almost out of time.

"Then what?" She asked her question quietly, dropping
to her knees beside him. He'd hoped she wouldn't ask, but
Lily had always wanted the truth, hadn't she? Silently, he
pulled off his T-shirt, wetting down the fabric again with
what was left of his canteen. He wished he had more to
give her. Wrapping the damp cotton around her head and
face, he pushed her down into the little hollow. She went,
no arguments, which told him she'd seen the shit-storm
bearing down on them.

"Then the body goes, Lilybell, and that's a mercy at that
point."

For a long moment all he heard was the whoosh of a
tree going up too close, followed by the ominous crackle
as the fire consumed its new fuel. Already that fire
sounded like a tidal wave pushing toward them. Overwhelming noise.

"Tell me," she said, "this contraption can't fail, Jack."

"Fiberglass and aluminum," he said. "Best the government has to offer. Shake-'n'-bakes—that's what we call
them." He wouldn't lie to her, and he didn't blame her for
the little quaver in her voice. The shelters weren't infalli-
ble, but it was the best he had to give right now.

Planting his boots on the back wall of the shelter, he
pulled the fabric over his head as he dropped down on top
of her and planted the other side on the ground, praying
like hell the entire time.

"God, Jack." She swallowed. "Next time, lie to me."

"There won't be a next time, baby," he promised roughly. One way or another, this would be the first and last time he trusted his life to a fire shelter. He was literally holding his future in his arms.

The boys joked that using the silver cocoon meant making a giant shake-and-bake of yourself. They always laughed, but they knew the odds. Fire shelters didn't always work. They could only withstand so much heat before the glue melted and the shelter started emitting toxic fumes. Gas yourself or burn alive. Not much of a choice.

Gently he forced her facedown into the little pocket he'd hollowed out. "Breathe slow and easy," he whispered, lowering his head to cover hers.

"Thank you," she said, surprising him. "Thank you for coming back for me, Jack."

A frown creased his forehead. He'd always come for her. Hell, he hadn't been able to stay away when they were growing up, and all he wanted to do now was grow old with her. And wasn't that a shocker? Bad boy Jack Donovan, who couldn't wait to shake the dust of Strong from his feet, didn't want to go anywhere. Didn't want to leave unless this woman was coming with him.

"This counts, Lily." He spoke low, into her ear. "I think this counts in the forever column. You said I never stayed put. I'm not going anywhere this time, not so long as I have you. This is going to get hot, though," he warned hoarsely. The shelter was already cooking at two hundred degrees inside, but what was outside was far worse. "And loud, baby. But I've got you. All you have to do is hold on to me, and we'll get through this, okay?"

"You never did lie well, Jack," she whispered.

He was fighting to hold the shelter in place, sealed to the ground, against high winds generated by the advancing fire. The heat prickled his skin, searing his lungs. He nudged her face farther down into the small impression he'd hollowed out. That space was a few critical degrees cooler for her.

"I need to tell you something, Jack."

"Whatever you want, baby." He fought to keep the shelter anchored as the wind pulled at the thin walls. God, he couldn't bear the thought of holding her, hearing her, as the fire consumed her. "I'm right here for you. I'm not going anywhere."

Her little snort of laughter surprised him. "This wasn't what I wanted, Jack."

"Yeah, well, the timing sucks." The first sudden blast of heat and wind made her flinch, an instinctive jerk she couldn't hide, not with him covering her. "You keep talking, though. I like hearing your voice." Her voice anchored him. She was right there with him. Trusting him. And that had him praying like a madman, because he'd pay any price to keep her safe. "You just stick with me, baby." Pressing a small, tender kiss against the back of her neck, he let himself breathe in the scent of her. This clearing wasn't a bad place to make a stand, so, if he held on long enough, she'd make it through.

Even if he didn't.

"It's a terrible thing to say, but I'm glad he's gone. How could he have started something like this?" The worry and fear in her voice was killing him.

Yeah, Eddie Haverley was gone, all right. The fire had seared his lungs from the inside out. Jack only hoped the bastard was roasting in an even hotter hell now. She didn't need those details right now, however. Not when that same fire was about to flash over them. "He's not hurting you again. Do you know how I felt, watching him pull a gun on you?"

"No," she whispered. "But I'll tell you how I felt, Jack. Scared."

"You don't have to be scared anymore," he promised.

"I was scared," she said, "because he could have turned that gun on you at any point. Scared because you'd just launched yourself out of a plane and right into his damn sights, Jack. I couldn't bear it if anything happened to you. You could have been safe. Not here."

"This is where I want to be, baby." He swallowed, listening to the sounds of the fire. Five seconds. Maybe less. Could be the last chance he had to give her the words he'd been keeping for her. For the right moment. Couldn't be any moment less perfect than this, but he wasn't going out of this world without telling her the truth. "I love you, Lily. That's the God's honest truth. I'm always coming for you, and I'll always be there for you. You need to do something for me now. No matter what happens in the next couple of minutes, you keep your grip on this shelter, and you don't let go. No matter what. Things are going to get real hot in here."

"God, Jack." Something between a laugh and a sob escaped her. The dampness on his arm where the side of her face pressed made him want to howl. She was scared, hurting so badly. And there was nothing he could do but hold on to her as tightly as he could and pray even harder. "I want so badly to turn around and kiss you," she whispered.

"Don't," he said, alarmed. He tightened his grip on her, tucking her farther beneath him. "Don't move, Lily. No matter what happens."

"I love you, too, Jack," she whispered.

Then the freight-train roar of the approaching fire drowned out everything else. He pinned her beneath his weight, all his attention focused on sheltering her with his body. Fire wouldn't get to her. Not while he was here.

Chapter Twenty-six

Yesterday, she'd come as close as anyone could to dying. She shuddered, but there was no shaking the memories. She'd never forget the thunderous roar of the oncoming fire—or the sudden, heated silence when the flames had surrounded their shelter. She was damned lucky to be alive today.

She stretched luxuriously in her bed. She'd had luck on her side—and Jack Donovan. He'd done exactly as he'd promised. He'd kept her safe, wrapped in his arms, anchoring her.

He'd held her for the longest hour of her life, until he was sure the fire had passed. When the wind and the heat had died down, he'd still held her. He'd wanted to be sure, he'd whispered against her hair. Eventually, when a chopper roared in, low and heavy overhead, he'd let her go. The chopper had dumped a jump team over the hill, where smoke still billowed, and then circled back. When it set down, they'd scrambled aboard.

"Close one" was all Rio said, but his tense face told her the truth. It had been more than close. The hillside beneath the clearing was a hot, smoldering wreck. The fire had swept through that area fast and strong, and there was nothing left of the hunting cabin other than a handful of blackened bricks from the foundation. As they lifted up and headed back toward Strong, she spotted the blackened skeleton of the truck, smoking on what had been the road out. She realized she was looking for some sign of Eddie Haverley, but he was gone.

"They'll send in a forensics team," Jack had said, raising his voice to be heard over the steady beat of the chopper's blades. "But he's not coming back, Lily. We both saw him go."

"Flashover?" Rio yelled from the controls, tossing headphones back to them. And, at Jack's tight nod, he'd muttered, "Hell of a way to go, cooking from the inside out."

The fire had been an angry orange quilt beneath them, still devouring trees and roads and landmarks. For the first time, she really understood just how close she'd come to losing Jack. And how much he'd sheltered her from, down there on the ground as the fire roared overhead.

Afterward, there had been the hours spent debriefing in the sheriff's office, after which Jack had bundled her home. Held her in the shower as those big, strong hands moved lazily, gently over her, wielding the soap and warm water with devastating efficiency. He'd finally tucked her into bed, exhausted, when she was clean and as smoke-free as he could make her. Last words she'd heard had been another promise. "Smoke will be gone in a few days, honey," he'd whispered against her damp hair.

Now, after sleeping through the night, she padded downstairs, pushed open the screen door, and went out onto porch. He'd put her to bed in one of his T-shirts. It was too large, the opening dipping down one shoulder, and she'd seen a shorter hemline on the last cocktail dress she'd bought. The way she was going through his clothes, Jack Donovan was going to be shirtless before too long. That wasn't a bad thing, though. The female residents of Strong would thank her.

Jack was waiting for her on the porch.

She sat down next to him, inhaling lavender and wondering what she should say. What she could say. Instead of saying anything, however, he just gently grabbed her wrist and turned her arm so he could see last night's damage for himself. The abrasions weren't bad at all and would heal up within a week or two. But the way Jack had fussed, you'd think both her arms had caught fire. While he made light of the burns he'd taken on a leg and arm. Protecting her.

"Is everyone else okay?" Standing on the front porch of the hunting cabin with Eddie, she'd seen Jack's team jumping.

"The boys are just fine." He shot her a small, amused frown. "Rio's swearing he'll never let Evan or me jump again, claiming that we took twenty years off his life, and Nonna's backing him up."

His hand touched her wrist, turning her toward the light so he could examine it. Again. "It's nothing." She pulled her arm free. "You'll be jumping again by next week, if another call comes in."

"You don't think fire season should be over for me? That I might have pushed my luck as far as it can stretch?"

She shot him a look. "I hope there are no more calls this summer, but if there are, we both know you'll be the first one out of the plane."

Jumping was simply part of who he was. That job of his wouldn't ever thrill her, but it was an intrinsic piece of him. That, she could live with.

"And you're okay with that?" The concern and tenderness reflected in his eyes was as shocking as it was unexpected. She didn't want to change who he was.

She nodded. "I'm okay with you, Jack. If you need to fight fires, then you do that." She managed a little smile. "Strong certainly needs you on our side."

He stood up. "Come with me," he said, holding out a hand, and she went. He took her to his truck.

"I'm not dressed to go out, Jack!" she protested.

"Won't matter," he said.

She got in, and he drove down the familiar road into Strong, a man with a mission. Impossibly, wonderfully, given yesterday's inferno, they were both alive. Eddie Haverley was dead, and he wasn't coming back, and she wanted to be getting on with the rest of her life.

He didn't break his silence during the five-minute drive. So she just sat there, her head against the beat-up headrest, watching him drive. She wanted to say something, but what? What did he want? What was he thinking?

He parked the truck in front of the old fire station. The building still listed like a drunk on Friday night, but there was a pile of roofing shingles and building supplies decorating the brown patch of front lawn. Someone had fixed the porch's sagging front steps and put a pot of geraniums on the railing. Right now, the flowers drooping from the unexpected transplant, but by nightfall the cheery red blossoms would have perked back up.

"This is what you wanted to show me?" Coming around the truck, he lifted her out. She let him, savoring the feel of his body pressed against her. What she really wanted, she decided, was to hook a leg around his denim-clad thighs and drag him back into the truck's cab. Even if half of Strong was watching. "Jack, the old firehouse has been here a hundred years at least. It's not going anywhere. Except, maybe"—she eyed the place critically—"the demolition heap."

"Yeah. She's a little rough around the edges." He shoved a hand through his hair. "But I bought the place and made the Realtor a damned happy man. I'm wondering if she wouldn't make a good home base for me and my team. If that was what you wanted."

Foolishly, her breath caught. "Do you want to stay here, in Strong?"

His fingers tangled in her hair. "I want you to be happy, baby, and Strong's part of you now. You've got your farm. You've got roots here."

"You've spent a lifetime running away from this place," she pointed out. "So what makes you want to come back and stay put now?"

He stared at her intently. "You, Lily. You tell me what you need, and I'll make sure you have it. You want Strong, you want us here in Strong, and that's what we'll do."

"All I want is you," she whispered.

He finally smiled, and she knew everything was going to be okay. A man like Jack Donovan never took to feeling—being—vulnerable. He wanted to protect, to defend. He wasn't going to give her the words twice a day, but he'd live them. "So I thought I'd base a jump team here. The mountains here are good terrain to practice on, and in our downtime we can man the fire station. Keep a truck or two for local fires."

"You're going to be a fireman," she teased. Tugging on the cotton of his T-shirt, she pulled him into her.

He went willingly, pinning her between his hard, lean body and the door of his truck. His thigh slid between hers, and an arm braced above her head.

"Only part-time," he grumbled. "I'm not giving up the smoke jumping, not if you can live with it. I love what I do, and I'm damned good at it. But I can base here and go out on jobs when I need to. But you need to be sure, Lily. Be very sure."

"And then what? We date while you're in town?" She was asking questions, but her hands were already sliding up his chest, over his shoulders. He was so big and strong and alive.

His hands slid up on a journey of their own, cupping her face. His gaze was fierce on her, giving her his weight as he leaned into her. Let her feel every inch of him. This was who she was getting. He'd never be tame, and maybe they'd butt heads too often, but she wasn't running, and he finally knew what he wanted. "I love you, Lily. I meant every word of what I said yesterday, and I'll say it again and again until you believe me. I want whatever you can give me. You want to date, we'll date, but I'm holding out for more. I want all of you, every day. Waking up in my arms. Going to sleep beside me. The rest of it, we'll figure out."

"What are you saying?"

"Marry me, Lily. I want to come home to you, make a home with you." Those big, strong hands tangled fiercely in her hair. Holding her still for a hard, deep kiss. Exploring her, relearning her. She reveled in the fierce heat and sensual promise of his body. "I love you," he promised.

"Yes." A smile spread across her face. "Yes, Jack."

"Thank God," he grunted. Something cool slid over her ring finger. "I drove like a madman to Sacramento to find a ring."

She completed him. Made him whole. He'd run from Strong, run from Lily Cortez, because he hadn't known what to do with those unfamiliar feelings. He'd thought he couldn't let himself love her. He'd been wrong.

"I love you, Jack." Her hands wrapped around his neck, pulling him down into her kiss. "Welcome home."

"Not yet," he said. "We're not home yet." Swinging her up into his arms, he headed purposefully for the staircase that led up to the second floor of the firehouse. "I ever show you the firemen's quarters? We've got ourselves an entire apartment."

"Now? Here?" A bubble of amusement lit up her face as she wrapped her arms tighter, pulling him closer. Those brown eyes of hers laughed up at him. Familiar. Right. This was his Lily, and damned if he was ever letting her go.

"Absolutely," he growled. "I'm taking you to bed, Lily, and I'm not letting you out."

"Hurry up," she ordered. Her fingers tunneled into his hair as if she didn't want to let go, either. She didn't have to. He was all hers.

"Whatever you want, baby." Pushing open the door with his foot, he carried her inside. "We have all the time in the world to get this right." He was so full of love and lust and laughter, he wasn't sure his feet were altogether on the ground. "We jump together now."

Hooked on Anne Marsh's wickedly sexy alpha heroes? Check out *One Hot Cowboy*, available now wherever ebooks are sold.

Blackhawk Ranch was running dry. Cabe Dawson had lost one well already and now the second had slowed to a trickle. There hadn't been enough rain this winter to fill the creek the ranch got its surface water from, and the two surviving wells fought to bring the water up nine hundred feet and into the baking, skin-drying heat of California summer. Now, as he steered his battered pickup over the dark dirt road, time seemed to slow to a heated, sensual shimmer with one driving urge pounding through them all: find water. Cattle needed it. Men wanted it. Cabe Dawson would be damned if he allowed a drought to take what he'd built here.

Making a living from the land meant fighting every step of the way. Fortunately, Cabe had never minded a good fight.

He'd planned for this day, already had the solution. There was water underneath the Jordan place. He held the mortgage on the neighboring ranch. All he had to do was foreclose and the land was his. He'd drill. The cattle would drink. They could all live happily fucking after.

Instead, he was waiting for Rose Jordan to bring her sweet little ass home so he could talk things out with her. For Auntie Dee's sake, he wanted to hand Rose a check and preserve the fiction he was buying her out—not spring the news about a reverse mortgage he was calling due after the older woman's death. He sure as hell didn't want to drag this through the courts. He didn't have the six months to wait. He needed that water now and he'd get it, but he didn't have to be a bully about it.

Unless Rose left him with no other option.

He owned this particular part of California and the ranch was feudal at heart. His word was law. He had the money—and the land—to back it up. Rose had her time to dally only because he'd decided to give it to her. Soon, however, he'd cut her off.

His cell buzzed and he flipped on the hands-free. "You track her down yet?" As always, Seth cut right to the chase. His brother had never been patient. Hell, he was more of a heat-guided missile, constantly seeking out his next adrenaline rush. That need made him a star on the rodeo circuit, but piss-poor at waiting for one woman to make up her mind to come back home.

The turnoff for the swimming hole appeared out of the nighttime shadows. Cabe guided the pickup over, the crunch of gravel beneath his tires threatening to drown out his brother's voice and then his own response.

"You know Rose. She's not picking up." Or answering her e-mail or the three registered letters he'd had the lawyer send her way.

There was laughter in Seth's voice now, his earlier impatience forgotten. "Yeah. She'll get here when she gets here, Cabe. Our Rose never was an early bird. Plus, if she knows how badly you want her to come, she'll just take twice as long."

That was certainly true. Rose had spent most of her high school years tormenting him. Teasing him. Worst part was, she'd had no clue what she did to him. What he'd wanted to do to *her*.

She'd seen him as an older brother.

A boring, play-by-the-rules, too-strict older brother.

"This can't wait any longer," he growled. The pickup emerged from a tunnel of trees and he killed the headlights, just soaking up the peace of the night. The pure quiet and the heat escaping slowly from the ground. "We can't wait any longer. The ranch needs that well, Seth."

"We've got two wells left," Seth pointed out, laughter gone.

"We had four." The prospect of losing one inch of the ranch had Cabe gritting his teeth. This place, this land, was *his*. He'd damn well hold onto it, keep it together. He had too many families depending on him for a living and he'd poured himself into building the ranch one acre at a time. Rose Jordan would not stop him.

Rose, he suspected, was a born procrastinator. Cabe knew the type. Sure, he hadn't been close to her before she'd up and left Lonesome—she'd been too damned young, for one thing—but he'd done a little watching. She was pure trouble, but good-hearted. She and his brothers had raised good-natured hell from one end of Lonesome to the other.

"She'll turn up, Cabe," Seth said again. "She always does."

"She'd better." He was bone tired from a day that had begun before sunrise and had only just ended. He was hot, he smelled like sweat and horse and probably a dozen other things as well. Right now, a swim sounded perfect, exactly what he needed to cool down and think things through.

"I'm going for a swim." Signing off, he tossed the cell onto the seat beside him and parked. The quiet surrounded him the second he got out of the truck. After a long day wrangling the ranch, he needed that. He needed to be alone.

Except he wasn't alone. Tucked into the edge of the

road was a beat-up Honda he couldn't believe had made it down the dirt track.

Christ, he was sick and tired of the trespassers who thought ignoring the signs and the fences was just a game. High school kids had always enjoyed sneaking onto the ranch for a swim. Never mind that all those kids had to do was ask and follow a few basic rules.

He'd have said yes. Scrubbing a hand over his head, he grabbed the Stetson from the passenger's seat and jammed it on. Somehow, he'd got himself a reputation for being a mean-ass, coldhearted bastard. Of course, he also didn't give a damn about what folks said, which probably meant his fan club wasn't all that wrong.

Getting out of the truck, he carefully closed the door behind him. No point in advertising his presence until he had to. Tonight's trespassers were probably just kids but, damn it, it wasn't safe to swim out here alone. He'd warned them not to come at night and never to come alone. He needed to know when there was someone on his land. Too many things could happen out here if a man wasn't careful.

It took just minutes to get through the fringe of cottonwood trees ringing the swimming hole. Older than any of them, those trees had seen plenty. His brothers had had a rope and a tire swing here. They'd spent hours whooping it up, letting go as soon as that swing got out over the center of the pond where the deepest water was. Cold as hell, too, because that water came from deep underground.

As soon as he reached the edge, his feet stopped moving; tonight's swimmer was unexpected. He'd *expected* to find a few high school kids. Maybe a cooler of beer or a couple a little too busy discovering each other.

Instead, there was a woman in the water.

A damned fine, completely bare-ass naked woman.

She cut through the dark water with slow, lazy strokes.

Not too tall and real damned curvy. He could see her sun-kissed skin even in the silvery moonlight. Water-slicked hair covered her bare shoulders and back. He should have been a gentleman, should have looked away. But damned if her swimming bare-ass naked in his swimming hole wasn't the sexiest thing he'd ever seen.

She dove beneath the surface, giving him a spectacular view of her ass. From where he stood, those curves looked soft as peaches and just as luscious. He wanted to cup both cheeks in his hands. Run his hands down that skin and explore every inch of her. Even the shadowed crease between her cheeks. Yeah, there, too, if she'd let him. He'd show her every dark, sweet pleasure.

A slow grin tugged the corners of his mouth. Hell, she'd have been safer if his hell-raising brothers had been the ones to find her.

He'd never pretended to be nice. He didn't have to. He owned this ranch. This world, this place, was *his* and here she was. . . .